ALL HELL BROKE LOOSE

as waves of North Vietnamese soldiers poured out from behind what seemed like every bush, rushing the camp carrying a bangalore torpedo amid open fire.

Unarmed and oblivious to the fighting going on around him, Alex leapt from his bunker carrying his medical-aid kit. First he pulled a wounded soldier behind the bunker for protection, then he carried another with him, stopping the bleeding of his wound. Then Alex dodged past NVA soldiers and heavy fire to retrieve another, and another.

The NVA sprung out of hiding places in the jungle, but Alex didn't see them. He was concentrating on stopping the blood from running into a wounded man's eyes, unaware of the soldier approaching him from behind. . . .

MAJOR DONALD E. ZLOTNIK (Ret.) was a Green Beret, paratrooper, and F-4 Phantom flyer in Vietnam, and was awarded the Soldier's Medal for Heroism as well as the Bronze Star. He is the author of six previous novels.

FIELDS OF HONOR #2

✪✪✪✪✪✪✪✪✪✪✪✪✪✪✪✪✪✪✪✪✪✪✪✪✪✪✪✪✪✪

DISTINGUISHED SERVICE CROSS

Donald E. Zlotnik
Major (Ret) U.S. Army Special Forces

A SIGNET BOOK

SIGNET
Published by the Penguin Group
Penguin Books USA Inc., 375 Hudson Street,
New York, New York 10014, U.S.A.
Penguin Books Ltd, 27 Wrights Lane,
London W8 5TZ, England
Penguin Books Australia Ltd, Ringwood,
Victoria, Australia
Penguin Books Canada Ltd, 2801 John Street,
Markham, Ontario, Canada L3R 1B4
Penguin Books (N.Z.) Ltd, 182-190 Wairau Road,
Auckland 10, New Zealand

Penguin Books Ltd, Registered Offices:
Harmondsworth, Middlesex, England

First published by Signet, an imprint of New American Library, a
division of Penguin Books USA Inc.

First Printing, February, 1991
10 9 8 7 6 5 4 3 2 1

FIELDS OF HONOR is a creation of Siegel & Siegel, Ltd.

Ⓢ REGISTERED TRADEMARK—MARCA REGISTRADA

PRINTED IN THE UNITED STATES OF AMERICA

PUBLISHER'S NOTE
This is a work of fiction. Names, characters, places, and incidents
either are the product of the author's imagination or are used
fictitiously, and any resemblance to actual persons, living or dead,
events, or locales is entirely coincidental.

BOOKS ARE AVAILABLE AT QUANTITY DISCOUNTS WHEN USED TO PRO-
MOTE PRODUCTS OR SERVICES. FOR INFORMATION PLEASE WRITE TO
PREMIUM MARKETING DIVISION, PENGUIN BOOKS USA INC., 375 HUDSON
STREET, NEW YORK, NEW YORK 10014.

Dedicated to the unconquerable spirit of the American paratrooper, past and present.

They were grand, glory days—weren't they, war buddy?

Army Regulations (AR) 672-5-1
Section II Criteria

2-7. Distinguished Service Cross

The Distinguished Service Cross is awarded to a person who, while serving in any capacity with the Army, distinguishes himself by extraordinary heroism not justifying the award of the Medal of Honor; while engaged in an action against an enemy of the United States; while engaged in military operations involving conflict with an opposing/foreign force; or while serving with friendly foreign forces engaged in an armed conflict against an opposing armed force in which the United States is not a belligerent party. The act or acts of heroism must have been so notable and have involved risk of life so extraordinary as to set the individual apart from his comrades.

(Actual extract from the military regulation.)

To the reader:

This novel was a tough one to write. If you served in Vietnam during the war, you'll understand some of the pain written between the lines. We've all lost war buddies to suicide because they couldn't get rid of their ghosts. Contrary to a number of popular myths that are circulating in the psychological community, it is rarely the *total* effects of war and battle that damage the human spirit, but the little things. I use Christmas cookies in this novel, but it could be anything from a funny-shaped cloud to a gentle odor.

I've placed the story in the flatland jungles surrounding Tay Ninh and the Black Virgin Mountain (Nui Ba Den). If you served in the border area north of the city around the Special Forces camp at Tong Le Chon, you might remember the huge bamboo thickets that could go on for miles and were so damn thick that a human would have to crawl *under* the matted mass because a machete would just bounce off the finger-thick bamboo.

You might have been there when Tong Le Chon was overrun by the North Vietnamese. If you were there, please excuse the liberties that I took in the story. I was more interested in developing my characters than giving an "accurate" description of the battle.

Some people gained from Tong Le Chon. Their after-action reports about themselves got them promotions and awards—and some soldiers did their jobs quietly and still carry the "ghosts." It was a good fight and deserves to be honored, even if it is at the end of my humble pen—twenty-odd years later and after the suicide of a good war buddy.

D. E. Zlotnik

CHAPTER ONE

✪✪✪✪✪✪✪✪✪✪✪✪✪✪✪✪✪✪✪

ON A COLD
WINTER'S NIGHT

She cocked her head to one side and looked down from her perch in the oak at the bright object that had been placed in the snow next to the shiny black marble wall. The late-afternoon light was fading rapidly but would break through the heavy snow clouds occasionally and send bright flashes sliding over the fresh snow.

A loud, raucous *jay-jay* cry came from her mate, followed by a long series of other calls that echoed over the small park. She couldn't resist. She spread her blue wings and landed only a couple of inches away from the object that had attracted her attention. She hopped closer, turned her head to one side, and stared closely to see if the shiny thing was edible, then risked a quick peck at it.

The activity drew the attention of a pair of cardinals. The male banked to his left and circled down, landing only a couple of inches away from the female blue jay. She hopped back away from the shiny object and flapped her blue wings, fluffing out her white chest feathers to seem larger than she was. The bright red male cardinal ignored her and hopped over to look at the object. The male jay saw the cardinal land and left his perch to join his mate as the female cardinal called in a rich *what-cheer, cheer, cheer, purty-purty-purty-purty*, followed by a metallic chip.

The man sitting cross-legged on the snow didn't

move as he watched the birds hop around the medal he had placed next to the black marble wall. A very slight curve appeared at each corner of his mouth as he realized the red cardinal and the blue-and-white jay made up the same colors as the medal's ribbon.

The female cardinal called again to her mate and he left to join her. The male jay started scolding the cardinal as it flew away.

The female jay looked over at the motionless mound she had mistaken for a rock pile and stared at the opening at the top. The slight movement of blinking eyes sent her flying off, giving her alarm cry. The larger male jay followed her back to safety in the oak.

The man shifted his shoulders underneath the poncho, and some of the snow that had built up over his back broke loose and slipped down in a mini-avalanche. He had been sitting facing the marble wall with the cold wind to his back for a very long time. He was warm except for the small exposed portion of his face around the eyes. A freezing rain had started falling less than an hour after he had laid the medal down on the narrow ledge under a long list of names and had taken up his vigil. The rain had frozen when it touched the black marble and left a sheet of clear shiny ice that reflected the streetlights' soft glow as they flicked on for the night. The man reached out from under the warm camouflage liner attached to the rubber poncho and used his thumb to light the Zippo in his hand. The falling snowflakes touched his warm skin and melted almost instantly. A soft flickering glow sprang from the wick of the lighter and reflected off the ice-covered wall. The man held the lighter up against a spot where a name had been carved in the marble and watched as the ice melted away from the letters.

"Hey! What the hell are you doing there?" The voice broke the peaceful quiet of the military park.

The man turned slowly from the wall and looked at the national-park guard walking toward him.

"I asked what in the hell you think you're doing?" The park guard pulled the fake fur collar on his uniform coat up tighter around his neck.

"Getting the ice off my buddy's name." The voice coming from the beard-covered face was surprisingly pleasant.

"Oh, well . . ." The guard looked over at the small portion of the black marble wall where the ice had been melted and saw that no damage had been done. "Do you know that it's Christmas Eve?" He looked at the man sitting in front of the marble wall and felt a deep sense of compassion. "Don't you think that you should find some shelter for the night?"

"I'm fine." The man pulled the poncho back together under his nose and peeked out through the small opening.

"I can't just let you stay here all night." The guard didn't know what to do. He had seen a lot of Vietnam vets visit the new memorial during the summer and had witnessed a lot of grief. Almost every day there would be a pile of medals that had been left behind and all sorts of bayonets and belt buckles and photographs. "Is that your medal?"

"Yes."

"That's a Distinguished Service Cross, isn't it?"

"Yes."

"Those were hard to come by."

The man didn't answer.

"Look, fella . . . I'm going off-duty in a couple of hours. You can stay here until then, but then you'll have to leave. My replacement doesn't like soldiers . . . you know what I mean? He was a hippie during the war and will haul you in for trespassing after midnight."

"Thanks." The single word was muffled.

"Just be gone by midnight." The guard turned to leave and mumbled, "Merry Christmas."

The man watched the uniformed guard disappear in

the swirling snow and lowered the CAR-15 submachine gun back down across his legs under the poncho. He looked back at the wall and saw that the white particles of ice had filled the black marble grooves in the chiseled letters of his war buddy's name: WILLIAM S. MILLS.

Tears flowed down the middle-aged man's cheeks and froze when they reached his blond beard, now streaked with gray. Soft sobs echoed off the long black marble wall back out over the snow and blended in with the Christmas carols coming from across the street. A large group of high school students were out caroling with their church group. He slowly shoved the poncho off his shoulders and stood up. The long green military overcoat covered his submachine gun and the belt of TNT sticks he had rigged around his waist. He bent, picked up his rucksack, and slung it over his shoulder before walking slowly away from the memorial, leaving his camouflaged poncho liner behind to gather snow. Only one side of the bronze cross and a small portion of the attached eagle were still visible as the snowflakes covered the United States Army's second-highest award for extraordinary heroism during combat.

He walked to the end of the ice-covered black marble wall and performed a slow military about-face before finding the first of the eleven names that had begun the terror of what the military labeled the Battle of Tong Le Chon.

"Jaxson! I'm coming in!" The coarse voice, between a whisper and an exhausted yell, was followed only seconds later by the sound of someone crawling through the rain-soaked undergrowth dragging something heavy.

Jaxson glanced up from the unconscious soldier he was working on and saw his senior medic slipping over the edge of the bomb crater, dragging another wounded soldier underneath him between his arms and legs.

"Fuck! I'm beat!" The sergeant first class unhooked the jerry-rigged carrying strap and propped the wounded Nung CIDG commando up against the side of the bomb crater they had turned into an emergency field hospital. "I can't crawl another fucking inch . . ." The sergeant's voice trailed off in a sigh.

"I'll go out this time." The younger sergeant looked up from his patient at the Green Beret senior medic. "Let me get this guy rigged up with a blood expander first." Jaxson reached down in his forty-pound medical pack and pulled out one of the small packages.

The older soldier dropped his head back against the muddy bank of the huge hole and rested with his eyes open. "Sorry to have got you into this, especially on your first combat patrol, Alex."

The younger medic shrugged his shoulders. "We knew it was going to happen sometime—might as well be my first trip out."

"It's not as bad as it looks"—the sound of a Soviet RPD light machine gun cracked over their heads and cut through the green vegetation on the lip of the crater, sending down a shower of green confetti on the wounded commandos—"we're holding our own perimeter and we've got some of the toughest fighting men in the world protecting our asses!" The RPD fired again, but this time it sounded closer and the senior medic reached for his pistol.

"Which way should I go?" Alex Jaxson used the back of his hand to wipe the sweat off his forehead, and only succeeded in smearing the crater mud out over his face. It had been raining steadily for the past five days and everything that wasn't sealed in plastic was saturated from the monsoons.

Sergeant Mills looked up from where he was resting and stared into Alex's green eyes. The young soldier looked a mess and his white eyeballs looked too *clean*. Mills pointed off to his side. "I heard calls for a medic

about thirty meters in that direction. Don't go much farther than that or you'll end up outside our perimeter."

Alex took the carrying strap from Mills and wrapped it around his waist a couple of times. He started reaching for his CAR-15 submachine gun and Mills grabbed his wrist. "You don't need that with you—it'll just get in your way. Rely on your pistol if you get in trouble, or crawl back here."

Alex gave a curt nod. He was trying not to act scared, but his fear had turned the inside of his mouth copper. If it hadn't been for the wounded keeping him occupied, he knew that he would have panicked when the first burst from the automatic weapon had signaled the beginning of the firefight less than an hour earlier, though it seemed much longer in his mind. He started crawling over the lip of the bomb crater that had been formed from a B-52 Arc Light mission the night before. The whole jungle floor was pockmarked with the giant fifteen-foot-wide craters. The soft earth allowed the two-thousand-pound bombs, set on delayed fuses, to bury themselves ten feet before exploding. The flatland jungles of III Corps were famous for their underground tunnel systems, and the bombs had been dropped in hopes of caving in and destroying a huge underground network of NVA tunnels that were said to occupy the Tong Le Chon area. In fact, the purpose of this patrol was to survey the bombed area and look for any tunnels the bombs had opened and seed them with powdered tear gas. They had found a tunnel system and a whole lot of pissed-off North Vietnamese soldiers. It was similar to opening a hornets' nest and not having enough bug spray with you.

Alex paused for a second on the edge of the crater and picked a direction to crawl. The instant he left the opening of the bomb crater, the jungle closed in around him. He stopped crawling five feet away from the edge of the crater and looked back over his shoulder and saw only a green curtain closing behind him. He would

have to be careful or risk getting lost and be in serious trouble. The battle was raging all around him. He could distinguish the M2 carbines from the AK-47's and tried crawling in the direction of the friendly fire. The jungle prevented him from seeing anything more than a few feet in front of his face. Alex wondered how the commandos could see a target to fire at and got his answer almost too quickly. His head and part of one shoulder broke through the jungle and he could see that he was in a small three-foot-wide tunnel cut out of the underbrush. Instinct, and the fact that the NVA gunner was changing drums in his RPD, saved his life. Alex ducked back by crawling backward and continued crawling backward for about five feet. The NVA gunner was an old soldier, and he fired a long burst about three feet back from the edge of the tunnel, hoping to hit the American soldier he saw sticking his head out in the fire lane.

A groan reached Alex from a spot to his left and he started crawling again. He ran into a warm body and quickly rigged it so that he could drag the wounded soldier between his arms and legs on the ground by the strap that went under the wounded man's back and arms and up and over his head. He could use his shoulder and neck muscles to lift the casualty a little bit off the ground when he crawled on all fours back toward the crater.

Mills reached for his weapons when Alex fell head-first into the crater on top of the man he was dragging. They both ended up in the muddy pool of water in the bottom of the hole. "Let me help you with him." Mills scooped up a handful of water to splash on the wounded soldier's face and tried stopping halfway through the act. The water drained out between his fingers. "This is a fucking NVA!"

Alex hadn't looked closely enough when he had picked up the wounded man. The mud covering the NVA's uniform had concealed the khaki cloth, and

the Oriental features were the same as their Nung commandos. It was a very easy mistake to make.

"Fuck it! Come on and help me with him." Mills had accepted the wounded NVA soldier as just another wounded man who needed help. "Cut his shirt away—it looks like he caught one in the gut."

Alex used the long-bladed medical scissors to cut through the wet shirt, and pulled back the cloth to reveal four neat holes in the NVA's abdomen. Pieces of undigested rice were oozing out of one of the bullet holes. "He took one in the stomach." Alex tilted him over on his side and saw that there were only two exit holes, which meant that two of the bullets had changed course inside the man's body. The prognosis for the man's survival was not good. "He's going to need surgery, and soon."

"Give him a shot of morphine and cover the wound." Mills handed Alex a Syrette with the plastic protective cap removed.

The sound of a single artillery round passing by overhead made both the medics duck instictively. Mills looked up at the jungle that allowed only a small portion of light to filter down from directly above the crater. "The lieutenant is fucking up! Artillery can't penetrate this jungle." He glanced over at Alex and added for the young man's sake, "The rounds hit the big trees and ricochet. You can end up having your own artillery land on your own men in this shit!" Mills picked up his CAR-15 from where he had laid it across one of the wounded commando's legs to keep it out of the mud. "I'm going to see if I can find the command section and find out if the lieutenant is still alive."

Alex injected the NVA soldier with the morphine and nodded his head in agreement. "You want me to stay here with the wounded?"

"Yeah—some of the platoon leaders know about this location and will be bringing their wounded back here, so be careful that you don't open up on them by

accident. But be *careful*—you hear?" Mills didn't want to leave the kid alone, but it was important for him to find out if the lieutenant had been killed, because he was the next-senior man on patrol and would have to take charge. He paused and looked back over his shoulder. "Keep your weapon close to you and *listen* for anyone crawling toward you. In this thick shit, you won't know who is who until they're on top of you." Mills disappeared into the jungle.

Alex looked around at the wounded CIDG commandos and the NVA soldier. The sides of the crater were covered with wounded and none of them could help him by pulling guard while he worked on the more seriously wounded. Alex tried separating the sounds of the battle from the softer sounds of the jungle and he tried tuning in to the slushy sound of someone crawling through the mud and undergrowth. For the first time since the fight had started, Alex felt very much alone and scared. He was alone, and in the middle of a firefight that could go either way. He kept telling himself that he was with a company of Chinese Nungs and they had *never* left a wounded man on a battlefield. The thought was consoling, and he busied himself by checking his supplies in his medical-aid kit.

The sound of the battle started dying down a little and Alex crawled up to the edge of the bomb crater to see if Mills was on his way back. A pair of Cobra gunships passed overhead and made a slow inspection of the area before leveling off and attacking a target a couple hundred meters north of the crater aid station. One of the wounded men screamed, and Alex drew away from the rim of the hole. He scrambled over to the dying commando and tried comforting the man who had lost both of his legs at the knees. The blood coming from the wounded was running down to the small pool of rainwater at the bottom of the bomb crater, turning the water a soft pink. Alex slipped down the side of the steep mud bank and rinsed out a

drive-on rag to clean the mud off the face of the dying commando. It was all he could think of to do.

Mills and another American flew over the edge of the crater and landed in the pool at the bottom. The newcomer, dressed in a tiger-striped camouflage suit, sprang to his feet and climbed back up the mud bank and opened fire down the closing path they had made.

"Motherfuck!" Mills backed up the soldier while he changed magazines in his weapon. He ducked just in time to miss the B-40 rocket that whistled over their heads and detonated in the side of a hardwood tree fifty feet away. Pieces of wood arched up in the air and rained down into the pool of pink water. "Alex! Grab your medical kit! We've got some work to do!"

Alex closed the flap on his kit and zipped it up. He could see his hands shaking. "Where are we going, Sarge?"

"Peters here"—he nodded at the other American—"has brought his SOG Hatchet Force to rendezvous with our company, and it looks like he brought an NVA company with him."

"Don't blame this shit on us!" Peters grinned at Alex and winked. "You're the ones who've wandered across the fucking border!"

"What border?" Alex was confused.

"It looks like the lieutenant's got us in Cambodia." A loud cracking from an A-6 light machine gun interrupted Mills. "Don't worry about that gun—it's one of ours. We brought an MG team back here with us to cover the aid station while we go patch up the American wounded with Peters."

"How many are there?" Alex started climbing back up the muddy side of the crater. "Any seriously wounded?"

Peters dug the toes of his boots in the mud up to their laces and reached the top before Alex. "Eleven wounded—I think two of them aren't going to make it. We've been fighting a rear-action fight since this

morning. Nothing can penetrate this fucking jungle! I've been up in II Corps and I Corps and I haven't seen anything thicker than this flatland shit!" Peters seemed extremely calm, considering all the explosions and gunfire going on around them. He grinned at Alex and winked again. The young medic's fear was written on his face. "Don't worry about all the noise. Bullets don't travel far in this thick shit. It sounds worse than it actually is. I'd say they have less than sixty men left."

Alex didn't say anything, but sixty men sounded like a lot of enemy soldiers to him. The control the Studies and Observation Group recon man was showing actually started to relax Alex, and he learned one of his first lessons in combat leadership: fear breeds fear and calm action breeds confidence.

The SOG leader led the way back through the jungle to where a small command post had been set up for the wounded. One of the RTO's was trying to stop the flow of blood from a hole the size of a half-dollar in one of the wounded American's arms. Alex eased him aside and looked at the bullet hole.

"Armor-piercing round—it went right through." The wounded man helped Alex inspect the gunshot. "I don't think it hit the artery."

"Good—it's clean. I'll put a pressure bandage on it and give you a shot of morphine."

"I'll pass on the drugs, Doc. Just in case I'm needed later on." The recon man patted his CAR-15, lying on the matted-down grass next to him.

"Fine." Alex bandaged the wound and moved on to the next man, who was in very bad shape. He had taken at least seven rounds and was fighting for his life after each breath he took. "Sergeant Mills, I've got to trake this man. He can't breathe properly." A tracheotomy would open an air hole directly to the man's windpipe.

Mills scurried over to where Alex was working on

the soldier and nodded in agreement after looking at the wounds. "Do it. I'm going with Peters to check our perimeter for wounded. The lieutenant says that we've just about sealed the area. He's moving the CP over to the high ground."

"What about these wounded?" Alex looked up from the man he was working on.

"They'll be safe here. We should be able to blast down a couple of those trees and bring in a Medevac as soon as the shooting dies down a little." Mills pointed back to the crater with the barrel of his weapon. "When you stablize these wounded, go back and start bringing the commandos here for evacuation."

Alex nodded and kept his attention on the man he was working on. The SOG medic had done a good job patching up most of the wounded recon men before he was killed.

"This your first patrol?" The recon man with the bullet through his arm spoke softly.

"Yeah—would you believe this shit!" Alex felt relaxed since the additional Americans had linked up with them. Normally, there were only two American Green Berets that would go out on patrol with a Civilian Irregular Defense Group—CIDG—company but the lieutenant was new in-country and so was Alex, so the captain had decided on a double team to break them in. Alex was glad for the small favor because he knew that if the lieutenant and he had run into the NVA alone, they would have been in very serious trouble. "How many Americans with your Hatchet Force?"

"Fifteen. We've only got seven assigned to the platoon, but we were attached a special All-American team of experts for a special mission." The young Green Beret looked around at the wounded. "Looks like most of us have been fucked up. We lucked out when we ran into your company. I didn't think CIDG were allowed to cross the border."

Alex searched the thick bamboo with his eyes and

tried listening for anyone approaching before answering the friendly recon man. "We didn't think we were in Cambodia either! This is some really bad stuff to orient yourself in." He was very good at locating himself on a map, but the miles of bamboo thickets mixed with giant jungle trees totally blocked out any major terrain features and you ended up having to orient yourself mostly through luck. If you could locate yourself on a map within a thousand meters, you were good, and it took months of practice to get that down to a hundred meters. "We tried calling in high-burst smoke and WP rounds to mark a spot for us to orient on, but we couldn't even see the rounds because of the bamboo overhead."

"It sounds like the NVA are pulling back." The wounded recon man lifted his CAR-15 and checked his magazine. "Shooting is dying down."

Alex lifted himself up into a half-crouch and agreed with the recon man's comment. There were only sporadic volleys of small-arms fire and an occasional rocket going off. "Would you mind keeping an eye on these wounded guys? I've got another bunch back over there in a bomb crater that I need to check on quickly."

"No problem, Doc. Go ahead and I'll tell your sarge where you're at when they come back here to cut out a landing zone."

"You sure you feel up to it? I can stay if you need me here." Alex zipped up his medical kit and looked directly at the wounded American.

"I feel great—just a minor flesh wound. You go." The recon man pushed his tiger-striped short-brimmed hat back a little on his head and a thick lock of bright red hair fell down on his forehead.

"You'd better tuck that back under your hat." Alex gave the recon man a wide smile. "It looks like a flag."

"Shit—just my luck to have been born with red hair—*bright* red hair." He took Alex's advice and

pulled his hat back down low over his forehead. The redhead recon man had an olive-drab triangular bandage tied around his head in order to cover the rest of his bright red hair.

"Why don't you cut it short?" Alex started crawling away toward the bomb crater.

"Shit! These locks get me lots of free pussy!" The recon man grinned. "You'd better hurry if there are more wounded back there."

Alex left the small clearing and crawled on his hands and knees through the thick bamboo. He was forced to stop a dozen times to free his gear. The firefight was just about over when he reached the bomb crater. Four more wounded had been brought to the safety of the defilade, and one of the Nung medics was working on them. Alex called a warning to alert the Nung that he was coming and slipped down into the familiar mud. He checked all of the wounded and saw that two of them had died from their wounds. The rest looked as if they would make it, if a Medevac arrived soon.

Alex busied himself checking the wounded Nungs and was just about ready to return to where the eleven American wounded were when he heard the sound of helicopters circling above their position, and then he saw one appear directly above the bomb crater. He stood up and waved with both arms to draw their attention. The crew chief leaned out of the open Medevac door and waved back down at Alex. There was a slight hesitation and then the chopper started desending slowly through the large hole in the overhead jungle that the two-thousand-pound bomb and its neighbors had made. It was a very close fit but the chopper pilot lowered his aircraft until the skids touched the edge of the crater.

The Nung medic helped Alex drag the wounded Nungs up to the edge of the crater and hand them to the waiting airborne medics, who laid them on the chopper floor. There wasn't enough time to strap them

into the cots, or even rig the stretchers to hold them. The pilot wanted to get all of the wounded from the crater in one trip so that he wouldn't have to make the very dangerous maneuver again.

The chopper lifted slowly back up through the trees and underbrush. A small bunch of bamboo sprang free from its cover and shredded itself in the rear rotor blade, nearly causing the pilot to lose control. Alex dropped down exhausted on the lip of the crater and looked up at the bottom of the chopper. The cool air created from the down wash felt good against his sweat-soaked uniform. He felt a strong sense of accomplishment knowing that the wounded Nungs were safe and had a chance of surviving the fight. The chopper continued climbing until it was a couple hundred feet above the trees and then the sound of the rotor blade changed and the aircraft disappeared from sight.

The loud sound of the chopper was replaced by the sound of explosions coming from the direction Alex had left the American wounded. He sighed and reached for his aid kit. They were blasting a landing zone to extract the rest of their wounded. Alex knew that Mills would need help, but his body refused to move. The effort he had expended hauling the wounded Nungs up the side of the crater had caught up with him and he needed to rest for a couple of minutes.

The Nung medic patted his thigh and spoke in broken English. "You good *bac-si*—very good American doctor!"

Alex smiled back at the Nung, and the drying mud on his face cracked and fell down in little pieces on the front of his fatigues. He was happy that the Nungs liked him and he knew that the Nung medics would spread the word to the other CIDG that he was a reliable medic in combat. "Let's go—many more wounded."

The Nung medic gave a curt nod and picked up his

kit to follow Alex through what was becoming a very familiar path through the bamboo thicket.

The sight that greeted Alex when he reached the small clearing where he had left the Americans at first was shocking and very confusing—and then it became terrifying. The redheaded recon man lay with his eyes open against a small mound of earth that propped him up. He had been bayoneted through the heart. Alex could see that there were shiny shell casings scattered around the dead Green Beret and that the man had put up a brief fight. He turned and saw that four NVA soldiers were caught in the bamboo on the opposite side of the clearing. Alex looked back at the recon man and noticed that his bright red hair was exposed— all of it—and then he saw where the NVA soldier had cut off the redhead's ears. His eyes moved slowly around the clearing, picking out the rest of the wounded Americans he had left. The NVA squad had bayoneted all of them before they disappeared back into the jungle.

Mills saw the look in Alex's eyes and hurried over to the young medic. "Where did you go?"

The voice seemed to be coming from inside a tin-lined tunnel. Alex blinked and kept staring at the dead Americans—eleven dead Americans—that had been his responsibility.

A sharp stinging sensation came from his face, and his eyes focused on Sergeant Mills. "What?"

"Where were you?"

"I went back to check on the Nungs"—Alex's eyes went back to the redhead recon man—"he said that he could guard them . . ."

"Fine! You did the right thing, Jaxson!"

Alex felt the stinging sensation again on his cheek and frowned. He couldn't understand why Mills was hitting him.

"Jaxson! Snap out of it! You did the right thing!" Mills could see that the young medic was slipping into

shock, and slapped him again. Alex's eyes focused. "I'm glad that you went back to check on the Nungs— they needed your attention more than these guys."

"I loaded the Nungs on a Medevac and then came here . . ."

"Great! You did good, Alex—*you did good!*"

"But I left . . ."

"No! Dammit—*no!* You did not leave them! What happened here could have happened to me or anyone else! Do you hear me! This could have happened to anyone!" Mills was nearly screaming in his attempt to reach Alex and break through the emotional barrier the junior medic was building.

Alex searched the faces of the recon men standing around the clearing and couldn't find the slightest hint of blame. His eyes locked with those of the Hatchet Force leader, and the man nodded slowly and mouthed, "You did the right thing." The sound of the arriving Medevac choppers prevented the words from reaching Alex's ears.

He reached up on the ice-covered black marble wall and ran the tips of his fingers over the grooves of the first man's name. He had made a special trip after his first major battle back to III Corps, C-team, in Bien Hoa to get the names of the eleven SOG recon men who had died during the fight. It had taken a lot of effort to find out their names, because the men had belonged to a supersecret operation headquartered in Saigon.

The ice-encrusted snow crunched under his boots as he walked slowly along the face of the wedge-shaped wall, stopping only to touch a name occasionally in the rows of names that listed the Vietnam dead. Someone had taped a picture of a loved one to the wall, and the ice storm had coated it. He passed it by and paused when he reached the name of the redhead. He smiled and recalled the man's bright red hair falling down over his forehead. At the time the redhead had seemed so much older and so much more experienced than he was, but now he realized the redhead had been just a young kid—no more than twenty years old—as he himself had been during the war.

A gust of arctic cold air hit him just when he reached the place on the wall where Sergeant Mills's name was carved. It reminded him of the slap on his face that Mills had given him, and he smiled again and angled away from the wall toward a brightly lit telephone booth.

The sides of the booth broke the cold wind blowing down the boulevard from the north. He shoved his rucksack against the door and leaned against the glass wall with the telephone receiver held up against his ear with his shoulder. The telephone at the other end of the line rang over a hundred times.

The automatic garage-door opener obeyed the command coming from the black Rolls-Royce moving slowly down the snow-covered street. All the evergreen trees lining the exclusive residential lanes were covered with Christmas lights.

"Dad! Hurry up!" The ten-year-old boy's voice was about ready to break from the excitement. The family's traditional present-opening ceremony always took place after midnight Mass.

"Robert! Now, don't get your father nervous! We're almost home!" The middle-aged woman smiled affectionately at her son sitting on the backseat. "The roads are so bad tonight, of all nights!"

"Daddy . . . I think Bobby is going to pee his pants if you don't hurry." The mature seventeen-year-old girl ran her hand through the hair on the back of her little brother's neck.

"I'm driving as fast as I can without going off the road." He looked back at the road through his rearview mirror and watched the headlights of the car following him wiggle back and forth on the freshly fallen snow. "I hope Alex can handle that car . . ."

"He's a very good driver, Sasha." The woman spoke automatically in defense of her handsome eldest son.

"I know . . . but I shouldn't have allowed him to drive the AC Cobra in this weather."

"Sasha! It wasn't snowing when we left for Mass." Mary chuckled under her breath at her husband's forgetfulness.

The middle-aged man turned off Lone Pine Road and entered the narrow lane that led up to the long driveway of the large estate. He reached up and pushed the button that opened the wrought-iron gates.

The rear door of the Rolls-Royce opened before the car came to a complete halt and the ten-year-old ran for the nearest bathroom.

Sasha smiled and patted Mary's leg. "I love the tradition of a Russian Orthodox Christmas Eve Mass, but the little ones are tortured when it ends up lasting over two hours."

"I know dear . . . but that's the price we must pay for being Russian, and the children might as well understand that when they're young." She patted her husband's arm.

The man parked his car and then looked back down the driveway for his eldest son. He saw the headlights turning up the driveway and sighed, relieved that his family was home safely.

"Dad! You're wanted on the phone!" The high-pitched adolescent voice of the ten-year-old reached him from the hall bathroom where the boy had taken the cordless telephone with him.

"Who would be calling us at this hour?" The mother's voice bordered on fear as she mentally reviewed the whereabouts of all her children.

"Maybe it's someone who wants to wish us a Merry Christmas." He took the telephone from his son's free hand sticking out the bathroom doorway and answered the waiting caller.

"Sash."

The single word released twenty years of memories flashing through the middle-aged millionaire's brain cells, back to the portion of his well-guarded subconscious memory that held the identity of the soft voice on the other end of the long-distance telephone line. The whole mental process had taken less than three seconds of real time, but had covered millions of thought miles.

"Alex?" The man walked away from the bathroom door and the sound coming from the flushing commode. "Is that you, Alex!"

There was a very long silence that was filled with static. Sash waved for his wife to fix him a drink from the bar and walked down the hallway into his private library, leaving the double French doors open behind him. "Alex, let me change telephones . . . these cordless inventions have too much static." He lifted the other telephone off its receiver before pushing the switch off on the cordless one. "Alex? Are you still there?"

"Yeah. You sound good." The voice quavered from the cold wind that blew in through the cracks in the telephone booth.

"Alex, is something wrong?" Sash was instantly alerted.

"I'm tired . . . real tired."

Sash took the crystal glass from Mary and smiled his thanks. "So what have you been up to? I haven't heard from you in . . . God! Eighteen? *Nineteen* years!"

"It's been *twenty* years, Sash." The statement wouldn't have made any sense to a listener, but Sash knew exactly what Alex was referring to. Alex continued, "In fact, tonight is the twentieth anniversary."

"The Battle of Tong Le Chon." Sash closed his eyes as a flood of violent scenes flashed in front of him. He had thought that those particular war experiences had been forgotten, but just the mention of the Special Forces camp had opened that sealed door. "Alex . . . are you okay?"

"Tired . . . real tired."

"Excuse me, sir. You must deposit an additional two dollars and twenty-five cents for three additional minutes." The metallic voice interrupted the two men.

"Sash, I've got to be going now. I just wanted to call and say good-bye."

"Wait! Alex . . . wait just a minute!" Sash knew something was very wrong. "Operator?"

"Yes, sir?"

"Will you transfer the billing for this call to my number?"

"Sir . . ."

"Please?"

"All right, sir . . . just a minute." A series of clicks filled the line and then the operator came back on. "Go ahead, sir, and have a Merry Christmas."

"Thank you." Sash sipped from his drink. "Alex? Are you still on the line?"

"Yes."

"Where are you calling from?"

"Washington, D.C."

"Washington? I thought you were living in New York."

"I was for a while, and then I decided to come to Washington to see the Vietnam Memorial." Alex inhaled a deep lungful of cold air before continuing, "Sash, do you remember Billy Mills?"

"Of course I do! He was the senior medic at Tong Le Chon!"

"Sorry . . . I thought you might have forgotten . . . it *has* been twenty years."

"Never!" Anger accented the word. Sash looked over at the head sticking in through the open French doors to the library and beckoned for his eldest son to

31

join him on the natural-colored steerhide sofa. "Hey, good buddy, I'd like for you to talk to your godson." Sash handed the telephone to his son.

"Uncle Alex?" The confident eighteen-year-old's voice spoke the words with powerful force.

The man at the other end of the line felt the tears flow from underneath his eyelids and swallowed before he trusted his voice to answer. "You *can't* be . . ."

The young Alex cut his godfather off in mid-sentence with a chuckled, "Sure am! You know I've received your birthday presents every year, but there never was a return address where I could send a thank-you note. I don't want you to think that I didn't care."

"I know that you did—it's just that I travel a lot." The older man bit his lower lip as he tried stopping its trembling.

"So when are you going to come and visit us?" The handsome young teenager grinned into the telephone. "Dad speaks of you often, and we're all dying to meet you."

The older Alex ignored the question. "Do you play football?"

"You've got to be kidding me, Uncle Alex! I'm a lacrosse man . . . *watch my lips* . . . la-crosse!"

A deep-throated laugh crossed the air waves, loud enough that Sash could hear it where he was sitting.

"What's so funny, Unc?" Alex frowned into the receiver.

"Who taught you that line about watching your lips?"

"Dad."

"Yeah? Well, tell your Dad that he's a W.D."

"What's a W.D.?" The teenager spoke into the telephone but looked at his father for an answer. Sash smiled and shrugged.

"Weak dick," the older Alex answered.

32

"Whoa! You're talking to the *stud* of Cranbrook High School." the younger Alex boasted.

"Who's a stud?"

Young Alex's head snapped around and his face turned red when he saw his mother standing in the doorway with a tray of Christmas snacks.

Sash bailed his son out. "We're talking about horses, dear."

"Oh . . . who's on the line?" Mary set the tray of homemade cookies on the coffee table—a sheet of thick glass supported by four antique Canada-goose decoys.

"Uncle Alex, Mom!" Young Alex smiled.

She looked over at her husband with a very worried expression. Sash waved her off and laughed. "It's all right, dear!" The words didn't remove the wrinkles around her eyes.

Young Alex changed back to his original question. "So, when are you coming to visit us, Unc?"

"I don't think that will be possible, Alex, but thanks anyway for the invitation."

"We've got plenty of room . . ."

"It's not that."

"Come on! We all would really love meeting you. A guy shouldn't have to grow up never having met his godfather."

"I'm tired."

"You're tired?" Young Alex frowned into the receiver. The comment didn't make any sense.

"Very."

Sash looked over at his son and joined his frown. He held out his hand for the telephone.

"Dad wants to talk to you . . . love you."

"What did you say?"

Young Alex's cheeks turned red. "I . . . I said that I love you . . . sorry."

"Don't be sorry. It's just that I haven't heard that phrase in quite a while. . . . I love you too, Alex."

33

Sash glanced over at his son and nodded toward the open French doors. Alex pulled them shut and took a seat in a high wingback chair across from his father. Sash's voice was somber when he spoke into the telephone. "All right, war buddy, what's going on?"

Alex rubbed his hand over his beard and blinked his eyes slowly. He could feel the cold penetrating the back of his military overcoat. He had been leaning against the glass wall of the telephone booth with the left side of his head resting against the storm-cooled glass. When he opened his eyes again, he could see the graffiti surrounding the front of the black pay telephone. FUCK YOU stood out from the rest of the words and initials. "I can't take another Christmas."

"Why?" The voice was commanding. Sash knew his war buddy was hurting.

"Do you remember what happened the morning after the NVA hit us and overran Tong Le Chon?"

Sash shook his head slowly from side to side, trying to figure out what Alex was driving at. "We cleaned up the mess?"

"No . . . Christmas cookies."

"*Christmas* cookies?" Sash's voice rose. "Alex, what in the hell are you talking about? Have you gone nuts on me?"

"Yeah . . . probably."

"Bullshit!" Sash adjusted his position on the couch and looked at his empty glass. "Alex, would you mind if I put you on the speakerphone?"

"Sure . . . go ahead."

"I'm in the library with my son . . . I'd just like to make a drink."

"Sure . . . make yourself comfortable."

Sash pushed the switch that transferred the conversation to the built-in speaker system in the telephone and replaced the receiver in its cradle. "Now, tell me this shit about Christmas cookies." Sash poured another glass of vodka from a crystal decanter.

34

"It sounds like you've done quite well for yourself, old buddy."

"The good Lord has blessed us, Alex. Do you remember when I told you my father had a small fresh-meat business that supported the family in Hamtramck?"

"Yeah, I do." He sounded pleased with himself at remembering that information.

"Well, when I returned from Vietnam, I got a few bank loans and expanded the business. We've done very well since then, and recently we've gone national with our line of fresh sausages and smoked summer sausage."

"Are you a millionaire yet, Sash?"

"Many times over, my friend." Sash didn't hesitate in answering his friend. They had talked openly to each other during the war and he didn't feel ashamed or apologetic about his answer .

"Good, if anyone deserves it, you do." Alex moved his cheek off the glass wall and looked over at a passing police car. The officer riding shotgun stared hard at him, trying to see if he was actually using the telephone or just occupying the booth to stay out of the winter wind.

Sash brought the conversation back on track. "Let's get back to your comment about the Christmas cookies."

"They flew in Christmas cookies and a complete Christmas dinner." The bearded Alex's voice lowered. "Don't you remember?"

"Yes."

The young Alex turned quickly away from watching the speakerphone to see his father's face. He had never heard that tone in his father's voice before.

"We sat on the side of the berm and ate—smoked ham, mashed potatoes . . . gravy! Remember the steam coming off the paper plates of food?"

Sash nodded. "We had been eating refried rice for almost a month . . . I remember."

"Yeah, buddy, yeah, so do I." Alex swallowed.

"Those were tough times."

"I can't get rid of them, Sash!" The words carried many different meanings with them over the telephone. Sash could feel his war buddy's pain. Alex sucked in a lungful of air and the sound filled the expensively decorated library in Bloomfield Hills. "*Every* fucking time I hear a Christmas song or see a fucking Santa Claus . . . and *especially* see Christmas cookies . . . I see all of those dead bodies again and *again*! Every fucking Christmas since Tong Le Chon!"

Sash raised his glass to his lips and drained it. He *had* forgotten.

"We sat there on the side of that fighting berm and laughed and ate Christmas dinner . . . surrounded by all of that death." A sob caught in the middle-aged warrior's throat and he had to stop talking and swallow. "Oh, Sash . . . *remember*?"

Sash was remembering. He didn't want to, but he was remembering the battle all over again.

The North Vietnamese had attacked the Special Forces camp with a regiment-size unit and the fighting had been extremely fierce during the hours of darkness on the night before Christmas. A North Vietnamese company had penetrated the northern barbed-wire defenses and Alex had been trapped on the berm as he tried administering first aid to the wounded American infantrymen who had been assigned to reinforce the under-strength Green Beret camp on the Cambodian border. A large fighting team of the elite NVA soldiers had destroyed the key fighting bunker on the north berm and had started bayoneting the wounded Americans that had been placed behind the bunker for protection during the battle. Alex had grabbed a machete that had been sticking out of the berm mud next to the bunker and had gone berserk.

Sash sighed as his mind raced over the battle thoughts. He drained the iced-down vodka from his glass and looked over at his eldest son. He could see love and support coming from the young man, and tried smiling. His thoughts slipped back to Tong Le Chon and his son's godfather. Alex had been surrounded by the NVA and Sasha had used his M-60 machine gun to keep the enemy from totally overwhelming his war buddy, but the distance and the battle raging in the camp between them had prevented him from joining Alex on the berm.

"I've relived that damn battle every year during Christmas, for twenty years." Alex's voice took on a tone of defeat.

Sash responded, "Buddy, we've all had to live with that shit." He had slipped back into a GI language. "Who the fuck cares?"

"Maybe a war buddy would care." Alex's words hit home.

"Yeah . . . maybe an old war buddy might." Sash glanced at the vodka decanter and decided he needed another one.

The voice coming over the speakerphone followed him to his bar. "Sash, I can still *see* those hacked-apart bodies lying in front of us as we sat there eating Christmas dinner!"

"Alex! If you hadn't done what you did . . ." He looked at his son, trying to temper the conversation for the young man's sake, and decided that maybe the truth would be a good lesson for the teenager: ". . . they would have bayoneted all of our wounded."

"I know that, Sash! But I can still *see* those damn bodies and I can't get Billy Mills out of my mind for more than a couple of minutes! It's been twenty fucking years!"

"Billy Mills did what you or I would have done if we had been in his place and thought of it." Sash skirted the rest of the answer.

"Bullshit!" The older Alex squeezed the tears out of his eyes and became angry with himself for allowing his emotions to show. "I wouldn't have had the guts to set myself on fire and run over to the fuel pods."

"Alex! He didn't set *himself* on fire. I saw what happened and I swear to you that he was torched by an NVA flamethrower. Maybe he knew there wasn't any hope for himself and then stumbled over to the fuel pods; Alex, nobody knows for sure, but whatever the reasoning, he saved all of our lives by doing it."

"Are you *sure*?" Alex's voice was pleading and filled with agony.

"I swear it!" Sash closed his eyes and rested his head back against the cool leather couch. He spoke with his eyes still closed, and for the first time he smelled the microwaved Christmas cookies his wife had placed on the coffee table in front of him. A flood of memories was released. "Shit!"

"What's wrong?" Alex's voice was hesitant. His eyes were on the returning Washington, D.C., police cruiser.

"I remember the Christmas cookies now . . ."

"Hold on a second, buddy, I've got some company." Alex held the telephone against his chest but Sash and his son could hear him speaking to the policeman. "Is there a problem, officer?"

"Might be . . . what in the hell are you doing in this phone booth?"

"Talking to a friend."

"Yeah, sure . . . all right, you fucking bum! Get your ass out of there and let decent people use the booth."

"It's two in the morning . . . I don't think any *decent* people are out on the streets in this weather, officer."

"Don't get smart-mouthed with me, you fucking burnout!"

Sash heard the officer yelling and the booth door open. He yelled over his speakerphone. "Alex! *Alex!* Are you still there?"

The police officer stopped when he heard the voice coming over the line. "You *are* talking to someone."

"I told you that, *officer*."

"Sorry, I thought you were faking it so that you could stay in the telephone booth."

"Would it have made a difference if I were?" Alex rubbed his right index finger gently up and down the warm metal trigger on his concealed submachine gun.

"We can't allow bums to take over the telephone booths at night. Decent people are afraid to use them."

"Merry Christmas, officer." Alex nodded for him to close the booth door again and lifted the telephone back to his ear. "Sorry about the interruption . . ."

Sash had been listening to the conversation and had pieced together quite a bit of information. It was obvious, even to young Alex, that the old soldier was down on his luck. Elizabeth, his daughter, and Bobby had joined them in the library, followed by his wife carrying a wrapped present for each of them to open. Bobby was overtired and Mary wanted Sash to get off the telephone and conduct the small family ceremony. Sash waved for them to get started unwrapping the presents.

"Sash!" Mary tried giving him one of her severest looks but was overruled by her husband's glare.

"Was that your wife?" came over the speakerphone. "Am I interrupting something?"

"No!" Young Alex spoke up, and frowned at his mother, who had missed the whole telephone conversation and hadn't a clue what was going on. "My little brother is getting anxious to open his present. We have a family tradition where we get to choose one present from under the Christmas tree that we can open on Christmas Eve after midnight Mass."

"I'd better go . . ."

"No, Uncle Alex! It would be fun if you would join us over the telephone." Young Alex looked over at his father for support.

"Yes, stay with us, Alex . . . it would be fun for the kids and I would enjoy it very much too." Sash didn't give him a chance to refuse. "You're first, Bobby."

The sound of wrapping paper being torn off a very large package filled the room, followed by a high-pitched adolescent's voice: "Just what I always wanted! How did you and Dad know, Mom?"

"It wasn't hard, Bobby. You gave us enough clues." The woman's soft voice countered the boy's.

"It's beautiful, Dad!" Bobby hugged his father and then ran over and hugged his mother.

"Well, tell Uncle Alex what you got, stupid!" Elizabeth shook her head over her little brother's conduct.

"It's a silver dirt bike with racing wheels and . . . and . . . everything on it!"

"It sounds really nice, Bobby." Alex smiled into the telephone. He was enjoying himself.

"You're next, Beth." Sash smiled at his daughter. "We're going according to age this time."

Young Alex left the room and returned a minute later carrying a small package. He took his seat again and waited until his mother had opened her selected gift, which was from Bobby. It seemed that she always picked the gift from under the tree that meant the most to the giver and always selected the homemade gifts first.

"Who's younger, Dad, you or Uncle Alex?" Young Alex smiled over at his father.

"Well . . . your uncle is, I believe." Sash chuckled. "How old are you, Alex?"

"Thirty-eight."

"You're younger!"

"I'm going to open your present for you, Uncle Alex." The man's godson carried the package near the speakerphone and opened it slowly. It was the gift he had bought for his dad. Sash smiled.

Elizabeth held her hands up to her mouth and sighed. "Oh, it's gorgeous!"

40

"Well? What is it?" The voice over the speaker sounded cautious.

"A Gucci wristwatch!" Elizabeth described the watch in detail. "It has a black lizard band and a black face with gold trim and gold hour and minute hands and a tiny 'Gucci' spelled out on the face. It's really nice!"

Alex spoke up over his sister's chatter. "Now you'll have to come and visit with us, Uncle Alex. So that you can pick up your watch."

"Thanks for the gift . . . I wish that I could send all of you something over the telephone."

Sash sat in his comfortable seat and thought what his friend must look like on the other end of the line if the police officer had mistaken him for a bum. "Maybe next Christmas, buddy."

"Yeah, maybe . . ."

"All right, kids! Off to bed now!" Mary reinforced her command by moving her hands toward the door.

"Good night, Uncle Alex." Elizabeth yawned and left the library after kissing her father on the cheek.

Alex followed suit and waved at the speakerphone. " 'Night Uncle Alex . . . visit us soon."

" 'Night, Godson, and Merry Christmas." The middle-aged man took in a lungful of cold air.

"Leave Bobby here, Mary, and I'll bring him up to bed with me. I want to talk to Alex alone for a couple of minutes." Sash brushed his son's hair out of his eyes and rested his hand on the boy's side. Bobby had curled up on the couch next to him and had fallen asleep, using Sash's lap for a pillow.

"All right." She removed a small lap blanket from the arm of a reading chair and covered Bobby with it before departing. She paused in the doorway and spoke to the speaker. "Merry Christmas, Alexander."

"Thank you, Mary . . . Merry Christmas."

Sash waited until his wife was gone before speaking to his friend. "Thanks for sharing part of Christmas

41

Eve with us. You've made this a very special night for me."

"She never has liked me, has she?"

"She doesn't understand, Alex. I don't think *any* woman can understand what happens on the battlefield —oh, I think some of them try, but it's too much for them so they get jealous, especially over war buddies. She's a very good woman, Alex, and I couldn't have asked for a better wife and mother for the kids. She just senses how close we are and that threatens her."

"Yeah, I think that from the very first time two cavemen chucked rocks at an enemy, women were jealous over war buddies." Alex adjusted the sling under his overcoat and rubbed his shoulder where it had dug in. "War has a way of cementing people together in a *mental* sort of way."

"Alex . . . you've got to beat this thing that's kicking your ass." Sash decided that he would attack directly now that the room was empty and Bobby was sleeping. He ran his hand along his son's side and stopped when he felt the boy's chest moving up and down slowly as the child slept deeply. Sash knew that he had been blessed and spared a great deal of misery. He glanced up at the Russian Orthodox crucifix on the wall and felt the warmth of Christmas.

"It's too late for that, Sash. I'm wired."

"Wired?"

"Yeah, twenty sticks of dynamite around my waist, one stick for every fucking year since Tong Le Chon, and I've got my CAR-15 . . . How about that shit! I shipped it back to the States piece by piece and there's no problem buying 5.56 ammo nowadays."

"Alex . . ."

"Sorry, buddy . . . it's over for me, but all of those *hippie* motherfuckers are going to know that I was here before I take myself out!"

Sash was shocked over the instant turn in the conversation, but somehow he had been expecting it. All during the telephone call he had sensed that something was wrong. "Alex, you're not going to suicide! That's dumb! Listen to me! Buddy, God knows, I'm rich enough! I'll get you the very best help there is . . . God! Alex . . . don't do this to me and to your godson . . . man, that boy has grown up loving you. He's heard me talk about you all the time and idolizes the ground you walk on. Not ever having met you makes it even more important that you don't go out this way. It would destroy him."

Alex had heard everything Sash had said, but he continued, "You know those hippie bastards *spit* on us as we walked down the street wearing our uniforms and now they're wearing three-piece corporate uniforms and making big bucks, while the Vietnam vets are fucking trying to hold their brains together!"

"I know that it's not fair, Alex . . . but you can't let them win the last battle! If you suicide, they win!" Sash looked over at the decanter of vodka on his open bar and desperately wanted another refill, but couldn't move with his son sleeping against him. He decided that the warmth coming from his youngest son was more comforting than the booze in the bottle and looked back over at the speakerphone.

"*They* ain't going to *win* the last battle. We lost one hundred and forty-three men at Tong Le Chon . . . I'm going to take one hundred and forty-three hippie motherfuckers with me when I go out!" Alex's voice was low and menacing.

Sash knew that Alex was capable of doing what he wanted. "Alex! You were trained to *save* lives. You were the best medic Special Forces ever trained! You know that!" Alex had graduated first in every phase of the long fifty-four weeks of Special Forces medical training, including the extremely difficult Dog Lab.

"They gave me a fucking medal for *killing* NVA, not saving lives, Sash!"

43

"We both know that you saved as many lives at Tong Le Chon as you took."

"But what did they give me the Distinguished Service Cross for? Saving lives or killing?"

"Both!"

"I called to say good-bye. You've been a good friend and I owe you."

Sash could tell by the tone of Alex's voice that he was about ready to hang up. "Alex . . . why take out a hundred and forty-three people with you? How can you *know* that they all were hippies during the war?"

"Random sample . . . let's call it a representative sample of humanity." Alex looked out at the blowing snow. "I'm going to do it over in Lafayette Park, across from the White House. They're going to have a pro-abortion demonstration there on Christmas morning . . . I figure that the only ones that will go with me will be ex-hippies, queers, and drug dealers. Hey, Sash! I'll be doing the country a fucking favor!"

"Alex! That's wrong!"

"Wrong? We fought that fucking war and that was *wrong*! We should have herded those fucking worthless hippies on ships and sent *them* over there and watched how long their asses would have lasted!" Alex was on a roll. "Wrong! They're having a fucking demonstration tomorrow . . . sorry, make that *this* morning . . . Christmas Day . . . a fucking demonstration for their *constitutional right* to murder their own babies! And they call *us* butchers!"

"Abortion is *wrong*, Alex. I agree with you, but let Reagan handle the politicians. He's the best President this country has ever had and the good Lord will use him to change that horrible law!"

"Sash, how can you believe like you do. A good God would never have allowed for all of this to go on . . . Christmas cookies with happy smiling Santa Claus faces . . . and all of that death surrounding them . . .

44

Christmas cookies." Alex's voice lowered as he slipped off in personal thoughts.

Sash felt the cold glass being put in his hand and looked up to see his eldest son standing next to the couch wearing his bathrobe and slippers. Sash nodded his thanks and took a long sip from the glass of vodka and ice. Alex took a seat next to his father on the couch and rested his arm over the man's shoulders. He could see that his dad was hurting.

A couple of minutes of silence went by before Alex's voice came back on the speaker. "It would only be right, Sash . . . one hundred and forty-three of them in exchange for the *good* men who died at Tong Le Chon." There was a pause, and Alex added, "Maybe I should add the North Vietnamese KIA's. They had five hundred and . . . and what? Fifty men die in that battle?

"Buddy, remember how happy we were to have survived that fight? Remember?" Sash felt the helplessness and frustration over the miles that separated him from Alex. He wished that he was there so that he could try to stop his friend from committing a horrible massacre. He felt his son's hand squeeze his shoulder and gained strength from the act to continue. "When we ate that Christmas dinner on the berm, we were happy to have just *survived*!" Sash inhaled a deep emotional breath. "Alex . . . I don't want to lose you, not now, not after all these years, buddy."

There was a long pause on the line.

Sash added to his statement. "Alex, what if just one . . . just one of those women demonstrating for pro-abortion brings one of her kids . . . a kid like Alex or Bobby or Beth . . . man, that would be so wrong, taking them out for something their asshole mothers are doing . . . Alex, you can't let that happen." Sash had hit home. Alex hadn't thought about kids being at a pro-abortion demonstration, but it was possible.

"Thanks, buddy . . . I'll think about it." Alex spoke very softly into the receiver.

"Alex, *please* . . . for me." Sash felt the tears running down his cheeks and he didn't care if his son saw them. "Promise me!"

"I promise you that I won't take out any kids with me. I'll promise that much. . . . Merry Christmas . . . buddy."

A dial tone filled the telephone line.

Young Alex used his thumbs to wipe the tears off his father's cheeks. "It's okay, Dad—you did your best."

Sash nodded his head slowly and cried harder.

CHAPTER TWO

✪✪✪✪✪✪✪✪✪✪✪✪✪✪✪✪✪

FROM OUT OF THE GHETTO

Alex pulled his collar together around his neck and lowered his chin as he stepped out of the telephone booth into the cold night air. The first blast of arctic air sucked all of the warmth off his bare skin, and he shivered. He leaned forward into the wind and walked back across the street to the deserted Vietnam War Memorial. A small portion from his camouflaged poncho liner was sticking out from under the white layer of snow. He reached down with one hand and pulled the tropical blanket free. The rubberized poncho, attached to the liner, had frozen and the loose ends cracked loudly in the strong wind, sending a cloud of dry powdered snow racing on the wind to the face of the black marble name stone where a mini-thermal updraft dispersed the particles.

Alex crossed his legs and dropped down on the frozen ground as he wrapped the liner around his shoulders and tucked the ends in under his buttocks. He ignored the cold and rested his eyes at the base of the black marble wall where he had laid his Distinguished Service Cross. Slowly his eyes crept up the long row of names and stopped when they reached the eighth name from the top. He was too far away to read what was carved in the stone, but there was no need for him to get closer because he knew the name by heart and where it was positioned on the wall among fifty thousand more names. He blocked out the thoughts that were trying to enter his rational mind. It was too late for rational thinking. Twenty years of suffering was enough for any man. He closed his eyes and fought harder not to think about Sasha and the telephone call. It had been stupid calling his old war buddy and had made it even worse. He had planned everything so carefully, so very carefully, and then he weakened and decided to call Sash.

Alex opened his eyes and stared hard at the wall. He ground his teeth and thought about the beginning, twenty-two years earlier in New York City.

He saw her coming up out of the subway. She was leaning against the railing for support. She was only twenty-nine years old, but looked forty. Alex let go of the window frame and dropped back down on his cot. His room overlooked the street and the subway entrance. He pulled his pillow over his head and tried shutting out the world.

The door to the apartment opened and then he heard five muffled footsteps before the knock on his bedroom door. "Alex? Alex, are you ready yet?"

He didn't answer.

The door opened. "Alex! Get your ass out of that bed!"

He felt his sheet being torn back and the pillow coming off his face. He held on to the pillow.

"Alex! Stop screwing around . . . damn you! You're going to be late!" She pulled harder.

Alex fought to keep the pillow covering his face so that the bright light of reality couldn't force him to look back outside at the real world going on around him. He would rather dream.

"All right, damn you! You want your fucking pillow!" She stopped tugging.

Alex smiled under the soft security of his pillow. He had won.

She straddled his chest in a quick maneuver and pressed down on the feather pillow, cutting off his air supply. Alex tried arching his back to buck her off, but he reacted too late. She was firmly seated.

"You want to hide under this fucking thing?" She increased the pressure. "Fine! Then fucking die!"

Alex struggled to shove her off, but failed to even budge her. He started to panic. His sister had gone crazy on him. Keena had finally lost it and was going to kill him. He felt dizzy and stopped struggling.

The pillow was lifted off his face and the sweet odor coming up from the street through his open window filled his nose. He sucked in a dozen deep lungfuls of great New York air before he could speak. "You fucking bitch! You damn near killed me!"

"Get your jeans on and move that cute ass of yours! We have less than an hour to get over to the Army recruiter's office."

"I decided that I don't want to go." Alex coughed and looked out the window.

She had looked tired walking up the subway steps, but anger replaced her worn muscles with generations of spirit strength. She grabbed for Alex and caught the waistband of his Jockey shorts.

"Keena! Stop pulling or you'll tear my briefs!" Alex slipped off the bed toward her.

"I said get dressed!" She kept a firm grip on his shorts.

"All right! Let go!" Alex glared at her. "Let go or you're going to see something so damn *big* it will ruin your sex life!"

"Oh, shit!" Keena released her hold. "Remember, stud-o, I was the one who changed your diapers . . . and there ain't *that* much down there!" She smiled, knowing that she was lying through her teeth.

Alex slipped on his Levi's and opened the top drawer of the dresser he shared with two of his sisters and pulled out a clean T-shirt.

"Aren't you going to wash?" Keena spat the words at him.

"What for?" Alex shrugged his shoulders.

"Brush your teeth, at least! Damn! Your breath will kill the fucking dentist!"

"I have to see a dentist?"

"Yes, asshole!" She shook her head. "That's what an induction physical is all about!"

"I ain't going!"

Keena caught Alex before he could reach the bathroom and lock the door on her. She got him in a headlock and dragged him over to the mirror on the wall above the sink. "Listen to me, boy!"

Alex tried breaking free, but his sister held him firmly and started cutting off his air supply again.

"I'm not fucking around with you anymore! Look!" She kept her left arm around his neck and grabbed the front locks of his hair. She forced him to look at his reflection in the mirror. "What do you see?"

Alex stared at his own face and then focused in on his sister's face behind his in the reflection. "What do you want me to see?"

Keena took a second to compare her face to her half-brother's. She had the thick lips and wide nose of her father. Her hair was worn in a popular Afro style. The only thing that matched her half-brother's face was her eyes; they both had sparkling emerald-green eyes. "You dumb fuck! Can't you *see*?"

"See what?" Alex was getting angry.

Keena released her grip on him but kept her body pressing against his so that he would have to stay in front of the mirror. She gently brushed his cheek with her fingertips. "You're a dipshit, Alex . . . a real airhead-dipshit!" The tone of her voice was affectionate. "You really don't see, do you?"

"What?" He tried frowning at his reflection in the mirror.

Keena laughed over his shoulder. She brushed her

fingers through his red-blond hair. "Look it . . . your hair has every damn color known to man! If someone could figure out a way to put that in a bottle, they'd be millionaires! I know that women would pay anything to have hair coloring like yours."

"Yeah, well, that's their fucking tough luck!"

"Mother says that your father was a Danish sailor she met down in Hell's Kitchen."

Alex shrugged his shoulders and used one of his sister's brushes to comb his hair.

"You don't care, do you?"

"Care about what?"

"Who your father is."

"No, not really. He didn't give a fuck . . ." Alex smiled to himself and then started combing his hair again. ". . . well, he did give *one* fuck, didn't he?"

The hurt showed in Keena's eyes.

"Sorry, Sis." Alex turned around to face her. "I'm here and that's all that matters. How I got here really doesn't make a difference to me."

Keena nodded in agreement. There were five kids in their family and all five of them came from different fathers. She was a mulatto. Only the youngest girl didn't know that their mother was a hooker and worked the docks, even now when she was well past fifty and had borne five children out of wedlock.

"Keena . . ." Alex smiled a wide grin at his sister, who was more his mother than his mother was. "I don't think I should show up at the Army recruiter's office. The military isn't what I want."

"What *do* you want, Alex?"

"I want to be a doctor."

"Not that shit again, Alex!" Keena felt the old frustration boiling up inside her again. She had failed him, and it hurt. Alex had done his part and had received straight A's throughout high school, but she just couldn't make enough money to get him into college. Every time she had saved a few dollars, something would come up with one of the other kids and she would have to spend it. Alex would be going to college now, instead of the Army, if she had worked harder.

Alex saw the hurt in his sister's eyes and knew what she was thinking. He reached over and wrapped her in his arms a second before the tears came.

"Oh, Alex . . . I tried . . . really tried!" Keena cried.

"I know, and I'm sorry that I'm being such a horse's ass this morning."

Keena pushed him away and wiped her nose with the back of her hand. "If there was another way, *any* other way, but there just isn't." Keena motioned for Alex to look back at his reflection in the mirror. "Look at yourself." She laid her hand gently on his shoulder. "I don't think that you really *see*, but you're one damn fine-looking young man."

Alex blushed. "Sis . . ."

"No! You are!" She turned him around so that she could look directly into his eyes. "How long do you think you could last down there on those streets?"

"I've made it for seventeen years so far."

"Right! With *me* laying the word that anyone fucking with you is one dead motherfucker!" Keena hissed out the words. Alex knew that his sister had been sleeping with the leader of the most powerful gang in the city and the only reason she had put up with the man was to gain protection for him. "Once my *friendship* is over with Raul, you're prime—and I mean *prime*—meat for every pimp in the borough."

"Keena! I'm not that kind of guy!" Alex was hurt by what his own sister was implying.

"Alex . . . oh, Alex . . . if only you had a choice." Keena patted her little brother's cheek. "You have to join the Army. It's your only escape from this shit life! And *our* only hope of ever getting out of here. Alex, if you can't make it, none of your sisters can."

Alex nodded. Keena was making good sense and he knew it. If he stayed in New York, it would be only a matter of time before he got into selling drugs or working as a gigolo—or worse. He looked back in the mirror at his reflection and rubbed his naturally tan cheek. "Do you think I have some black blood in me?"

Keena started laughing and slapped his rear. "God only knows."

"Let's go or we'll miss my sub." Alex nodded toward the door.

"Where are the girls?" Keena looked into the kitchen as they passed it.

"Over at Mrs. Goldstein's, like you told me."

"Did you pay her in advance?"

Alex turned the doornob and opened the door a crack. "Yes."

"I told you not to!" Keena opened her purse and removed a hidden twenty-dollar bill she kept in the lining for emergencies.

"No!" Alex pushed the door closed. "I don't want your money. Once I'm in the Army, I can make do. After all, they'll feed me and put a roof over my head."

"You'll need a little something . . ." She tried forcing the money into his closed hand.

"No!" Alex opened the door and started to leave.

"Wait, Alex . . . wait a minute." Keena's voice was very soft. "Close the door for a second."

Alex obeyed and looked back at her, puzzled. She reached up and wrapped her arms around his neck and gave him a long kiss and then wiped the lipstick off with her fingers. "I just wanted to give you a good-bye kiss in private before we left, and I want to tell you how much this old nigger bitch loves you."

Alex blinked back the tears and left the apartment ahead of his sister. He took the steps four at a time out to the street and landed at the base of the stoop two floors ahead of Keena. He waited on the sidewalk for her to catch up to him and then whirled around to face her. "Keena, I want you to promise me one thing before I leave for the Army."

"Sure, Alex . . . anything."

"Don't you ever call yourself a nigger bitch again . . . ever! You're not a nigger—you're one of the smartest people I have ever met. I know why you quit school . . . and as for being a bitch—that'll never happen!"

Keena stared at her handsome little brother and felt as if her heart was going to burst from the love she felt for him. "I promise . . . just for you, little brother."

"Let's go see the Man!" Alex pulled his folded bandanna out of his back pocket and tied it around his forehead.

Keena shook her head and grinned. The bandanna wasn't Alex. She knew that he wore the red railroad handkerchief because all the Puerto Rican kids who weren't members of a Latino gang wore them. Not to have worn a headband bandanna and not have been a member of a gang would have been too much for any of the street kids. Alex would never have made it to school, let alone survived through a whole day.

Alex stepped into the subway car and made room for Keena on one of the nearby seats. He stood and held on to the railing running the full length of the ceiling.

Keena took the seat and watched her younger brother sway as the subway car started moving along the underground rails. She took her time inspecting him with her eyes. Alex was a little bit too thin, but had a solid frame. He looked good in Levi's and usually drew stares from women and girls his own age. Keena rested her eyes on his face and wondered if he had ever been laid. He was seventeen and almost all of the kids in their ghetto had sex before they reached fourteen, but she wasn't sure about Alex. She knew that if one of the local girls had seduced him, it hadn't occurred very often. Alex had worked hard for the local pharmacist since he turned twelve. He had started at the drugstore as a drug runner. Alex had made a reputation for himself, delivering legal prescription drugs to old shut-ins. In a normal neighborhood the task would have been an easy one, but in the ghetto the runner usually got mugged and the drugs were resold for ten times their value. Alex had been so good at outsmarting the older boys that senior citizens would ask for him by name.

Keena smiled.

"What's so funny?" Alex smiled back at the woman who was more of a mother to him than his mother.

"Just feeling real proud of you."

Alex blushed and looked around to see if anyone had overheard their conversation. "Yeah, thanks, Sis, but a lot of guys are joining up right now."

"I know, but I wasn't feeling proud about that."

"What, then?"

"You in general." Keena's face took on a serious look. "I want you to remember what we talked about."

Alex nodded.

"Take anything but the infantry, if they give you a choice." Keena looked worried. She had heard stories about minority-group men being shoved into the infantry and then forced into battle.

"I'm going to try to get in the medics. The recruiting sergeant said that my scores were high enough for me to pick anything I wanted."

Keena nodded and stood up. They had left the last stop before the one that was nearest to the induction center. "I'm going to stay on the car . . . you don't need a sister tagging along. They might make fun of you, and then I'd have to kick some ass."

Alex grinned and nodded. "Thanks, Sis . . . I'll write."

" 'Bye, Alex. Remember, this old nig . . . *girl* loves you."

Alex paused in the open doorway to the subway car and winked. "I'll write as soon as I can . . . and send you whatever I can afford out of my pay."

The doors closed impersonally behind the Army recruit.

"Jaxson! . . ."

"Here."

"Jackson, Henry!"

"Yeah."

"Sanchez!"

There was no answer.

"Sanchez!" The medical sergeant looked up from the clipboard at the four Puerto Ricans standing together in the back of the reception hall.

"Do you mean me, man?"

"Is your name Sanchez?"

"Yes."

"I mean you." The sergeant smiled out of the corner of his mouth. He couldn't wait until tomorrow when they had all sworn in and had become *legal* members of the United States Army. "Martinez!"

"Here, man."

"Costello."

"Ugh."

"Lopez."

"Here, *sir*!"

The four Puerto Ricans all started laughing at the sergeant.

"Get off the man's case. He's only trying to do his job." Alex spoke before he had thought the situation through.

"Well-well-well! What in the fuck do we have here?" Sanchez slipped into his street voice.

"That's enough!" The sergeant slapped his clipboard against his thigh. "You'll have your fill of fighting once you get your asses to Vietnam!"

Sanchez pointed at Alex. "Later, man . . . *later*!"

"You"—the sergeant pointed at Alex—"lead these men to the dressing room, and I want all of you to strip down to your briefs; no socks and no T-shirts."

"What if I'm not wearing any underwear, *man!*" Sanchez hiked up his trousers.

"Then you'll be walking down the halls naked." The sergeant sneered. He was hoping that the wise-ass was telling the truth.

"Sorry, man! I wear boxers." Sanchez rib-punched his buddy. "I need room for my *stuff.*"

Alex looked down the hallway and saw a sign hanging over a door: "Station One," and under it in large block letters: "START HERE." "Let's go." He didn't wait for the four street hoods to follow him, but started walking over to the open entrance.

The sergeant watched the hoods strut slowly to the dressing room and felt bad about assigning the smaller kid as their group leader for their induction physical. He knew that he had set the kid up for a very tough day.

Alex was already undressed to his shorts and had his gym bag and clothes locked in one of the lockers when the small gang entered the room. The recruiter had told him to bring a lock with him for the induction physical and he had spent his last three dollars on the Master lock. The key hung around his neck on a thin fake silver chain.

"Hey, man! Let me have your lock!" Sanchez stopped inches in front of Alex's face. He was short for his age, but was still an inch taller than Alex.

"Sorry, man." Alex stared the hood down. "If you have any valuables, I'll put them in my locker for you, but I'm keeping the key."

"Fuck you, man!"

Alex shrugged and tried bluffing his way. He felt very vulnerable standing in front of the four punks wearing only his Jockey shorts.

"What colors you with, man!" Lopez asked the question. He wanted to make sure they weren't going to beat someone's ass who was a member of a friendly gang.

Alex knew that he was going to get his ass kicked regardless of how he answered the question, so he told the truth. "None."

"Man! You live in the burrello and you don't wear colors?" Costello was shocked that anyone would be so damn dumb.

"I don't live there. I'm from downtown." Alex felt his face blush. He was embarrassed to tell them that he wasn't a Puerto Rican like they thought he was; it would only make matters even worse than they were.

"We're Aztecas." Sanchez spoke the gang's name with pride. "We didn't wear our colors here because they said we'd get in a lot of trouble and not be allowed to join the Army."

"Why would you want to join the Army anyway?" Alex tried smiling as he asked the question.

Sanchez started laughing and was joined by the other three hoods. "Because, man, we are *wanted* by the law, man, for . . . let's say a misunderstanding about a Black Lord's, disappearance, if you know what I mean?"

Alex nodded. He could guess what had happened.

"I want your locker key, *man!*" Sanchez's face contorted into his best hate mask.

"I'll wait for you outside." Alex stepped over the bolted-down bench and tried walking past Costello and Martinez to the doorway.

"Grab that punk!" Sanchez barked the order and his flunkies obeyed.

"The sergeant is just outside that door, Sanchez." Alex tried bluffing his way again. He remained calm.

"Fuck you, asshole!" Sanchez sneered. "I saw him going back into the office before we came in here." Sanchez pointed to the bench. "Put his skinny ass down there on his back!" The three hoods obeyed their leader and shoved Alex down on the worn wooden bench. Alex kicked Lopez in the chest and the small punk fell backward and hit the row of lockers, tripped, and fell down on the gray-painted floor.

"You're dumb, man . . . real fucking dumb!" Sanchez balled his fist, ready to bury it in Alex's stomach.

"Wait!" Lopez was looking under the wooden bench. "Get me that Coke cup!" He pointed over to an empty sixteen-ounce cup someone had left on the bench.

"What in the fuck are you doing, Lopez?" Sanchez snarled at his man.

"Give me the cup! Hurry!" Lopez held out his hand and Costello gave him the cup. "You'll like this, Sanchez!" Lopez looked back under the bench and shoved the cup up against the wood and then moved it about a foot to his left before using his free hand to tap the side of the waxed surface. "Hold that motherfucker down tight!"

Sanchez, Martinez, and Costello were holding Alex stretched out on the bench.

Lopez rushed the cup over Alex's stomach and turned it over. A large black-widow spider dropped out and landed directly on Alex's belly button.

"Look at the size of that bitch!" Sanchez instinctively loosened his hold on Alex's right arm and Alex took advantage of the opportunity. He pulled his arm loose and grabbed the spider. The other gang members released him and stepped back away from him.

"Are you *bad*, Sanchez?" Alex opened his eyes wide. "*Really* fucking bad?"

Sanchez looked at Alex as if he were nuts.

"Do this, then!" Alex opened his hand and held it up to his cheek, allowing the large black-widow spider to crawl off his hand onto his face.

"You're crazy, man! Fucking crazy!" Sanchez felt a shudder ripple along his backbone.

"What's wrong, Azteca! No fucking guts?" Alex felt the spider creeping over his ear and reached up to gently scoop it back up in his hand. He squatted down and held his hand up against the underside of the wooden bench and let the spider crawl off.

"You're a nut case! A fucking nut case, man!" Sanchez screamed.

"Move your ass to Station Two and get started with your physical." Alex took advantage of his new position. *"Move!"*

Sanchez obeyed, followed by the three other Aztecas.

Alex leaned over and checked out his new friend. He puckered his lips as if he was going to kiss the spider. It was too much for Lopez. "The man's fucking going to *kiss* that bitch!"

Alex waited until he was alone before he started laughing. He had noticed almost immediately when they had placed the black-widow spider on his stomach that the creature had exceptionally long legs. Only male black-widow spiders had long legs in proportion to their bodies and male black-widow spiders did not bite. He had learned that from working at the pharmacy. A lady had brought one of her kids in who had been bitten by a black widow and she begged the pharmacist to give the child an antidote. One of the little girl's brothers had caught the spider in a mayonnaise jar and had brought it with them. The little girl was crying hysterically, and cried even harder when she saw the jarred spider. The pharmacist took one glance at the captured black widow and smiled at the little girl. He told the mother that the girl had not been bitten by *that* spider. After the little girl had been calmed down, she told her mother that she hadn't been bitten. The spider had scared her and she had started crying.

Alex gained control of himself and stepped out into the hall. The four gang bangers were already standing in line at Station Two.

"That was quick." The sergeant nodded at Alex.

"No problem, Sergeant. These guys are in a hurry to join the Army." Alex winked at Sanchez and smiled.

"Take a seat and lay your arm down on the table." The Army medic spoke the sentence in a bored voice. "Make a fist and don't pull away." He took one of the empty needles and tubes off the stack on the table behind him and waited while Alex opened and closed his fist until the veins stood out on his forearm. The medic found a fat vein near his elbow joint and shoved the large needle through the skin. Blood flowed immediately into the clear receptacle. Alex had felt a slight stinging sensation as the point of the needle went through his skin, but after that it only *looked* painful.

"Fuck this shit, man!"

Alex looked over to where Sanchez sat at the next table. The medic held a needle over Sanchez's arm.

"You aint sticking that fucking thing in me, mother-fucker!" Sanchez was terrified.

"You got a problem, Sanchez?" Alex grinned and pushed the small cotton ball against the bend in his elbow from where his blood had been drawn. "Would you like me to show you again how a non-color-wearer does it?"

"Fuck you, man, an Azteca ain't afraid of nothing!"

"I thought so." Alex left the station and headed for the next one down the hallway. "Hurry up or you'll end up staying here all day."

Station Fourteen was the next-to-last one and Alex could see that he wasn't going to like it. Three doctors, wearing rubber gloves, worked their way down the lines of recruits, who were bending over. Alex turned away as the doctor nearest to him shoved his rubber-coated index finger up the rectum of the last man in line.

"What's going on in there?" Sanchez had taken the place behind Alex in the line and couldn't see into the room.

"You're going to love this one, Sanchez. This is what Aztecas do to each other for thrills."

"What?" Sanchez looked into the room and saw only three rows of sheepish-looking men.

"You'll see. It's our turn."

One of the enlisted medics waved Alex into the room. "Line up on the yellow lines and face the front of the room. When a doctor approaches you from the back, lean over and drop your shorts." The medic took the stack of medical records from Alex, who had been promoted to group section leader as the day had progressed. The sergeant had noticed that the four gang members were listening and obeying everything Alex told them to do. He wondered what had gone on in the dressing room.

Sanchez watched as the doctor ran his finger up the rectum of the man next to him. He started shaking his head. "You call the fucking police . . . I don't give a fuck! But you ain't putting nothing up this Rican ass, man! Nothing!"

The sergeant smiled. Every once in a while they had a case like Sanchez that broke up the boredom of the job. "Recruit, you either let the doctor do his job, or we'll call in some female nurses to hold you down while a female doctor does the anal check." The sergeant grinned. "Would you like that better? Huh? But you'll have to promise us that you won't get hard while she does it."

"I'm going to kill you! Motherfucker!" Sanchez's face turned red.

"Bend over like everyone else and get it over with!" The sergeant's voice was filled with contempt. "Do you think we *enjoy* checking your smelly asses?"

All the men in the room had been checked and were watching Sanchez. Even his buddies had cooperated with the doctors and were finished, and no one had really seen anyone else getting the finger wag until Sanchez. He had every eye in the room watching him as he stiffly bent over and grunted as the doctor jammed his finger deep into his rectal cavity and spoke loudly.

"This is a very *loose* one. What have you been doing back there, young man?"

The room filled with laughter. Sanchez pulled his underwear back up and glared his hatred at Alex. He had chosen the object for his revenge.

CHAPTER THREE

⊗⊗⊗⊗⊗⊗⊗⊗⊗⊗⊗⊗⊗⊗⊗⊗⊗⊗⊗

BASIC BLUES

Alex shivered. The storm wind was penetrating the layers of his clothing. A sliver of light appeared above the buildings to the east, alerting him to the new day. He moved his jaw left and right and then wiggled his lips. His beard was frozen.

The headlights from an approaching vehicle reflected off the ice-glazed black marble wall in front of Alex. He flexed his shoulders, trying to get some warmth back in his body by moving. Time had slipped by quickly while he had allowed his memories to occupy his mind. The headlights became stationary and then were turned off. Alex heard a car door slam shut, and then the sounds of boots crunching on dry snow reached his ears. Someone was approaching him from his right rear.

"What in the fuck are you doing out here?" The voice was muffled.

Alex didn't move.

A gloved hand knocked the accumulated snow off Alex's right shoulder. He turned around slowly and pushed his poncho liner back away from his head so that he could see. A National Park Service guard stood behind him.

"I asked you what in the hell you are doing out here!" The man's face was surrounded by the lowered flaps of his two-tone brown NPS winter cap. The flaps had been tied together under his chin. He looked very warm.

"I'm keeping a friend company." Alex's voice was almost drowned out by the wind.

"Oh, shit! Another fucking Vietnam vet who's gone fucking nuts!" The park guard shook his head and continued talking to a nonexistent third person. "How much more of this fucking shit am I going to have to take?"

"Why don't you just get back in your vehicle and leave?" Alex returned his attention to the wall.

"What did you say?" The guard's face turned red. "*You* are the one who's going to leave!"

"This is a public park and I'm part of the public." Alex didn't look back at the guard.

"This national park wasn't built to house fucking burned-out vets! Now, get your ass moving or I'll call in and have you arrested!"

"If this park isn't for *vets*, who's it for?" Alex turned his head slowly and glared at the guard.

"You fucking vets think we owe you a fucking living! Bullshit! Now, get out of here!" The guard placed his gloved hand on the butt of his pistol.

"You're the ex-hippie, aren't you?"

"Who told you that?"

"Your buddy told me earlier that you would be coming on duty at midnight."

"Yeah . . . I was in college during the war."

"The war lasted ten years."

"I took my time getting through school!"

"Hiding."

"What the fuck did you say?"

"You were *hiding* in college so you wouldn't have to serve your country. I find that ironic, a *hippie* guarding the Vietnam War Memorial."

"Funny, huh?" The guard was angry. "You want to hear something really funny, asshole?" He didn't wait for Alex to respond, but continued, "I skipped over to

Canada and lived there for six years. How about that shit, asshole vet? I would have stayed there until hell froze over before I went to Vietnam, but good ol' President Nixon pardoned us. I like him, even though a lot of people said that he was a crook."

The guard failed to see the glow in Alex's eyes.

"What in the fuck do you think about that, vet? Look at you, sitting there freezing your ass off and I'm guarding *your* memorial. . . . I like that!"

"How did you get the job?" Alex's voice was becoming husky.

"Friends, man! Friends working at the National Park Service. Don't forget, while you assholes were over there getting your asses shot off, *we* were going to college. We're educated." The guard reached into his thick winter overcoat pocket and removed a hand-rolled cigarette. "Here, man, get a little high on me . . . call it a Christmas present from the enemy." He started laughing.

Alex grinned, and if the guard had been paying attention, he would have realized that he was in serious trouble. "I don't know what I should give you in return."

The guard stopped laughing long enough to choke out, "Hey, G.I., you could give me that poncho liner you're wearing. Those are collector's items."

"I can think of something a lot better."

"What's that?"

Alex pushed the front of his poncho back and lifted the barrel of his CAR-15 off his lap. The guard's eyes widened as he realized what was going to happen. Alex used his thumb to push the selector switch to semiautomatic and pulled the trigger. The single explosion was lost on the wind. The ex-hippie rocked a little and then collapsed down on his knees. He looked at Alex, disbelief covering his face, and then fell over on his side. His left leg began shaking and a dark spot appeared in the crotch of his uniform pants as his bladder released itself in death.

Alex lowered the barrel of his weapon and pulled his poncho liner closed again. He shivered from the cold and looked over at the black marble wall. He let his mind return to the past.

Sanchez sat across from Alex. The top of the picnic table was covered with M-16 parts. Volleys of rifle fire could be heard coming from the rifle qualification course a few meters away.

A drill sergeant wearing a wide-brimmed WWI-style campaign hat approached the dark green table where Alex sat. "You men are the next line to qualify. You have fifteen minutes to assemble your weapons." He looked over at Alex. "Have your platoon in the assembly area on time, Sergeant Jaxson."

"Yes, Sergeant." Alex started putting his M-16 back together again, hardly looking down at the pieces.

Sanchez stared at the dark blue armband on Alex's right arm. The staff-sergeant stripes sewn to the armband were a contrast in golden yellow against the blue. Sanchez ground his teeth. Alex had been chosen as the acting platoon sergeant for their basic-training platoon, over him. Alex had also been chosen senior recruit on their bus ride down to Fort Dix. Sanchez hated Alex.

"Hey, Jaxson!" one of the other platoon members called from a nearby table. "How many of us do you think will bolo the course?"

"None. We've all qualified during our practice runs and there shouldn't be any reason to screw up now." Alex looked across the table at Sanchez.

"All it takes is a ten-dollar bill left under a sandbag to qualify." Sanchez sneered.

"No one in the Second Platoon is going to bribe a scorer!" Alex glared at Sanchez.

The gang member grinned back and shoved the pin

through his M-16, locking the last parts together. He pulled back the charging handle and lifted the weapon to his shoulder. Sanchez placed his front sight between Alex's eyes and squeezed the trigger. "Bang, motherfucker! You're dead!"

The M-16 was snatched out of Sanchez's hands so hard that his finger got caught in the trigger guard. Blood ran between his index and third fingers.

"Don't you *ever* pull that shit again, recruit!" The drill sergeant held Sanchez's M-16 by its barrel. "Do you hear me?"

Sanchez struggled to his feet. "Yes, Sergeant!"

"You're a fucking idiot, Sanchez, and I'm going to keep my eyes glued on you the remainder of this cycle!" The sergeant hooked his thumbs over his pistol belt and rocked back on the heels of his highly shined boots. "Now, get your ass over to the assembly area!"

"I cut my hand, Sergeant." Sanchez held his wounded hand up so that the NCO could see the blood.

"Go see the range medic and get that bandaged, and you'd better not miss your qualification run!"

Sanchez nodded and slipped his rifle over his shoulder before he started jogging toward the ambulance parked next to the range hut. He flashed a look of pure hate at Alex before he left.

Alex was the last one to take up a position behind one of the foxholes on the firing line. A cadre scorer sat on a small seat just to the rear of the foxhole with a clipboard and scorecard. The range was designed with olive-drab pop-up targets silhouetted to look like the top half of a man. The targets would pop up at different ranges and the trainee would have to first identify one and then engage it. A range controller in the tower overlooking the firing line gave the fire commands and sequence of targets.

A loud voice came over the speakers. "Firers, get in your foxholes!"

Alex looked down the line at his platoon members and watched as they obeyed.

"Lock and load one magazine of five rounds!" The voice was too loud coming over the speaker behind Alex's position.

The scorer watched Alex carefully. He was waiting for the recruit to slip a ten-dollar bill under the sandbag his rifle was resting on. The money would ensure that Alex qualified on the range. Alex took up a good position and waited for the first target to appear.

"It's your ass, recruit." The voice came from the scorer. "Are you sure?"

"I'm *sure*." Alex spoke with his cheek pressed up against the stock of his weapon.

"Fine. I'll see you back here again after they recycle your ass."

The first target appeared fifty meters in front of Alex. He sucked in a lungful of air and held it in as he squeezed the trigger. He watched the silhouette flip backward. Immediately he lowered his weapon and looked down the range over the sights until he identified another target. Alex spent the next thirty minutes concentrating on the targets appearing and disappearing in his lane. At three hundred yards, the targets were very difficult to detect, especially if there was any green vegetation surrounding them. The advantage the trainees had was that the ground in front of most of the targets was plowed up from the hundreds of rounds that had impacted around them.

The training committee would rotate ranges, and usually the first couple of basic-training companies who fired on a newly opened range would do very poorly, unable to detect the targets because of the overgrown vegetation. That was also part of the political game that was played between the training cadre and the cadre who ran the ranges. If one of the training-battlion commanders gave the rifle-range commander any trouble, he almost always would find his battalion qualifying on a newly opened range. Scores were a very important part of an officer's efficiency report, and a political war was always going on between the line officers and the training-committee cadre.

Alex was in question over two of the long-range targets when they were told to clear their weapons and hold them, butt-first, over their shoulders for one of the range officers to check them before they could leave the firing line.

"You fucked up really bad there, *Acting* Sergeant." The NCO scorer sneered at Alex.

Alex turned around and looked at him. He knew that he had qualified as an expert rifleman; it was just a matter of how *high* his score was. He wanted to have the highest score in his company. "How did I do?"

"Bolo."

"What?"

"I said that you fucking boloed!"

"That's bullshit!"

"Watch your mouth, *Acting* Sergeant!" The NCO held out his clipboard for Alex to see the red marks that represented misses. The card was filled with them.

"You're trying to screw me!"

"Hey, asshole . . . no pay, no play."

"Bullshit!" Alex started taking a step toward the corrupt NCO.

"What's going on here, soldier!" One of the range officers ran over to support his range NCO.

"This sergeant is trying to screw me over." Alex stood his ground.

"He's lying, sir. The dumb-ass recruit boloed and now he's trying to blame me."

"Get back over with your company, soldier." The lieutenant glared at Alex. "Now!"

"Yes, sir." Alex obeyed and walked stiffly back to his company's assembly area.

The Second Platoon's drill sergeant was waiting for

71

Alex to join them. He smiled when his acting sergeant approached the formation. "How did you do, Jaxson?"

"Bolo."

The sergeant's smile widened. He knew that Alex had qualified at least in the bottom range of an expert rifleman. The young soldier was one of the best shots he had seen coming through the training center. "Right, Jaxson. Now, unless you want to do push-ups for the rest of the morning, you'd better stop trying to bullshit me."

"I'm not bullshiting, Sergeant. I boloed." Alex flexed his jaw muscles and looked back at the smiling scorer, who had been watching from the firing line.

"I can't believe that!"

Sanchez watched from his place in the formation and grinned. He was enjoying himself. He had qualified as an expert rifleman.

"It's true, according to the scorer." Alex glared at the range NCO. "But I *know* that I hit all but two targets, and those two I couldn't see because of all the dust in the air."

"Are you sure, Jaxson?" The sergeant's voice was deep and angry. "Did he ask you for any money?"

Alex kept quiet. He knew that a lot of his fellow recruits had bribed the scorers and he wasn't going to be a squealer.

"You don't have to answer that!" The drill sergeant pointed at the platoon. "All of you wait right here!" He stalked off toward his company commander, who was drinking coffee with the range officer-in-charge.

Sanchez waited until the drill sergeant was out of hearing range. "The big, bad *acting* sergeant fucking boloed! How about that shit!"

Alex ignored Sanchez and watched where the drill sergeant was going. He could see the sergeant's hands reinforcing whatever he was saying to the officers, and then the sergeant pointed to where Alex had fired from. His company commander said something to the range officer and the two of them got into a heated argument. The scorer from Alex's lane was called over and the argument continued until finally the battalion commander's jeep pulled up next to the range hut. Alex could see the officers standing in a semicircle around the lieutenant colonel. The range officer lowered his head and then looked up again red-faced. Alex's drill sergeant came running back to the platoon with a smile on his face.

"Stack arms. Sanchez, you stay here and guard our weapons. The rest of the platoon is going to pull all of the targets!" The drill sergeant grinned over at Alex. "I hope you're right, soldier, or we're going to be in a hell of a lot of hot water!"

"Right about what, Sergeant?"

"Right about hitting those targets in your lane. The battalion commander has demanded that all of the targets be pulled in and a count of the holes in each target be made and checked against *all* of the scorecards.

"What in the fuck is that going to prove, Sergeant!" Sanchez was scared. He knew that he had bought his score with the ten-dollar bill he had left under his sandbag. "A lot of guys shot at those targets!"

"Wrong, Sanchez! All of the targets were changed right before the Second Platoon went up on line. You guys were the *first* ones to fire at them, so hits on the targets will match, or let me say, *should* match the scorecards." The drill sergeant winked at Alex. "Our battalion commander has been trying to catch the range cadre taking bribes for a couple of months now. He's an honest man and hates cheaters."

Alex felt the pit of his stomach turn sour for a second and then he regained his courage. He *knew* he had hit his targets, and had nothing to fear.

The scorer in his lane glared at Alex as he started walking down-range with him to gather the targets. "You're a troublemaker, recruit!"

"Well see when we get the targets." Alex increased his pace.

"Where are you going?" The NCO had stopped at the first pop-up pit.

"Out to the three-hundred-yard targets and work my way back. There's no sense in carrying the targets out there and then back again."

"Listen, punk! You do what I say. Now, pull this target." The range NCO wanted to screw with Alex as much as he could.

"Whatever you say, Sergeant." Alex wasn't going to give the NCO an opening. He knew that he had him by the balls and he wasn't going to give him a chance to press charges against him.

Alex's drill sergeant had been watching what was going on in Alex's lane and started jogging down the path to catch up to the scorer and his man.

The training-battalion commander stood behind the range shack and watched as his trainees stacked the targets in piles according to what lane they had been in. The range officer glared at the lieutenant colonel and kept looking down the dirt road. He had placed a call to the range-cadre commander and to the training center's commanding general; both of them were on their way out to his range. He had wanted to hang this asshole lieutenant colonel ever since the man had run his first cycle through the ranges.

"I'd like to wait until my colonel arrives before we start counting holes in the targets." The captain ground his teeth as he spoke to the lieutenant colonel, who was standing in the shade of the building.

"That's fine with me, but as long as we're waiting, I'd like for you to assemble *all* of your scorers back here with us."

"Why?"

"I think we should all be together when your colonel and the general arrive, don't you?"

The captain shrugged his shoulders. "Whatever will make you happy, sir."

"Good, then get them back here."

The training center's commanding general arrived in his helicopter. He had brought the training cadre's colonel along with him. The range officer met them at the helipad and was talking rapidly to the general when they approached the range shack where the targets were stacked.

The brigadier general looked hard at the lieutenant colonel before he spoke. "The captain here has said that you've made some very strong accusations."

"I've asked for the targets to be brought here, sir, and for the bullet holes to be counted in each of them and compared to what the scorers have put down on their scorecards, sir."

"Do you suspect cheating?" The general's eyebrows rose slightly. "You know how I feel about cheating, and all of you also know how I feel about accusations that damage an officer's reputation!"

The range officer smiled. "Sir, if it's all right with the lieutenant colonel, we can drop this matter right now and get back to qualifying his company. I'll hold no hard feelings because I know the pressure the line officers are under to score well."

The general looked over at the battalion commander. "Well? That sounds reasonable to me. We all have things we can be doing besides counting holes in targets."

"General, if it's all right with you, I'd like to finish this. We won't have such a good opportunity again to match target holes with scorecards."

"If you insist, but I want you to understand that I will not take this matter lightly if you're wrong!"

"I understand, General." The battalion commander glanced over at Private Jaxson; he was staking a lot on a recruit's word. "But first, sir, I would like to request that all of the range scorers empty their pockets on the tops of those picnic tables."

"What?" The range officer's face turned red. "This is absurd!"

"Why do you request such a thing?" The general looked shocked.

"The rumors are that it takes a ten-dollar bill under a sandbag on the firing line to ensure that you qualify." The lieutenant colonel glared over at the group of NCO's standing under a cluster of scrub pine trees. "They have been out here all day and one of my other companies fired this range this morning. If they have been taking bribes from the recruits, they'll still have the money on them."

"I . . . well . . ." The general didn't know what to say.

"General! I must insist that you prevent that from occurring. It would be humiliating to my cadre to go through such a foolish, degrading experience!"

"If I'm wrong, Colonel, I'm quite sure the general will take corrective action."

"That's true." The brigadier general glared at the battalion commander. "Very corrective action!"

The range officer grudgingly went over to his assembled cadre and told them to go over to the picnic tables and empty their pockets. Alex's platoon sergeant slipped away from the platoon and went over to where the cadre had been standing.

The battalion commander watched as the sergeants slowly emptied their pockets. About a half-dozen of them were smiling and didn't hesitate. "Would you please empty *all* of your pockets?"

"I have, sir."

"What about your top-left shirt pocket?" He was speaking to the NCO who had been working the lane Alex had fired from.

"There's nothing in there, sir. We never break starch in our shirt pockets."

"Really? Then you won't mind doing it just this once for me, will you?"

"Sir! This is getting to be too much!" The range officer tried intervening for his NCO, but the battalion commander moved too fast.

"What is this?"

The NCO's face turned red.

"Five ten-dollar bills and two fives?" The battalion commander dropped the wad of money down on the table.

"I was going to pay a bill after work!"

The battalion commander turned around to face the rest of the NCO's. "I'll strip every damn one of you down to your bare asses if I have to! Now, empty your pockets!"

Wads of small-denomination bills appeared on the picnic tables. The general looked over at the range officer and then back at the money. There was just too much cash for it to be circumstantial.

"Sir?" The Second Platoon's drill sergeant approached the group of officers. "You might be interested in this." He dropped several wads of money on the table nearest to the general. "I found this over there where they had been standing. Money must just grow on the ground out here on the ranges."

"Well?" The brigadier general waited for the range officer to answer him.

"Sir, the trainees bribed my men. They should be punished too!" The officer was trying desperately to involve as many people as he could so that the general would be forced to drop everything. "Even those line cadre knew what was going on! They're involved!"

"That is true. The trainees did the bribing." The colonel tried supporting his captain.

"Sir, this whole case broke open because *one* trainee tried earning his own score and they intentionally disqualified him because he wouldn't bribe them. They are at fault." The battalion commander's voice carried a great deal of contempt in it.

"Can you prove that?"

"Yes, sir, Private Jaxson fired on lane thirty-seven. We can count the number of hits on the targets and compare them against the scorecard."

"Do it . . . now!"

The officers stood in a circle around the stack of silhouettes and watched as the holes were counted and marked with a Magic Marker. The number of holes was compared with the scorecard. Alex had fired well into the top portion of expert on the range and even he was surprised when he saw that he had hit all of the three-hundred-yard targets, even though two of them had been ricochets. The holes in the long-range targets were perfect silhouettes of the side view of the rounds. The bullets had hit in the dirt directly in front of the targets and bounced up to knock them down with enough force to punch their way through the heavy cardboard, counting legally as a hit.

"Very well done, Private Jaxson." The battalion commander's face reflected the victory he had won over the corruption that had been going on for a long time.

"Thank you, sir."

"Now, let's go over and compare your hits to your scorecard." The lean lieutenant colonel looked over at the brigadier general, who was staring at the training brigade's commander.

"There's no need for that right now. I've seen enough!" The general could see for himself that Jaxson's scorecard was filled with red marks that signified targets missed. "I want all of this evidence saved for their courts-martial." He turned on his heel and started walking back toward his helicopter. "Colonel, let's get back to my office! We have a lot of things to talk about!"

* * *

The ride back to the company area seemed to take longer after the hard day at the range. The company had been woken up at three in the morning and had eaten breakfast before daylight. They had been on the range putting up targets before six in the morning, and now it was already starting to get dark.

Alex sat by himself in the back of the open-bed five-ton cattle car on the ride back. Most of the men in his company had paid the ten-dollar bribe to qualify and were divided over what Alex had done. They knew he was right, but they had given in to the system and were feeling guilty.

The trucks pulled up in front of the company barracks and idled their engines while the recruits unloaded. The strong smell of diesel fumes filled the heavy summer air. It had cooled off at least twenty degrees the minute the sun went down, but it was still in the mid-seventies. Alex marched his platoon over to the weapons-cleaning area behind the supply room. The tables had already been equipped with cleaning rods and patches and the fifty-five-gallon drums, cut lengthwise in half, were filled with cleaning solvent. The company's first sergeant had sent the morning sick-call detail over to the supply room to set everything up for the returning company. Alex was happy that they could get their weapons cleaned early and their gear put away so that he could get to bed. He had gotten up an extra hour earlier so that he could square away his gear before the rest of his platoon was up.

The company cadre left the barracks at ten-thirty and Alex dropped down on his cot exhausted. He was wearing only his military-issue boxer shorts. The warm breeze coming through the open window behind his head felt good as he slipped into a deep sleep.

Sanchez watched Alex sleeping, five double bunks down from where he was sitting on his footlocker. The platoon sergeant had told them that they would all have to requalify on a new range in the morning. He was sure that he would end up boloing the course, and that meant he would have to be recycled back to a training company that was just beginning its rifle training. All infantrymen had to qualify with the M-16.

"Lights out!" the company charge-of-quarters stuck his head in the squad bay and yelled as he turned out the lights. A soft glow coming from the single fire light above the exit doorway filled the long open area where forty recruits were bunked.

Sanchez waited until the sound of snoring filled the room before slipping off his bunk. He was still fully dressed and wearing his combat boots. He paused at each one of his buddies' bunks and tapped the foot of the bed. The four of them slipped down the center aisle towards Alex's cot.

"Did you bring a bunk adapter with you?" Costello whispered to Lopez.

"Naw, I'll use my fucking belt."

"Shut up!" Sanchez hissed the words between his clenched teeth. He was carrying a heavy wool olive-drab blanket he had taken off a sick-call bunk.

Alex was sleeping so soundly that he hadn't moved from the position he had fallen asleep in.

Sanchez and Martinez crept up the left side of Alex's bunk, while Costello and Lopez went up the right side. Sanchez handed a corner of the blanket over to Costello and then slowly started lowering it over Alex's head.

"I wouldn't do that if I were you." The voice came from the top bunk directly across from Alex's.

Sanchez looked up at the shadow figure that was watching them from across the aisle. "Man! You shut the fuck up and go back to sleep, or you'll be next!"

Costello raised the bunk adapter so that the man lying on the bunk could see it silhouetted in the dim light.

"I think *you* better get back to your bunk . . . now!" The voice was soft.

"Fuck you, man!" Sanchez dropped the blanket over Alex's face and brought his knee up against his side. Alex grunted in his sleep and rolled slightly to his left.

The dark shape left the top bunk and had grabbed Lopez before the other three Aztecas realized it. A soft thud and air hissing out of Lopez's lungs reached Sanchez only a second before Lopez's dark shadow flew up against the barracks wall and slipped down on the floor. Costello tried swinging his steel bunk adapter at the moving shadow but felt it stop in midair as a powerful hand grasped his wrist. He felt himself being lifted off the floor and moved out to the center aisle. The next thing he realized was that he was flying through the air, and then he felt the pain as his body hit the exit screen door, tearing the screen out. He landed on the dirt below the steps.

Sanchez stopped punching the struggling Alex and turned his attention to the dark shadow. "You just fucked up, big time, motherfucker!" He reached down in the top of his boot and pulled out a spring-loaded stiletto. "Get the motherfucker!" he screamed at Martinez.

The dark shadow brought up its knee and Martinez doubled over, holding his groin. "Oh, mother fuck me!"

"You're dead meat!" Sanchez attacked, holding the shiny blade out in front of his body. He moved the knife in small circles, looking at the same time for an opening.

The large shadow reached down at the foot of Alex's bunk and effortlessly lifted the full footlocker above its head. "Put the knife down." The voice was still soft.

"Fuck you, man!"

The shadow threw the dark green footlocker at the man holding the knife. It struck his chest and then tilted up and smashed its top edge against Sanchez's mouth.

"Mu teef . . . yu muffer fuakur! Yu nock ou mu fuckin' teef!" Sanchez dropped the knife and held his mouth.

"You'd better get over to the dispensary and see what they can do for you." The shadow bent down and picked up three small ivory-colored teeth off the waxed floor. "Take these with you. They might be able to put them back in your mouth."

Sanchez ran out of the barracks holding his missing teeth in his closed fist.

"You all right?" The shadow spoke to Alex.

"Yeah, just got the wind knocked out of me. The blanket acted as a cushion."

"Let's go outside and let me look at you under the porch light." The shadow went over toward the back door, which was torn off its hinges. Costello was still lying in the dirt.

Alex slipped off his bunk and followed the shadow outside. He could see under the light that his rescuer was the guy who slept across the aisle from him in his platoon's second squad. The big man rarely spoke unless someone spoke to him first. Alex recognized him as a very hard worker. "Thanks .. . . that's Maleko, isn't it?"

The big man nodded.

"Thanks, Maleko. You saved my ass from a good kicking. Sanchez has been wanting to get ahold of me ever since the induction center back in New York."

"You look all right." Maleko's eyes checked out Alex's face and bare chest for bruises.

"Like I said, the blanket sort of cushioned the punches." Alex rubbed his side where Sanchez had kneed him. "It doesn't look as if Sanchez's boys fared too well, though." He nodded down at the still body of Costello. "Do you think he's dead?"

Maleko left the small porch and went down and

rolled Costello over on his back. The Azteca groaned and spat out a mouthful of blood. Malcko looked back over at Alex and nodded. "He'll come around in a couple of minutes."

Alex sat down on the freshly painted wooden top step. "It's nice out here."

"Yeah." Maleko took a seat next to Alex.

"Everyone in the Army calls each other by their last names. What's your first name?" Alex looked over at the man sitting next to him. He didn't look as big as he had before, but Alex could see that he was very well-built.

"The same as yours."

"Alexander?"

"Sasha."

"That doesn't sound the same as mine." Alex smiled.

" 'Sasha' is 'Alexander' in Russian."

"Oh." Alex didn't say what he was thinking.

Maleko read his thoughts. "It sounds like a girl's name, but it is a very popular boy's name in Russia."

"Are your parents from there?"

"My father is. My mother is a first-generation Polish American."

"Where are you from?"

"Hamtramck, Michigan. We own a small meat market there."

"I understand now how you got that build on you."

"My father and I work hard. He's old now, so I do all the heavy work at the shop."

"Why are you in the Army?"

Maleko paused for a couple of minutes before answering. "I was drafted."

"Sorry."

"Why be sorry? It's a privilege for a man to have the opportunity to defend his freedom." Maleko smiled. It was the first time Alex ever had seen any emotional expression on the man's face. "My father hired a boy to replace me until I return home."

"I like what you said, but I'm afraid there are a lot of people who don't agree with you."

"I'm the one who has to live under this skin." Maleko patted his chest with his open hand. "Malekos fight for their freedom." The statement was delivered in an absolute tone of voice. No room left for questions.

"Do you mind if I call you Sasha?"

"Sash." The big man looked over at Alex. "You can call me Sash."

"Do you think I did the right thing today out on the rifle range?"

Sash shook his head before answering. "Most of the men in the company paid the ten dollars."

Alex looked down at the step between his feet. "Yeah, I guess I fucked up."

"You've read me wrong." Sash's voice rose. He knew that the men inside of the barracks were listening to them talk through the open windows. "If there's one thing a soldier must learn, it's how to operate the weapons he'll need in war. I don't know if you remember, but there's a war going on right now." Sash looked out over the empty wood-chip-covered bayonet pit behind the barracks. "You probably saved a lot of lives by what you did out on the range today. Don't think about our platoon alone; think about all the other basic-training companies that are going to have to go through here in the future." Sash stood up and took a step toward the open doorway. "Personally, I think you're a fucking hero." He entered the dark barracks.

Alex sat by himself for a couple of minutes and thought about what Sash had just said. There *was* a lot more to it than a couple dozen men buying their way through a qualification course.

"What in the hell is going on here?" The duty officer stepped around the corner of the building, followed closely by the company CQ.

"Some of the guys got in a little fight." Alex stood and saluted the second lieutenant.

"Who?"

"Sir, I don't really want to have to squeal on them."

"Private! I don't give a damn what you want. Tell me their names!"

"Yes, sir. Privates Sanchez, Costello, Lopez, and Martinez." Alex remained standing.

"Anyone else?"

"No, sir. They got in a fight about something after everyone else had gone to bed."

"Who's that?" The officer pointed at the unconscious soldier.

"Private Costello, sir."

"I want a full report in the morning."

"Yes, sir. May I be excused, sir? We have an early reveille in the morning."

"Yes." The lieutenant looked over at the sergeant. "Take care of that soldier!"

Alex went back into the dark barracks and sat down on his bunk. He could hear Martinez groaning on his bunk. The rest of the barracks was quiet; too quiet. Alex knew all of the men were awake and had been listening to the fight.

Alex looked over at the dark shadow lying on the bunk across from his. "Thanks, Sash . . . I owe you a big one."

The head of the shadow nodded slowly in agreement.

CHAPTER FOUR

✪✪✪✪✪✪✪✪✪✪✪✪✪✪✪✪✪

DOG LAB

The wind seemed to have warmed up a little when the first rays of morning sunlight reached the base of the black marble wall. Alex looked over to his right and saw the Washington Monument sparkling in the new day's light. The original ice storm that had started the very rare blizzard in Washington had thinly coated the tall obelisk on two sides in a transparent layer of God's crystal.

Alex pushed his poncho back away from his face and watched the sun melt through the layer of ice on the black marble wall, and then, without giving any warning, he stood up and walked away. He didn't look back at the wall and he completely ignored the dead National Park Service guard lying in a pool of bright red blood. The frozen red crystals looked like a giant snow cone that had spilled next to the ex-hippie.

Snowplows and salt trucks were racing down the main boulevards, trying to get the streets clear. Alex took his time walking to Lafayette Park. The street was lined with small shops and fast-food stores. A car honked its horn and veered away from him as he staggered into the street and regained his balance. He looked up at the driver, a well-dressed woman in her mid-thirties. Alex smiled and shrugged. He felt foolish. She raised her right hand and slammed it up against her windshield, making an obscene gesture with her middle finger.

Alex smiled and waved. He yelled loud enough for her to hear, "Merry Christmas!"

The woman rolled down her window and screamed back at him. "You fucking bum! You damn near made me wreck my car!"

"I love you too, bitch!" Alex turned around and started walking away. He tried ignoring her as he crossed the street. Traffic was light, but even for early Christmas morning there were a number of cars on the roads trying to get to their critical operation centers and replace the night shifts.

The sound of the woman's horn honking followed Alex down the snow-covered street until the stoplight changed and she took off, sliding left and right as she gunned her engine.

The snow looked beautiful piled up on the iron railings and storefront canopies along the boulevard. Alex took his time and stopped often to look at the Christmas displays in the windows. He paused in front of an antique toy store and watched a toy soldier move its head left and right as it beat on a drum. A soft whine caught his ear and he listened intently until he could locate the sound. He sidestepped and looked down a narrow alley next to the toy shop. A fast-food chicken outlet occupied the next building over. Alex could see a German shepherd standing on its hind legs, leaning against a dark blue Dumpster. The dog was looking back at Alex and whined again, but this time a little louder. He was asking Alex to come and help him.

"What's in there, boy?" Alex slipped down the alley and stopped when he reached the dog. "Something good to eat?"

The dog whined again and this time barked three times.

"You don't have to *beg*!" Alex lifted the steel lid on

the container and looked inside. A large frozen-chicken shipping box had been thrown on top of the other trash. It contained pieces of fully cooked chicken that had been thrown out. "Hmmm . . . it looks good." Alex reached in and took one of the top pieces from the box. "It's cold, but not frozen yet." He looked back over at the fast-food restaurant's back door and could see that there was someone inside cleaning up. "I can't believe they have people working there on Christmas Day."

The dog whined again, as if in answer to Alex's comment.

"Hold on there, old boy, and let me tear some of this chicken off its bones. You don't want to get a bone stuck in your throat, do you?"

The German shepherd sat back on its haunches and huffed a deep throaty sound of agreement.

"You're a smart dog . . ." Alex tore large pieces of white meat off the chicken bones and dropped them down at his feet. The dog just watched what he was doing and cocked his head to one side. Alex had the meat torn off twenty pieces of chicken before he stopped and reached down to scrape it into a neat pile. "All right, fella . . . it's yours."

The dog leapt forward and started devouring the food.

"You *were* hungry, weren't you!" Alex reached back into the box and selected a barbecued drumstick and gingerly tasted it, then took a big bite out of the leg. He figured it was too cold outside for the meat to have spoiled. The dog finished off the chicken and looked up again at Alex.

"You want more?" Alex laughed.

The dog licked his jaws and whined.

"All right, but this is going to be the last. I've got some business to take care of this morning." Alex tore the flesh off another couple dozen pieces of chicken and threw the meat over to the shepherd.

There were only a couple pieces of chicken left in the box when the back door to the restaurant opened and a tired-looking Indian wearing a turban stepped outside carrying a box filled with wilting vegetables from the salad bar. "Get out of here! You, beggar! *Go!*" He used the box to motion toward the entrance of the alley. Alex's hand slipped toward the butt of his CAR-15, hanging by its sling underneath his overcoat. The German shepherd growled and the hair on the back of its neck stood up. The Indian lifted the box, getting ready to throw it at the dog.

"Hold on. We're going." Alex started toward the entranceway and patted his leg. "Let's go, boy, we're not wanted here!"

"Find yourself a job!" the Indian yelled after them.

Alex paused to look back over his shoulder. "I've got a job this morning." He smiled. "I'm going to do a little consulting work."

Alex looked down at the large dog that walked next to his left heel. Someone had trained him well. Alex stopped walking and looked both ways on the street before he lifted the CAR-15 away from his side and laid it across his lap and squatted down in front of the dog. He pulled his coat together in front so the steel wouldn't show. "Are you feeling better now that you've eaten?" Alex scratched behind the dog's ears. He felt a chain collar under the thick winter coat on the animal. "What do we have here?" Alex pushed aside the thick hair and read the name on the I.D. tag. "Fang?" The dog responded to its name and nuzzled his hand. "I will say that's an aggressive name, old boy." Alex turned the tag over and read a street address and telephone number. "It looks like you've got a home, Fang." The dog nuzzled the palm of Alex's hand. "Come on, let's see if we can find a telephone and make a call."

Fang followed Alex down the street until the man stopped in front of a glass box and started kicking snow away from the folding door. The dog darted away from the swinging foot.

"Fang, come back here, fella."

The dog responded to its name and cautiously approached the open door, sniffing the air inside. Alex lifted the telephone off its hook and punched the button for the operator. He dropped down in a squat and patted his leg for Fang to come closer. The dog responded slowly, expecting some kind of trap, but trusted the human who had fed him.

"Operator Twenty-three, may I help you?"

"Yes, ma'am, I would like to place a collect call to the following number . . ." Alex turned the dog tag over and read the number over the telephone.

"Who may I say is calling?"

"Alex Jaxson. Tell whoever answers the telephone that I have their lost dog."

The phone at the other end of the line rang a half-dozen times before it was answered by a sophisticated woman's voice.

"Will you accept a collect call from a . . . Mr. Alex Jaxson?"

"Who?"

"A Mr. Jaxson. He says that he has your lost dog."

A sharp cry echoed over the telephone lines and then Alex could hear the woman calling to a boy. "Brandon! Brandon! . . . They've found your dog, son!" She came back on the phone. "Yes! Yes! I'll accept the call!"

"Thank you ma'am." The operator sounded pleased.

"Hello?" The woman was excited.

"Yes, ma'am, I think I've found your dog."

"Where are you?"

Alex looked around the telephone booth. He knew that he had wandered up Connecticut Avenue, but he didn't know exactly where he was. "I'm not sure right now, ma'am, but if you could meet me over in Lafayette Park in, say, an hour."

"Yes! I'll send a limousine over right away!" There was a pause and then she added, "Oh, darn! I let the help off this morning!" Her voice cheered up. "*I'll* drive!"

Alex shrugged and looked over at the dog. So, she'll drive. He grinned.

"Lafayette Park, right?"

"Across the street from the White House."

"Yes! I know how to get there . . . now, please, be waiting. My son is sick over losing his dog."

"I'll be there, just make it in an hour."

"There'll be a five-hundred-dollar reward for you. Just have the dog . . . please?"

"Fang and I'll be waiting." Alex hung up and looked over at the shepherd. "So you're a *rich* mutt?"

Fang whined as if he were apologizing to a bum for his social position.

"I know it isn't your fault, but you could have told me before I gave you all that good chicken!" Alex felt his stomach growl.

Fang took another step into the telephone booth and licked Alex's face. "Don't try to apologize! I'll still get you back to . . . what's his name? Brandon?"

At the sound of the boy's name, Fang's tail began to wag.

"So you like your master?" Alex ran his hands over the large dog's shoulders and felt the powerful muscles ripple under his touch. The animal had been well-cared-for and hadn't been out on the streets very long. He looked into the German shepherd's eyes and suddenly his thoughts went back to another German shepherd that had lived twenty years earlier.

The soft hum of the large diesel engine tried lulling Alex into a much-needed sleep. He was too excited to give in to the bus's lullaby. He had finally made it back to Fort Bragg after almost a year training with Army medics and an internship under a medical doctor.

"Who you with?" The voice came from a soldier sitting across the aisle from him.

"S.F." Alex said the abbreviation for Special Forces with pride.

The soldier looked at Alex out of the corner of his eye. A lot of new troops lied about their assignments to make themselves look big to their peers. "Where's your beret?"

Alex smiled at the new paratrooper. "I'm just finishing up my training. I start Dog Lab in the morning, and then Phase III."

"What's Dog Lab?"

"That's the last phase of my Green Beret medical training." Alex rested his head against the seat back and looked out the smoke-colored windows at the businesses that lined Bragg Boulevard from Fayetteville to the large military post.

"I thought you got your beret when you joined Special Forces."

"No . . . only when you finish all of their training. I should have mine in about five more months."

"Five fucking months?" The paratrooper shook his head. "Man, I could hardly wait to get through jump school, and that was only three weeks long!"

"It's going to be worth it." Alex looked down and carefully crossed his legs near the tops of his highly shined boots. He had spent hours working on his Cochrans and he didn't want to mar them accidentally against a seat post.

The paratrooper looked down to where Alex was looking and commented, "Nice boots!"

"Thanks."

"It looks like you've burned wax."

"I have." Alex turned his head to one side and looked over at the young paratrooper for the first time. The soldier was an obvious new replacement with the 82nd Airborne Division. "You with the 82nd?"

"Yeah, how did you know?"

93

"Your haircut sort of gave you away."

The replacement rubbed the bristles that were starting to appear along the sides of his bald head. "I hope my hair grows back quick. Man, it's cost me a lot of pussy!"

Alex smiled. He understood what the paratrooper was saying. Everyone was letting his hair grow down to the shoulders now out in civilian life, and a soldier or a marine stood out like a creature from another planet, and was treated that way by the girls. The hippie movement on the college campuses was beginning to take a firm hold.

"Hey!" The bus driver kept his eyes on the road and called back to the passengers. "Does anyone want to get out on Smoke Bomb Hill? Or do you all want to ride down to the bus station?" Normally, he didn't make the stop, but he liked the young guy who had gotten on the bus downtown and wanted to give him a break.

Alex saw the statue of the World War II paratrooper flash past his window and raised his rear off the seat so that the bus driver could see him in his rearview mirror. "I'd appreciate it, driver!"

The man nodded back at Alex through his mirror. "You've got it, fella!" He had already made the turn and was starting to brake the bus for the light on Honeycutt Avenue.

Alex watched the cars pulling into the drive-in restaurant across the street. The civilian-style fast-food operation was very popular on the large military base and was packed with normal Sunday-afternoon traffic.

The large bus stopped in front of a row of dull yellow buildings that had been erected during World War II. The driver left his seat with the diesel engine idling and opened the baggage doors in the belly of the bus. Alex pulled his green duffel bag out and nodded to the driver. "Thanks, I appreciate this."

"No problem." The middle-aged man reached up and touched the bill on his company cap.

Alex stood back to allow the bus to pull away from the curb and could hear one of the paratroopers going to the 82nd Airborne Division ask if the driver would make a stop over there for them. Alex smiled when he heard the driver reply that he had a schedule to meet. The bus pulled away from the curb, leaving a black cloud of diesel fumes behind it. Alex tucked the large envelope that contained his records under his left arm and picked up his duffel bag. He used his right hand to cover his mouth as he coughed; he hated the smell of diesel fumes.

From the window in his office, the company sergeant major had been watching Alex get off the bus. He smiled. It wasn't often a soldier could convince a bus driver to drop him off at his door.

Alex dropped his duffel bag just inside the orderly-room door and shifted the brown envelope containing his records into his right hand. The company clerk stopped typing and looked at the trainee. The clerk was not Special Forces-qualifed. He had dropped out of the communications course, and rather than get transferred to the 82nd Airborne Division, he volunteered to stay with the company as a clerk. Alex handed the specialist his records.

"I'll take those." The sergeant major stood in the doorway of his office.

"Sure, Sergeant Major." The clerk raised his eyebrows and handed the package to the senior NCO.

The sergeant major frowned. "Come on in here, Jaxson."

Alex glanced over at the clerk, whose expression was noncommittal. Both of them knew that the sergeant major rarely wasted time talking to Special Forces trainees. The senior NCO was a living legend. He had served with the Ranger Battalion that had landed at

Anzio during WWII and was one of the few men who had escaped from the Germans after the survivors had been captured. Then he had served with the 3rd Ranger Company during Korea, and was one of the eleven survivors from the company when the Chinese overran their position. To top it all off, the sergeant major was one of the team that had opened and designed the first A Camp in Vietnam.

The first thing Alex noticed when he entered the knotty-pine-paneled office was the half-empty bottle of Jim Beam sitting on the desk, its cap missing.

The sergeant major used the glass in his hand to point with. "Take a seat."

Alex obeyed. His eyes were trying to adjust to the dim room. The curtains had been pulled shut and the room was lit only by a single brass banker's lamp on the desk. Alex noticed that there was another person in the office, sitting on the dark green couch against the wall with his legs crossed out in front of him.

"This is Sergeant First Class Billy Mills"—the sergeant major took a long pull from his glass—"the best damn medic to wear a beret!"

Alex noticed that the sergeant first class was wearing his beret pushed down low over his eyebrows. A 3rd Special Forces Group crest, made up of four colors, reflected in the light. The NCO nodded slightly and then looked back over at the sergeant major.

"This will take only a minute, Billy, and then we can get back to some *serious* war stories." The sergeant major returned his attention to Alex. "He just got back from Nam and he's debriefing me."

Mills laughed into the glass he was holding up to his mouth. "Getting drunk, is what you mean to say."

The sergeant major dropped down in his chair and tore open Alex's orders. "I don't know what we're going to do with you, boy!"

"Have I done something wrong, Sergeant Major?" Alex tried to think of something that might have upset the senior NCO, but couldn't come up with a single incident.

The sergeant major twisted the end of his handlebar mustache and leaned back in his chair as far as it would go. "We try to produce quality soldiers out of this school. I mean, we bust our asses!" The sergeant major glanced over at Mills, who was finishing his drink and reaching over for the bottle. "You know what I'm talking about, Billy, people we can rely on in the fucking field!"

Mills nodded and concentrated on pouring another drink without spilling it.

"We bust our asses, and all we ask is that you fucking trainees just maintain a seventy-percent average on your fucking tests!"

Alex's expression became puzzled. He was well above seventy percent in every course.

"Look at this shit!" He held Alex's records up and shook them in his hand. "Look at this shit, Billy! Basic training . . . honor graduate . . . advanced individual training, medics . . . honor graduate . . . jump school . . ." The sergeant major dropped the package of papers on his desk. "Yup! Fucking honor graduate! The little fucker comes here, and instead of being like everyone else, what in the fuck does he do?" The senior NCO was talking to his friend.

"Honor graduate!" Mills dropped his head back against the couch and shook it. "Top, you've got yourself a fucking problem!"

"You're telling me!" The sergeant major glared over his desk at Alex. "You probably think you're going to be the honor graduate in Dog Lab, don't you!"

Alex looked down at the floor, trying to break the penetrating stare coming from the living legend.

"Well?"

"Probably." Alex whispered the word.

"Probably! Ha!" The sergeant major stood and leaned forward over his desk. "Not in *my* fucking company!

You have to earn that fucking title here, not look cute for some queer-assed medics down in Fort Sam Houston!" The sergeant major looked over at Mills, but spoke to Alex. "Get the fuck out of my office!"

Alex didn't need to be told twice. He pulled the door shut behind him and looked over at the clerk, who shrugged and raised his eyebrows before going back to his typing. Alex felt his face getting red with embarrassment.

The clerk stopped typing and looked over at Alex. "Hey, don't be upset. He likes you!"

"*Likes* me?" Alex felt like screaming. "Did you hear what was going on in there?"

"Right through the walls." The clerk hit the return lever on his typewriter and smiled.

The sergeant major waited until the door shut behind Alex, then smiled over at Mills. "That boy is going to be a better medic than you, my friend."

"Bullshit!" Mills sipped from his glass. "Punk kid!"

"I'm telling you, he's good, really good. The boy has aced everyone of his medical tests, and the commanding general of the training center at Fort Sam Houston has personally called our general and told him that Jaxson turned down an Army scholarship to med school."

Mills looked at his friend over the top edge of his glass. "he turned down an Army full ride to med school?"

"Ha! A full ride to four years' college *and* med school." The sergeant major shook his head. "Do you know why?"

"Why?"

"He said he would like to put it all on hold until he serves a tour in Vietnam to pay back everyone for giving him a chance."

Mills staggered to his feet and stumbled toward the door. He paused with his hand on the handle. "You're not shitting me, are you?"

"I'd rather be a leg!"

Mills opened the door and saw Jaxson standing near the clerk's desk. *"Bullshit!"* He screamed the single word out at Alex and slammed the door shut.

Alex stared at the door for a couple of seconds before commenting, "They *like* me?"

"Yep . . . a lot more than I thought." The clerk looked over at the billeting chart on the wall and added, "You're going to be in the Third Platoon . . . four buildings back, counting this one."

"Thanks." Alex picked up his duffel bag and looked back at the door. He couldn't believe what had just happened.

The screen door to the orderly room slammed shut behind him. What had just gone on was crazy; if he could get a transfer out of Bravo Company, he would. A voice followed him down the steps: "Believe me, the sergeant major likes you."

"Sure," Alex mumbled to himself as he walked up the sidewalk to his barracks.

The barracks sergeant showed Alex where he could bunk and assigned him an empty wall locker. He was happy that his bunk was the last one upstairs near the back fire exit. He was next to his own window. There was a wooden divider built next to each of the bunks, breaking up the floor into individual cubes. Alex had his uniforms hung up and was arranging his footlocker when he heard someone coming up the stairs.

"Shit!" The man slipped and hit the wooden wall with his shoulder.

Alex stood so that he could see who it was coming down the aisle, and recognized the sergeant first class who had been drinking with the sergeant major. Alex sat back down on his bunk and finished unpacking his socks and underwear.

"So they put you in *my* barracks." The voice came from the other side of the divider.

Alex shrugged. He had already decided that he wasn't going to take any of the NCO's crap, even if it meant that he got kicked out of the training group.

"Don't worry about me. I'm not part of the training cadre." Mills chuckled to himself. "I'm just passing through."

"To where?" Alex kept looking down in his footlocker.

"Back to Nam. Fuck . . . I can't handle this chickenshit place for more than a couple of weeks."

"I thought you just came from there."

"True, but I volunteered to go back. After all, that's where the fucking war is . . . right?"

"I guess so. It's the best war we've got right now." Alex tried acting cool.

"Fuck you, boy! What do you know about war?"

"No much . . . yet."

"You are one cocky little shit!"

Alex stood up and faced the NCO. "I try hard."

"Really?" Mills smiled and then left Alex standing by himself. He went over to one of the senior NCO rooms at the other end of the floor and unlocked the padlock with a little difficulty and entered without looking back.

Alex grinned, using only one corner of his mouth, and shook his head. It was obvious that the man was a burned-out alcoholic. He wasn't going to waste any more time thinking about him.

The door to the NCO's room opened and Mills stepped out wearing a pair of light brown PT shorts and carrying a Vietnam-style rucksack in each hand. "Come on, boy!"

"Where are we going?" Alex smiled, trying to humor the drunk.

Mills ignored Alex's question and asked his own. "Do you have any PT shorts?"

"Yes." Alex looked at the rucksacks and could see that they were heavy.

"Slip them on . . . and wear your boots."

"Where are we going?"

"We're going to take a little run before supper." Mills dropped one of the rucksacks down on Alex's bed. "With rucksacks . . . if you don't mind."

Alex looked into the red-rimmed eyes of the NCO standing in the aisle and smiled wider. "Maybe we should wait until morning; it's pretty hot outside right now."

"It's hot in Vietnam too." Mills nodded with his head at the rucksack. "Deadweight . . . fifty pounds of sand inside."

Alex shrugged and started undressing. He was going to enjoy running the loose-lipped NCO into the ground.

Mills walked over to the window and looked outside at the small stand of loblolly pines behind the barracks. "We'll do the MATA Mile."

"Fine with me." Alex had heard about the Military Advisory Command Training Area's (MATA) Mile when he had first reported into the Special Forces training group. The course was called a mile, but it was actually three-point-two miles that ran through the woods and was no more than a sandy trail crisscrossed with small streams and loose sand pits that made running extremely difficult. Alex picked up the rucksack on his bed and hefted it to guess how much it weighed. He agreed with Mills: it was close to fifty pounds.

Mills slipped his rucksack over his shoulder and shoved his right elbow under the padded shoulder strap. "We've modified these a little to reduce some of the rubbing." Mills showed Alex where they had added extra padding around the shoulders and in the back where the pack rested just above his hips. "Use your belly strap and the chest strap we've added." Mills stepped behind Alex and pulled all of the straps very tight, as if he were rigging him for a parachute jump. "I don't think the sergeant major will mind if you use his pack."

"This is the sergeant major's?" Alex didn't like the

idea of borrowing the senior NCO's gear without asking first.

"Believe me, he won't mind as long as you're running with me." Mills led the way to the stairwell and hustled downstairs and out the door before Alex could answer.

Out in the company street, Alex ran to catch up. "Where's your car?"

Mills grinned. "I haven't bought one. I told you that I'm going back to Nam very soon."

"I thought you said that you wanted to run the MATA Mile?"

"I did."

"That's a couple of miles away."

"I said we were going for a little run, didn't I?"

"Sure, but—"

"Are you ready?' Mills adjusted the drive-on rag he had tied around his forehead. He wasn't wearing a T-shirt, just shorts, boots, and a drive-on rag. Alex had dressed exactly the same.

"Whenever . . . Sergeant." Alex was beginning to feel like he'd been sucked into something that he couldn't handle. The only thing that gave him some hope was the fact that the NCO had been drinking so much.

Mills nodded and started jogging up the hill in the opposite direction, away from the MATA Mile course. Alex fell in behind the NCO and settled down to a level jog so that the rucksack wouldn't bounce as much.

Sweat broke out all over them before they had reached the corner. Alex knew that he would run the NCO into the ground because the man had to be dehydrated from the booze. They crossed over Gruber Road and headed downhill through rows of small barracks until they reached the thick North Carolina forest that bordered that side of the base. The forest was made up mostly of Scotch and loblolly pines, but Alex

102

could see a large stand of pocosin pines in the background, and that always meant there would be swamps nearby.

"How are you feeling, boy?" Mills smiled back at Alex.

"Fine . . . just got my second wind." He smiled back and felt the sweat dripping off his chin. The top half of his light brown shorts was already saturated with sweat. Mills's shorts were soaked almost entirely through, except for a very small spot on each side of his hips. "Are we going to take a break at the start of the MATA Mile?"

Mills looked back over his shoulder and grinned before answering. "*You* can if you want to. I'll wait for you back at the barracks."

"Bullshit, you will!" Alex tightened his jaws. He had planned on stopping as soon as the sergeant fell flat on his face so that it wouldn't be too embarrassing for him, but now he was going to run the son of a bitch to death!

Mills ran along the edge of the piney woods until he reached the entrance to the MATA Mile. Yellow slats of wood had been cut on one end into wedges and stamped with red letters to lead the way.

Alex felt the salty sweat run between his eyebrows and fill the inside corners of his eyes. He kept his hands on his shoulder straps and shook his head. Mills had increased his pace on the trail, and Alex had to push himself to keep up with the senior NCO. He smiled and licked his salty lips; it would be just a matter of time before the sergeant quit. Alex could feel the hot air passing through his wet hair; he was losing a lot of body fluid but he was feeling good.

A shallow sandy bottom stream crossed over the path, and Mills made a sharp right-hand turn off the marked path and started running down the center of the six-inch-deep waterway. Alex was surprised that the NCO would risk such a maneuver, and pushed himself to catch up. He was running only a couple of feet behind Mills and was trying to pass him on the left. Mills heard Alex behind him and smiled to himself. The boy had a lot of guts. Mills started edging to his left side to force Alex to stay behind him or run into a large stand of purple loosestrife growing along the banks of the stream. Mills looked up ahead and saw the water change color. His smiled widened and at the last possible second he cut sharply to the right and stayed on the wet sand around the three-foot hole. Alex couldn't stop in time and ran into the water trap. He stumbled, trying to maintain his balance, and then pitched headfirst into the water. He was back on his feet instantly, but Mills had already turned the bend in the stream and was out of sight. Alex adjusted his pack and cursed under his breath. The fall in the water hole wasn't so bad; in fact it was refreshing, but what had really screwed him up was the water that had gotten into his rucksack and soaked the dry sand. The weight on his back had almost doubled. Alex leaned forward and started running again. He felt his cheeks burn from the anger he was feeling. He wasn't going to let some drunk-assed NCO make a fool of him, not on his first day back in the training group.

Mills stepped out of the stream and slowed his pace going up the gentle slope that would take him back to the marked trail. He was almost forced to stop running until he had gained control of his laughter.

Alex saw the water marks on the dry bank and looked up. He stopped running just long enough to figure out that Mills had left the stream to pick up the trail again. He followed the contour of the slope with his eyes and guessed that if he stayed with the stream and ran hard, he could get ahead of Mills on the trail. It was taking a big risk, but he knew that he would never catch up to the sergeant by following behind him. Alex grabbed his shoulder straps, pulled down hard to keep his pack from bouncing, and started running downstream. He made his first bend in the stream and saw why Mills had taken the trail instead. Mills and the sergeant major must have reconnoitered the area on prior runs. The stream widened and turned a muddy brown where another stream intersected it. A large flat marshy area went off to the right side of the watercourse. The two-acre flat was covered with four-foot-high purple loosestrife in full bloom. Thousands of bees and hornets flew from plant to plant, one collecting pollen and the other hunting for small spiders that lived on the plants.

Alex didn't hesitate. He followed the stream to his right and started running through the wildflowers. He could feel the marshy ground beneath his feet, but he couldn't see his boots because of the plants. Alex thought of water moccasins for the first time. There had to be some living near this stream. His thoughts left the snakes and centered on his bare chest, just below his left nipple. A bee's wings had gotten stuck on his wet body and the small insect fought desperately to break free. One of its wings broke loose and it stung Alex.

"Fuck!" Alex released his grip on his rucksack and brushed the dying bee off his skin. The stinger and part of the bee's intestines remained hanging from his chest. Alex was distracted when another bee stung him . . . and then another. He started running faster, until he cleared the marsh and felt solid ground beneath his feet. The trail could be seen only a few meters to his front. Alex didn't pause, and ignored the pain coming from the bee stings. It could have been worse; just one of the hornets would have caused much more damage, because it would sting until you killed it.

Mills looked back over his shoulder at the trail and slowed his pace. He had lost the kid.

Alex panicked. He couldn't see Mills ahead of him. The trial had widened and he could see a couple hundred meters to the parking lot behind one of the committee group-storage areas. Mills must have gotten a tremendous lead on him. At first Alex was going to give up and start walking. He had made an honorable effort and the water-soaked sand was a very good reason to walk. His pack was tearing his shoulders apart. Alex took one walking step and then started running again. He wasn't going to let Mills gloat back at the barracks. He might be beaten, but he was going to close the gap as much as he could before Mills reached their billets.

Alex didn't realize the spectacle he was making as he ran alongside the paved road back to his barracks. Cars slowed down while the occupants stared at the young soldier running with water dripping out of his pack and splotches of mud covering his bare legs. It was quite obvious to everyone that the soldier was pushing himself extremely hard.

Mills broke out of the woods and turned to head back to the barracks. He was still wearing his smile until he saw Alex make the turn onto the main road. The kid had somehow gained a half-mile lead on him! Mills stopped running, shocked into a standstill, and then he took off running at a pain-racked clip. He wasn't going to allow some trainee to beat him at his own game. He hadn't told Alex that he held the record for running the MATA Mile; he had planned on letting the kid find out for himself.

Alex felt the pull of the hill in his muscles. He wanted to stop running. He had had enough of this macho bullshit for one day. He closed his eyes and leaned forward. He was not going to be seen *walking* into his company area. He should have quit back in the woods and rested before trying to make it back, but now that he was out in the open where everyone could see him, he had to finish the run.

The sergeant major sat on the dark green picnic table and inhaled the smoke from his cigar. He saw

Alex make the turn down the company street and struggle to keep his balance. Mills was nowhere in sight. The senior NCO grinned and took another lungful of smoke.

Alex blinked to clear the sweat out of his eyes and saw the sergeant major sitting on the table. He flexed his jaws and increased his pace slightly. Mills must have already gone into the barracks and probably taken a fucking shower!

The sergeant major shook his head from side to side. Mills had just made the turn onto the company street. Alex was going to beat him by almost a half-mile.

Alex saw the sergeant major shaking his head and thought that the senior NCO was making fun of him. He started running harder, and nearly fell on his face. The sergeant major left the table and started walking toward Alex.

"Drop your rucksack over on the table and walk it off for a couple of minutes."

Alex was too tired to answer and only nodded in agreement. The instant the rucksack came off his back he felt as if he was going to float up in the air, and grabbed hold of the table. "Shit! That was a mother-fucking *bear*!"

"Good run, huh?" The sergeant major turned his head away from Alex when he exhaled the blue smoke from his lungs.

"Oh, shit!" Alex took a couple of deep breaths before asking, "How much did he beat me by?"

The sergeant major's mustache twitched and he started laughing. The kid didn't know that he was ahead of Mills!

"I don't think it's that funny, Sergeant Major!" Alex gasped for air. He still hadn't recovered from the run.

"I'm not laughing at you . . . shit, soldier! You beat him!" The sergeant major pointed back down the road at Mills.

DONALD E. ZLOTNIK

Alex whirled around and stood with his mouth open. He couldn't believe his eyes!

Mills tried pressing his lips together but was forced to open his mouth to breathe. He stopped near the picnic table under a stand of pines and dropped his rucksack next to Alex's. "Good run." He wasn't a bad sport, but he hated to lose at anything. He flashed a warning look at the sergeant major.

"I *beat* you!" Alex's face lit up.

"No shit, kid!" Mills used the palm of his hand to wipe the sweat off his face.

"*I beat you!*"

"You're making a big deal out of a little thing." Mills glaced at the sergeant major, who was reaching up to pull a bee stinger out of Alex's arm.

The sergeant major raised his eyebrows at Mills. The kid had guts. "What happened here?"

Alex looked down at his arm. "I ran through a field of wildflowers next to the stream and got hit by a couple of bees."

Mills and the sergeant major knew instantly what Alex had done to get ahead. They had run that course enough times to know every foot of it. The shortcut Alex had taken required guts—even though he didn't know about the six-foot cottonmouth that claimed that section of the steam for its home.

"Go on inside and take a shower. You look like shit!" The sergeant major patted Alex's shoulder.

Mills watched the seventeen-year-old slip behind the screen door and waited until he was out of hearing range before commenting, "That kid is going to make one damn fine Special Forces medic, if he can get through Dog Lab."

The sergeant major agreed, and reached over to reclaim his rucksack. The weight surprised him. "Damn! What happened to my rucksack?"

Mills hefted the pack that was rigged exactly like his but was at least double the weight. "Waterlogged."

He looked at the barracks door where Alex had disappeared with an even greater respect in his eyes.

Alex fell asleep right after his shower and didn't wake up until three the next morning. He had been exhausted by the bus trip and the run. He laced his hands behind his head and looked out his window at the bright moonlit sky. A soft summer breeze had cooled off the heat of the day. Alex spilled off his bunk and went over to the fire escape. The door had been left open. He stepped out onto the small second-floor porch and looked out over the open training field behind his barracks. He saw a dark shadow on one of the tables under the pines and waited to see if it would move. The red tip of a cigarette came up from the shadow's side and stopped where the man's mouth was located. The glow brightened and the hand went back down to the side.

Alex climbed down the fire-escape ladder, wearing only his undershorts. He was barefoot and took his time picking his way across the cinders and small rocks that lined the sides of the narrow asphalt road behind the barracks. He recognized Sergeant Mills as soon as he reached the moonlit center of the pines. "You're up late, Sergeant."

Mills took another pull from his cigarette and flicked it back onto the asphalt, where it could burn itself out.

"Am I bothering you?" Alex stopped walking toward the NCO.

Mills reached down between his legs and brought a bottle up to his mouth. He took his time drinking and then set the bottle back down on the seat. "Naw . . . not really. Have a seat." Mills patted the top of the table next to him. "I like it out here at night. It's so peaceful. Listen. . . . A whippoorwill must be hunting moths over there in the woods."

"When are you leaving for Vietnam?"

Mills kept looking out over the open field. "This

afternoon I catch my flight for Oakland Army Depot in California."

"So soon?" Alex was shocked. He didn't know why, but he had thought that Mills was going to be around for at least a couple more weeks.

"I've some business to take care of on the way, and then I'll ship out."

"What are you going to do over there?"

"I don't know, I guess whatever the action is this time. Maybe one of the Greek projects, or back to an A camp. I guess working in an A camp is the best place for a medic."

"You really are a medic?"

Mills looked at the trainee. "What in the fuck did you think I'd be?"

"I . . . I . . ."

"You didn't think that I was smart-looking enough to be a Special Forces medic?"

Alex felt his face getting warm. That was exactly what he had been thinking. "Not really, it's just that you look more like a weapons man." Alex had been right in that assessment. Mills had the solid build of an infantryman and looked like he should be handling mortars and heavy weapons, not a scalpel.

Mills chuckled. "Don't worry about it. I started out as an infantryman with the 82nd, up the street. I ran into a good NCO, who convinced me that I had a fucking brain in my head, so I joined S.F."

"What do you think about Dog Lab?" Alex asked the question that had been bothering him for months. He had heard all the rumors, but what he needed to hear was the truth from someone who had gone through the course.

"Dog Lab is going to be the hardest training you've ever gone through in your life. Some people say that it's even tougher than med school."

"How do people graduate from it, then!" Alex's voice rose.

"I started out in a class of seventy-three men, and eleven graduated. That's no disrespect for those who flunked out, either, they're damn good medics over in the 82nd or one of the leg divisions."

"I couldn't handle that." Alex was telling the truth. He had set his heart on becoming a Special Forces medic and had told his sister Keena that he was going to be a Green Beret. There was no way he could face her again if he failed.

"I don't think you're going to have much of a problem except maybe with the dog." Mills's voice lowered and he glanced over at Alex to see his reaction in the moonlight.

"What do you mean?"

"You know about the dogs, don't you?"

"I've heard rumors, but you know we're not allowed to visit the lab until we graduate from our internship and return here."

"There's a reason for that. You see . . . Shit, I shouldn't be telling you this!" Mills lit another cigarette from the one he had burning.

"I don't want to get you in trouble." Alex gave Mills a chance to back out.

"Fuck, it won't get me in trouble. I just don't want to scare you off." He inhaled deeply and spoke as he exhaled. "'You know that you're going to be assigned a dog. They get them from the Humane Society pounds right before they're gassed." Mills was trying to justify what he was going to say next. "You're going to have to either shoot your dog or surgically amputate one of its legs or allow for gangrene to set in."

"Why? Can't we learn about that stuff without hurting an animal?"

"No, dammit!" Mills's voice rose in anger. "Would you rather it be a human? Man, in war you have to *know* what to do as a medic. Believe me, when the shit hits the fan, they'll look to you to patch them up, and that includes the officers. You've got to know your shit cold."

"What do they do with the dogs when we're finished?"

"They all die."

"All of them? Even the dogs that get well?"

"*All* of them, and I don't have to tell you that after you've nursed your dog back to health, you can get very attached to him." Mills looked hard at Alex. "I know. I've been there. Just remember that *human* lives depend on how much you learn in Dog Lab!" He changed the subject. "Memorize your *Merck Manual* from cover to cover."

"I've already started."

Mills looked at the trainee sharing the top of the picnic table with him and shook his head. The kid was sharp. "Learn your medicines too."

"I've worked in a pharmacy since I was a little kid." Alex tried mumbling the words a little, because he was getting embarrassed.

"You've been around, kid!" Mills was becoming more and more impressed. "If I told you: 'Emetine hydrochloride, 65 mg. a day, followed by tetracycline, 250 mg. four times a day, and then di-iodohydroxyquin, 650 mg. orally three times a day for, say, twenty days . . . what kind of disease am I treating?"

Alex frowned and looked down at his bare feet resting on the wooden bench attached to the picnic table. Mills smiled. Alex looked up and answered, "Dysentery? I'm not sure of the dosages of medicine, but it sounds like you would be treating acute amoebic dysentery."

"Shit! You are one sharp little punk! You learned all of that living in fucking New York?" Mills was very impressed. He knew a lot of medics who couldn't have answered his question.

"We *are* civilized in New York, Sergeant. Besides, I read a lot." Alex didn't tell him that he had studied

Asian diseases on his own when he was assigned to Fort Sam Houston.

Mills hopped off the table and stretched. The sun was breaking over the treetops. "They should be sounding reveille soon."

"Yeah, I'd like to get cleaned up and shaved before the rest of my fellow trainees are up."

"Shaved?" Mills shook his head.

"Get off my ass, Sergeant! I shave!"

"Right, kid . . . right!" Mills climbed up the fire-escape ladder and entered the screen door as quietly as a ghost.

Alex sat in the back of the classroom and looked at the stack of medical books neatly arranged on his desk. He glanced around the room and counted the new trainees. He remembered what Mills had said about the dropout rate and wondered how many of them would be there in sixteen weeks.

"Check your books against your list and sign your payroll signature at the bottom before you turn it in to me!" The instructor's voice boomed in the large room. "Which one of you is Jaxson?"

Alex felt his face getting red as everyone turned to look at him. "I am, Sergeant."

The NCO took this time staring at the small-framed trainee and then a slow smile spread across his face. "Did you beat Sergeant Mills yesterday on the MATA Mile?"

"It was a little longer, Sergeant. We ran from Bravo Company there and back."

"Oh? I heard you took him on the course." The NCO's voice revealed his respect for the trainee. "Do you know that Sergeant Mills holds the record for running that course?"

"No, I didn't, Sergeant."

"You must be really fast."

Alex didn't answer.

"You didn't cheat, did you?"

"I don't cheat at anything, Sergeant!"

"Good . . . we don't like cheaters here at the Dog Lab." The NCO held up his hand to suppress a grin. He couldn't believe Mills let a little kid like Jaxson beat him on the course. "All right! Enough bullshit! Everyone leave your books on your desk. Remember where you were sitting and follow me. We're going to introduce all of you to your best friend for the next sixteen weeks."

Alex waited until everyone else had left the room and got at the end of the line. He could hear dogs barking as soon as they had passed through a double set of swinging doors. The NCO opened a door marked "KENNEL" and held it open until Alex had passed. The instructor stared hard at Alex and watched his reaction when he saw the cages containing the dogs. He knew the rumors that had been going around about the lab and he was watching for any signs on the faces of the trainees that would give him an early warning.

Alex's eyes slipped from one cage to another and rested momentarily on each of the animals. He hoped he would be assigned a mean, vicious animal, even a rabid one that would be easy to put to sleep when they were done.

The instructor assigned each one of the trainees a dog and wrote the student's name on the dog's cage card. Alex was the last one to get assigned a dog, but all of the other cages were empty. The instructor looked over at Alex and then down at a large cage on the floor. "Jaxson, you'll have this animal. He's out in back, but they'll be bringing him in soon."

"Yes, Sergeant." Alex had to swallow. He hadn't realized how dry this throat was. He closed his eyes when he heard the door to the outside dog runs open. He prayed that the dog would be rabid.

"Here's your animal, Jaxson." The sergeant's voice was neutral.

Alex opened his eyes and stared at the most beautiful silver-and-black German shepherd he had ever seen. "This dog, Sergeant?"

"Yes."

"He doesn't look like a dog someone would send over to the dog pound."

"He was a champion, but he's suffering from a severe hip displacement."

"Oh." Alex felt his heart starting to beat faster. He couldn't kill that dog in sixteen weeks. That was something he already knew. The dog stepped toward Alex and licked the back of his hand. "Oh, shit!"

"What did you say, soldier?" The instructor had heard him clearly.

"I said, 'Oh, shit,' Sergeant."

"Why? Don't you like your animal?"

"I like him just fine, Sergeant."

"Good, because you're going to be operating on that animal's hip, and I hope by then you'll have learned enough to keep him alive. This is one dog that the owner wants back!"

Alex's heart pounded in his chest. There was hope. He looked down at the dog and smiled. He would give it his best effort.

CHAPTER FIVE

✪✪✪✪✪✪✪✪✪✪✪✪✪✪✪

COWBOY

Sash slipped a throw pillow under his youngest son's head and eased himself off the couch. His right leg had fallen asleep. He walked over to the stained-glass window in his library and stared at the antique rendition of Saint Jude holding a staff in his left hand and a picture of Christ in his right. He enjoyed having his morning coffee in the library because the morning sun brought the stained glass to life.

"Dad, you have to go."

Sash turned and saw his eldest son standing in the entranceway to the library, wearing his goose-down ski jacket and holding one of the insulated picnic bags they took with them to lacrosse games when young Alex played.

"Mom has packed us some sandwiches and a thermos of coffee." Alex nodded back toward the kitchen. "Grab your wallet and stuff and let's get out of here."

"Where?" Sash frowned and looked back at the couch where Bobby lay sleeping peacefully.

"Washington, D.C."

A light flashed in Sash's eyes. Mary always knew what was in the back of his mind. He hadn't even considered going to Washington, since it was Christmas morning. It would have been too much to ask of his family—but as with all good gifts, it was not too much for them to give. "I can't go and leave all of you, not on Christmas . . . not before Bobby opens his presents."

"If you wait until daybreak, it'll be too late, Dad." Alex started turning around. "Bobby'll understand, and Elizabeth has already agreed. She helped make the sandwiches. Let's go."

"What do you mean, *let's*?"

"I'm not going to let you drive all the way there alone." Alex smiled. "Besides, I want to meet my godfather."

"We'll never be able to find him in Washington, son. Do you know how big that place is?"

"Dad! You're not thinking. Uncle Alex mentioned that he was going to Lafayette Park. I checked the road atlas and its a little over five hundred miles to Washington by interstate. With a little luck, we can make it there by noon. I don't think those demonstrators are going to get there too early, especially if they want to draw the press."

Sash liked the idea. They might have a chance of stopping Alex. It was a very small chance, but at least they would be doing something, which was a lot better than sitting around waiting to hear it on the news. "Do you think a plane might be faster? We can rent a Lear jet."

"Good idea, Dad! Whom are we going to call at two in the morning?"

"You're right! Let's go!" Sash looked back at his sleeping ten-year-old son. "Sorry, Bobby . . . but I'll make it up to you." The boy wiggled his nose and pushed his face against the cushion.

Mary was sipping from a cup of coffee and looking out the window when Sash entered the kitchen. He went over and gave her a hug.

"Git before I change my mind! I still don't think that bum is worth it, but you'll end up making the whole family depressed if I don't let you go!"

Sash gave her a peck on the cheek. "Thanks."

Young Alex was leaning over the driver's door of the AC Cobra and removing something from under the front seat.

"What's that?" Sash opened the door of the Rolls-Royce.

"Something we might need for our trip." Alex hurried around the back of the Rolls and slipped in on the passenger's seat. "Did you bring some cash?"

Sash patted his pocket and felt his money clip. "Enough to get us there, plus I have my credit cards."

"Let's go." Alex felt the excitement rising from his stomach. He removed the cigarette lighter from the console and plugged in the radar detector.

"Where in the heck did you get that?" Sash flashed a suspicious look at his son.

"Dad, join the eighties! A guy can't drive a Cobra and not have some protection."

"We'll talk about this later!" Sash agreed with his son that they would probably need the detector if they were going to make it to Washington in time, but he didn't like what a radar detector signified. He changed the subject. "Did you plot a course?"

"Yes, sir! Down to Toledo and pick up the turnpike, head east until we hit U.S. 76, then the 46 intersection until we hit U.S. 270 into Washington. Easy route."

"Alex . . ." Sash blinked and stared hard through the windshield. "I appreciate this . . . you don't know how much that *bum* means to me."

Alex reached over and squeezed his father's leg. "I know, Pops . . . I know."

Alex rubbed his frozen beard and tried pulling out some of the ice, using his fingers as a comb. "Well, Fang, I think we should be strolling over to the park. I don't think your young master is going to want to wait."

The dog whined softly and nuzzled the middle-aged vet's hand.

119

Alex inhaled a deep lungful of cold air and sighed. He looked up at the crystal cold blue sky and scratched the German shepherd behind the ears. "It's a good day to die."

The park across the street from the White House was famous as a protest site because of the view it had of the President's quarters. Over the years the park had also picked up a very bad reputation for being a place to get picked up, if you were looking for male companionship. Alex entered the park from the corner opposite where the Mercedes Benz was parked. He could see the exhaust curling up in the still air and guessed that Fang's owner had arrived and was waiting for them. Alex skirted a line of snow-covered benches and looked around the area for the pro-abortion demonstrators. The park was empty except for a small group of bums sitting together on one bench, wrapped in newspapers and cardboard boxes to hold in their body heat.

Fang paused and looked over at the black windows of the Mercedes. He sniffed the air.

"Go on, dog!" Alex smiled down at the beautiful animal. "I think someone is waiting for you."

Fang took three quick steps and then stopped to look back at Alex.

The back door of the Mercedes opened and a young boy's voice carried all the way across the park. "Fang! Fang! Come here, boy!"

Alex nodded and smiled. He watched as a tall, extremely well-dressed woman left the driver's side of the car and walked around the front. She waited until Alex got within a few feet of her before she spoke. "Are you Mr. Jaxson?"

Alex nodded.

"You don't know how much this means to my son, Brandon. He absolutely *loves* that animal. We bought the dog as a means of security for Brandon." She glaced around the area and shivered. Alex couldn't tell if it was because of the cold or the bums sitting on the nearby bench. "Fang is trained to protect Brandon. He is a very expensive animal."

Alex nodded again, but remained quiet.

"I mean, they are so close that the dog sleeps in the same bed with Brandon, not that I approve of such a thing, but the boy sneaks him into his room at night." She reached into the pocket of her coat and removed a small folded bundle of money. "Here . . . I told you five hundred dollars reward—right?"

Alex nodded again. He was watching the reunion between the dog and the boy.

"Well, I hope you have a Merry Christmas. We've got to be getting back home . . . my husband is having some people over for brunch."

Alex stared directly into her eyes and grinned. "Your husband should spend a little more time with your son."

"What?" She looked shocked. "What did you say?"

Alex remained smiling.

"Do you know who my husband is?"

Alex shook his head slowly from left to right. "No . . . and I really don't care."

"Well!" She whirled around and picked her way through the slush to her car door, mumbling under her breath, "The ungrateful creature!"

Alex watched the car pull away from the curb. He couldn't see into the back smoked windows, but he knew that Fang was watching him. Alex waved and turned toward the bench housing the bums. "Hey, fellas . . . how would you like to spend Christmas Day in a hotel room, with a lot of good booze?"

A white-haired bum without any teeth glared at Alex. "Get away from us! What are you doing, tripping out on some of that crap you hippies smoke?"

Alex smiled and handed the old man the five one-hundred-dollar bills the woman had given him. "Have a good time."

"Holy shit!" The old man gasped and turned around to show his buddies. "Thanks, mister." There was a long pause as Alex walked away. "Hey, mister! God bless you!"

Alex stopped walking and turned around to stare at the white-haired, white-bearded bum. He felt the tear leave his eye and turn frigid as it slipped down his face next to his nose. His mind slipped back to another time and to something he had loved very much—a dog named Cowboy.

The humidity was already at a level that left your skin clammy, and it was only four in the morning. Alex threw his medical books into the small rucksack issued for that purpose and slipped one of the straps over his shoulder. He moved quietly so he wouldn't wake the rest of the men sleeping on his floor of the barracks. The fire-escape door creaked when he pulled it open and slipped out on the painted wooden porch. He looked down at the picnic table where he had sat and talked with Sergeant Mills. It seemed like years ago, but was only a couple of months. Alex smiled as he recalled the letter he had received from the sergeant. Mills had just been assigned as senior medic for a new A detachment in III Corps. He said they were going to build a new camp on the Cambodian border near a place called Tong Le Chon.

Alex adjusted his rucksack on his shoulders and decided that he would walk over to the Dog Lab rather than run this morning. He didn't want to have to sit through classes all day wearing a sweat-stained uniform. He was supposed to march over to the lab with the rest of his class, but the senior instructor had assigned him to the morning kennel detail and he had been excused so that he could shovel up the dog scat and hose down the runs before everyone else arrived for class. The job took only a half-hour, but he always arrived early enough to take his dog out for a walk before it got too muggy. Late summer in North Carolina was surely the origin of the term "dog days."

The soft call from a late hunting owl caught Alex's attention. He paused and tried locating the bird in the tall pines next to the road, but failed. He was angry at himself. If he couldn't locate an owl, how could he ever locate a North Vietnamese soldier in the jungle? The owl blinked and turned its head, giving away its location.

"There you are!" Alex smiled and started walking faster.

The dog heard him coming before Alex turned the corner of the building. He had been waiting patiently for the young soldier to arrive for their morning walk. A number of the other dogs were barking at Alex, but Cowboy just sat there waiting.

" 'Morning, Cowboy. Let me hose down the runs and then we'll go." Alex set his book bag down on the top step next to the rear door and turned on the faucet. He grabbed the nozzle end of the black high-pressure hose before the pressure had built up and opened the nozzle a little. The dog runs had been designed with gutters running along the base of the slanted decks so that when the concrete was hosed down, all of the scat and food scraps would be washed into the gutter and carried down to the far end, where it went into a large underground cesspool. Once a week, Alex had to dump a couple bags of lime in the concrete holding tank to help speed up the decomposing process.

The sound of the hose sent all of the dogs running through their flap exits back into the lab's kennel. Alex finished his work and curled the hose up next to the door.

"Come on, Cowboy, let's go, fella." Alex unlatched the Cyclone gate and let the large German shepherd out. "Let's check out the back meadow today." Cowboy gave a throaty huff, as if he had understood Alex and agreed. The dog explored the path about twenty meters ahead of his friend and would occasionally look back to see if Alex was still there. Alex had selected a walking stick from a pile of dead branches and had dropped it when he felt the sap sticking to his palm. He was squatting down trying to wipe the sticky tree blood off his hand when Cowboy gave one of his warning barks. Alex looked up and saw one of the largest skunks in the world walking down the trail directly toward him.

"Shit!" Alex sprang up and started running into the woods. "Come on, Cowboy!"

The dog skirted the skunk and then started running hard to catch up to Alex. He felt the pain in his hip joint and whined. Alex stopped running and spun around. "You all right, Cowboy?" Alex looked back at the skunk on the trail. It was waddling its way toward the row of troop barracks and the mess halls, looking for a free breakfast. Cowboy nuzzled Alex's hand and whimpered.

"Soon, fella . . . very soon." Alex was referring to the hip operation he was going to perform on the dog. He had been studying hard ever since he had been assigned Cowboy and knew that his final test for graduation from the Special Forces medical course was a successful operation on the dog. He had already lost a couple dozen of his classmates because their animals had died during operations or during medical treatment. A number of his classmates had already flunked out or just quit because they refused to operate on animals. Alex couldn't understand that kind of reasoning, and wondered what they expected to train on. Humans? "Come here." Alex sat down on the sandy soil and scratched Cowboy behind the ears. "You're going to be chasing rabbits very soon, and then you'll think you're a stud."

Cowboy shoved the back of his head against Alex's hand and groaned from the pleasure he felt.

"Look over there." Alex pointed at a family of cottontails feeding next to the trail near a bright orange butterfly weed. Cowboy made a loud huffing sound and leaned forward. "No, Cowboy! I said you can chase rabbits after your operation." Alex gently held the dog's collar. "Did you know that the Indians used to treat pulmonary ailments with the root of that orange-flowered plant?"

"No, I didn't know that."

Alex spun around and looked directly into the eyes of the sergeant major, who was squatting five feet behind him. "Damn! Sergeant Major! You scared the shit out of me!"

"You're going to make a fine soldier in Vietnam, Jaxson . . . a really *fine* specimen of a Green Beret!"

"Come on, Sergeant Major . . . give it a rest." Alex blushed over being caught totally off-guard and talking to a dog.

"So that plant really is good for chest colds?" The sergeant major stepped over and looked closely at the bright orange flowers.

"Sure is. The roots are ground and then chewed."

"Hmmm . . . interesting. I'll have to remember that." He nodded back up the trail. "Let's get on back to the lab. There's someone I want you to meet this morning before class starts."

"Am I in some kind of trouble?"

The sergeant major glanced at Alex from the corner of his eye and grinned underneath his heavy handlebar mustache. "Far from it. You've made yourself quite the reputation here in the training group. The only way that you won't make honor graduate is if you totally—and I mean totally—fail your final exam."

"What about Cowboy?" Alex looked over at the well-groomed shepherd. "What if he—?"

"That's what we're going to talk about this morning. We've set up the operation for tomorrow morning."

"Tomorrow? So soon?" Alex felt a lump growing in his throat.

"Your class starts Phase III training in less than a month, and the dog has to be healed by then."

Alex nodded in agreement.

The three of them walked down the narrow trail in single file, with Cowboy leading the way back to the building that housed the Dog Lab and medical classrooms. The sergeant major reached up and pushed Alex's cap down over his eyes from where he had shoved it on the back of his head. "Fix your cap before we get there."

Alex stopped on the trail and checked his gigline and removed the olive-drab cap from his head to check the blue band that signified he was a trainee with the training group's Bravo Company.

"Good, he's already here." The sergeant major nodded at a yellow Corvette in one of the visitor parking spaces next to the building. "Put Cowboy in his run and meet me in the staff office in five minutes."

"Yes, Sergeant Major." Alex always addressed the living legend formally when they were near any of the other cadre or trainees, even though everyone in the training group knew that the sergeant major had nearly adopted Jaxson. The old warrior and the trainee ran together every day after Alex got out of class, carrying their fifty-pound rucksacks; Mills had left his as a gift for Alex. The sergeant major also had Alex over to his home for dinner every Sunday after Mass. That was a new experience for Alex, going to Mass on Sundays, but the sergeant major and his family had eased him into it slowly. Alex was shocked at first that a living combat legend would go to church, but there were a lot of things about the elite Special Forces troopers that surprised Alex. Mills listened to classical music, and most of the instructors at the school were well-read and had college degrees or were very close to getting them. The Army's Special Forces had gained a reputation as ferocious fighters, which they had earned, but they were also well-educated and compassionate men.

The door to the staff office was open when Alex entered the building. He could see the rest of his class marching at the far end of the street. They should be arriving in a couple of minutes and would take a fifteen-minute break before the first session started. Alex stuck his head in the open doorway.

"Come in, Jaxson." The sergeant major beckoned for Alex to enter the cadre sanctuary, which was normally off-limits to students. "I want you to meet Dr. Redman, one of the best veterinary surgeons in the United States Army—and the best surgeon at Fort Bragg."

The doctor smiled at Alex and shook his head. "I wouldn't say I was *that* good."

Alex could see the silver eagle attached to the officer's collar underneath his white smock. "Pleasure meeting you, sir."

"I've heard some really good things about you, young man, and that comes all the way from Fort Sam Houston!"

Alex glanced over at the sergeant major, who shrugged.

"Well, let's go take a look at this dog that *we're* going to operate on."

"We?" Alex looked at the sergeant major.

"You bet your skinny ass, soldier!" The sergeant major was smiling. "Do you think I would let a damn trainee operate on my dog all by himself?"

"*Your* dog?"

"Cowboy's former owner thought that three hundred dollars in the hand was better than the five thousand dollars he might see if the operation is a success, but he still can't breed, Cowboy, so he sold him to me." The sergeant major gave a curt nod. "Now, show the doctor where the dog is kept."

"Yes, sir!" Alex shot ahead of them and opened the door to the kennel. He was sure he could have performed the operation by himself, but just knowing that the surgeon was there had taken a great weight of responsibility off his shoulders.

Alex and the sergeant major watched while the veterinarian examined the dog. The doctor looked at Alex and nodded his agreement. "I go along with your assessment, young man. He'll require steel pins to hold the joint in place."

Alex beamed. He had written a detailed report on what was required for Cowboy's operation that included a recommended procedure for the operation and annexes attached that detailed medicines and rehabilitation procedures. The report was so well done that the instructors used it as a guide for the rest of the classes, which caused more than a little jealousy.

The vet stood and looked back down at the dog. "He's very healthy; it was a good idea, taking him for those walks every morning to prepare him for the operation. His muscles and ligaments are well-developed."

Alex looked away from the doctor. He hadn't taken Cowboy out in the mornings to build him up for the operation, but because he had grown extremely attached to the dog. The sergeant major had foreseen that, which was the reason he had assigned Cowboy to Alex. If he hadn't intervened, Cowboy would have been put to sleep along with all the other dogs in the lab program. The sergeant major knew Alex's reputation in Special Forces and recognized that he was probably the only trainee who could save the animal.

The operation took all morning. Alex had spent the entire night before reviewing the procedures and making sure that absolutely everything in the operating room was perfect. He had even sterilized all the equipment they might be using, twice, just to make sure.

The veterinary surgeon watched over Alex's shoulder. "You can close now, Alex." He stepped back from the operating table and nodded to the sergeant major, who had been watching the whole operation with the rest of the class through a large window.

The sergeant major went into the cadre lounge and opened a drawer in one of the cabinets. He removed a full bottle of Jim Beam and three beakers that had been designed for some kind of medical test. Alex and the veterinarian entered the room still wearing their bloody operating smocks.

"Good work there, soldier!" The sergeant major held up his beaker of bourbon in a toast. "Have some, Colonel."

The vet smiled and took a courteous sip from the beaker offered to him.

"Jaxson?"

"I've got to get over to post-op, Sergeant Major. I can't be drinking during class."

"I'll cover for you." The sergeant major winked.

"Thanks, anyway . . . but I've got to take care of your dog." Alex smiled and slipped back out of the room.

The sergeant major finished his drink and slammed the beaker down on the table. "There goes the best medic in Special Forces!"

Alex heard the comment from down the hall and beamed with pride.

"Hey, Alex! We heard that everything went all right with Cowboy. Congratulations!"

"Thanks, Luke. I was worried for a while back there, but he's a tough dog." Alex liked the smiling Californian, who was also going through Dog Lab. "How's your mutt?"

"Tarzan?" Luke's lip curled and his eyes twinkled. "He's almost healed, and ready to take over again as the kennel stud. And speaking of stud duty—how about joining us downtown tonight?"

Alex glanced back to the recovery room.

"Don't fucking tell us that you've got to baby-sit Cowboy tonight! We've all got dogs in Recovery, and it's time that we went down and got our ashes hauled."

"Ashes hauled?" Alex frowned.

"Yeah, get laid . . . fucked."

"I don't know about leaving Cowboy."

"When was the last time you got laid, Jaxson?" Luke nudged Alex's side and waited for an answer.

"It's been a while." Alex tried to recall his last bout in bed. "Quite a while. Dog Lab has kept me busy."

"Ditto for all of us. We're leaving right after our last lab. Be ready by five." Luke started walking toward their next classroom.

"Five in the afternoon? Where are we going to find women that early?"

"Don't worry, paratrooper—I was assigned to the 82nd up on Gruber Road before joining S.F. I know the *lay* of the land!" Luke hooked his thumbs behind his lab-coat collar and strutted through the open doorway.

Alex checked his watch. He still had plenty of time to check on Cowboy, and if the dog looked all right, he decided that he would join his classmates for a little fun downtown. A couple of beers sounded good after all the weeks of studying and worrying about operating on Cowboy.

Luke and two more trainees were waiting in Luke's car in the student parking lot when Alex stepped out the side door of his wooden barracks.

"Hurry the fuck up, Alex!"

Alex jogged down the sidewalk past the sergeant major's office to the parked car. "You said five—it's a quarter till."

"Fuck, let's go. I'm so fucking horny that I'm going to come in my pants just thinking about it." The normally quiet trainee riding in the back with Alex pressed his head against the seat and groaned in mock ecstasy.

Luke glanced back at his classmate and shook his head. "If you're that bad off, you should have stroked it before going out tonight."

"Why? I want pussy, not palm."

"These girls charge by the shot. You come—you pay."

"Each time?" The trainee leaned forward on his seat so that he could hear Luke.

"Each time. If you want to play machine gun with them, you'd better have a wad of money."

"Fuck!" The trainee dropped back down against the scat and wished that he had taken care of business earlier so that he could last longer with the prostitute. He sulked the rest of the way downtown.

"I didn't know we were going to pick up prostitutes." Alex had lost interest in the trip.

"You don't like whores?" The big trainee riding up front with Luke spoke over his shoulder. He had to yell to be heard, because the convertible top was down.

"My mother's a prostitute."

Luke looked away from the road and back to see if Alex was joking, but caught only the side of his face as he turned away.

"Man! You shouldn't be talking about your own mother like that!" The big trainee leaned forward with his nose almost touching the windshield so he could light a cigarette.

Alex ignored his remark. He had never been with a prostitute because it reminded him of his own childhood. He had tried going to bed with one back in jump school, but he couldn't even get an erection because the only thing he could think about was if the woman had any kids stashed away in some dumpy apartment somewhere. It reminded him too much of his own mother. He shrugged his shoulders and contented himself with sipping a few long-neck bottle beers and listening to some music.

Bragg Boulevard was like any other main drag that linked a civilian town to a military base. It was lined with pawn shops and Army-Navy stores that bought TA-50 gear from the troops for rock-bottom prices and sold it back to other troops who were rotating for triple the price. A few car dealerships dotted the ten-mile stretch, and dozens of small bars sprinkled the strip.

"So what do you guys want to do first?" Luke yelled over the wind.

Alex shrugged. He would go wherever the others wanted to go.

"How about making a pit stop at the Shangri-la Lounge and see if anyone else is downtown." Luke glanced back over his shoulder. "You ever been there, Alex?"

"No."

"You might like it. A retired S.F. trooper owns it and it's a stopping-off place where all of the guys rotating from Nam go to bullshit and meet up with their buddies. It's one of the few S.F. bars in Fayette-ville."

"Sounds good to me!" The trainee sitting in the backseat with Alex liked the idea.

Alex watched Luke take the right fork in the road where Bragg Boulevard split by the Martinizing Cleaners. He slowed the convertible down, avoiding a well-known Fayetteville Police Department speed trap and pulled into the parking lot of the Shangri-la Lounge.

"Get out so that I can put the top up." Luke pushed a lever and the convertible top rose slowly into place. "Last month some motherfucking egghead from the 82nd threw a tear-gas grenade through the door of the Shangri-la and the cigarette smoke was so thick inside that it took ten minutes before anybody felt the gas!" Luke brushed his bleached blond hair back out of his eyes. He wore it at the maximum length allowed in the training group, and twice he had been called up front during class and one of the instructors had actually measured it with a ruler. Luke trimmed his hair as carefully as someone else would trim a mustache. He was proud of his surfing background and played the role to the hilt for the eastern girls. It got him a lot of pussy.

"Let's go, *legs*!" Luke pushed the tall trainee toward the door. "Or are you fucking afraid to bump elbows with *real* S.F.-ers?"

"Fuck you, Luke! Who are you calling a leg? I've got fifty more jumps than you have!" The superhorny trainee talked from behind the group.

"Let's stop bullshitting and get drunk!" Luke was the first one to walk through the doors, followed by Alex, who stopped in his tracks once he had entered the dimly lit bar. A half-dozen men glanced over at them from the bar and then went back to talking to each other. All of the tables near the back of the bar were filled, and Luke turned to take a table near the main entrance. "Are you coming?" He looked back at Alex.

"Look at what's going on at the bar!" Alex couldn't believe his eyes. An Oriental woman was sitting on the bar with her legs spread apart and a huge bear-shouldered man was sitting on a bar stool in front of her with his face buried in her crotch.

"Oh, they're having another pussy-eating contest tonight." Luke shrugged it off and sat down. "What are you guys drinking?"

"Beer all around," the tall trainee answered.

"I've got to tap a kidney—I'll be right back." The horny trainee started walking toward the johns.

"Don't take more than ten strokes!" Luke chuckled, knowing what the trainee was planning on doing to save himself some money.

"Fuck you, Luke!" The dark bar hid the trainee's blushing face.

One of the guys who had been sitting at the bar wandered over to Alex's table and leaned over with his knuckles pressing down on the Formica top. "You guys want a piece of the action?"

"For what?" Alex couldn't take his eyes off the man who was eating the woman's pussy in public.

"He's trying to set a new record for pussy-eating." He nodded over at the bar.

"What's the old record?"

"Three hours and fourteen minutes—with piss and beer breaks allowed every fifteen minutes."

"How long has he been at it?" Luke shook his head at the huge back of the man at the bar.

"Two hours and about five minutes."

"Give me ten dollars' worth."

"Of what?"

"That he'll break the record."

The man grinned and shook his head. "Keep your money. Are you guys trainees?" He had been testing them to see if they were S.F.-ers or paratroopers from the 82nd.

"Bravo Company—Dog Lab."

The man nodded and walked away. "Enjoy yourselves."

"What was that all about?" Alex watched the man leaving.

"Sometimes some rowdies from the division come in here to start fights with the S.F.-ers, or they'll wait out in the parking lot to jump them when they leave drunk on their asses."

"Why? I thought paratroopers got along."

"There's a lot of jealousy from the guys over in the 82nd. I mean, you can rot in that division for years without getting a promotion. Guys have left the division buck sergeants after ten years active and within two years are sergeants first class in Special Forces.

I'm an E4 right now, but the day we graduate from Dog Lab, we're sergeants, and within six months we're staff sergeants. That makes for a lot of jealousy in the regular Army."

"But fuck! We've been in school for a year and a half!" Alex didn't think it was fair for the guys in the 82nd to be jealous of them. "And if we flunk out of any phase of training, we end up in some fucking leg hospital pushing bedpans because the medics are jealous of us! Fuck all of them!"

"When you're the best, you've got to expect jealousy from those who are afraid to try." Luke saw the horny trainee returning from the john. "*That* didn't take long, and it saved you thirty dollars."

"Give me a fucking break, Luke!" The trainee couldn't help laughing. "It *did* save me some money—that was a *long* piss."

"Let's drink up and head down to Combat Alley and hunt us up some pussy!" Luke chugged his beer and slammed the bottle down on the table. "We can always come back here and get drunk if we don't score."

"I think I'll stay here and wait for you guys." Alex sipped from his beer bottle.

"Bullshit! We all came together and we'll leave together. Who knows what kind of hot shit we might find downtown!" Luke was reinforcing the code of sticking together.

"Come on, Alex. Don't forget that we're celebrating graduation from Dog Lab!" The tall trainee threw back his head and howled as they left the lounge. It had been a long haul getting through the Special Forces medical course, and that was all they had ahead of them before they were issued their green berets and given a unit assignment in Phase III, but that was ninety percent physical and very few medics flunked out of that portion of the training.

'I'll come along to watch after you kids." Alex

chugged his three-dollar beer and hurried to catch up to his classmates.

"Like hell you'll *watch!*" Luke leered over at Alex as he unlocked his car.

"The chances of the four of us finding girls are almost nil, and the chances of the four of us finding *four* women who will fuck on the first date *is* nil." Alex dropped down on the passenger's seat.

"I told you that tonight we're going to buy it." Luke waited until the convertible top had dropped down in place before backing out of the parking slot and jinked around a couple of barriers so that he could pull out onto Bragg Boulevard. "Combat Alley, here we come!"

Hay Street was infamous for its crime. Paratroopers wandered up and down its sidewalks looking for sex or a fight, and it really didn't matter which one they found. They came to Fort Bragg, North Carolina, from all over the nation, and the street was a blending of big-city toughs and country farmboys, all wearing buzzed haircuts and looking for some kind of action before going back to their units three-quarters drunk. Either they get laid or into a fight, but it was unacceptable for a paratrooper during the Vietnam War to go downtown and come back without either. The bus stop next to the railroad tracks was the last place to fulfill their quest. Soldiers stationed at Fort Bragg who were not paratroopers stayed clear of Hay Street and Combat Alley after dark unless they were *very* good at bullshitting their way past the paratroopers and knew more about parachuting than they did.

"What are we doing down here?" Alex kept his eyes on the gangs of troopers roving the street. "This place is looking for trouble!"

"And pussy—don't forget the pussy!" The horny trainee rubbed his crotch.

"If you found some pussy down here, you'd have to fight guys off while you were fucking her!" The tall trainee saw Alex's point. There were a hundred para-troopers for every girl on the sidewalk.

"Trust. You've got to trust me, guys! I told you that I was with the 82nd Airborne Division before joining S.F. I know my way around this place." Luke grinned. "Do I look like I'm pussy-starved? Me—a sufer from sunny California!"

"Fuck! I need another beer after that." The horny trainee rested his arm on the side of the car and wished that Luke had left the top up.

Luke turned off Hay Street and onto a side street that looked even worse than Hay Street, if that were possible. He parallel-parked in front of the most run-down bar Alex had ever seen in his life. Even the signs nailed to the side of the building were old and adver-tised *canned* tobacco: Prince Albert.

"Is this going to be a fucking treat!" The horny trainee was losing his interest in getting laid and was starting to worry about surviving the night in one piece. "Are we actually going inside this place?"

"Yeah, and you're going to *love* what you see." Luke knocked on the closed door and a small eye port opened and shut quickly before the door opened.

"Luke! It's been a while man." The six-foot-five black bouncer shook hands with Luke.

"Yeah, been studying hard. Speaking of hard . . ."

"They're in the back room, my man." The bouncer nodded to the closed door behind the almost empty bar. "The twins are back from Georgia."

"Ow!" Luke looked at his partners. "You are going to meet two of the finest fucks ever to come out of the South! Get your money ready!"

Alex braced himself for a pair of two-hundred-pound mamas.

The door to the back room was opened for them from the other side. A strikingly beautiful girl ran out into the bar with a muscle-bound paratrooper hanging on to her raven-black hair.

"Porky! Help me!"

The bouncer reached the paratrooper in three strides and felt the six-inch fighting knife enter his lower intestines all the way to the hilt. The big black gasped and reached down to keep the paratrooper from twisting the blade inside him.

"How do you like that, nigger?" The trooper tried pulling the knife back out but ended up losing all of his front teeth from one powerful punch before Porky dropped down on his knees.

Two more high-bred paratroopers came from the back room to help their friend, and the first one in the bar ran into Alex. There was no talk. Alex stepped as close to the paratrooper as he could and used his elbows to punch with. After the third powerful blow the trooper sank down slowly to the floor. Alex sidekicked the next man out of the back room and ended up by kicking him twice in the face. The third trooper held out his hands and shook his head. "Let me get my buddies, and we're gone."

"They owe us a hundred and fifty dollars." The second black-haired girl appeared in the doorway.

"Here!" The third paratrooper reached into his front pocket and removed a small bundle of twenties and then rolled his buddy over on the floor and removed some more money from his pockets. "It's all we've got!"

"Get the fuck out of here and don't come back!" Porky growled from the floor.

"Lie down on your back—I'm a medic." Alex tore open the huge black man's shirt and gently pushed his hands back from the wound. "Nice and clean, Porky."

The black bouncer stared into Alex's eyes to see if the kid was trying to bullshit him.

Alex smiled. "You've got yourself another cheap scar to impress the girls with. The knife missed all of your vital organs, and I doubt if it even cut through any of your intestines."

"He shoved the motherfucking thing all of the way in!" Porky couldn't believe he wasn't all cut up inside.

"It's too low for any of the vital organs, and you'd be surprised just how hard it is to stick intestines with a knife. I'd go see a doctor if I were you, though. I'm just a medic." Alex stood up and looked for something to wipe his hands on. The first black-haired girl handed him a bar towel.

"Where in the fuck did you learn to fight like that!" Luke was shocked at how fast Alex had neutralized the drunk troopers.

"I was raised in New York." He had learned early in life that once you committed yourself to fight, then the execution had to be violent and relentless, especially when you were outnumbered.

"Fuck! It happened so fast!" The horny trainee was stunned.

"They tried cheating us out of our money. They paid and then forced my sister to give it back to them." She spat down at the trooper with the missing teeth. "It's not my fault you came in ten seconds!"

Luke winked over at the horny trainee. "You saved yourself some money!"

"How can we repay you?" The raven-haired beauty batted her eyelashes at Alex.

"It wasn't a big deal. Just a few drunks."

"They took out our bouncer—it could have gotten real nasty if you hadn't been here." Her voice purred, and the horny trainee felt his pants getting very tight in front. "I know"—she glanced back at her twin sister, and the girl nodded slowly in agreement—"we can repay you at our place."

"Carl! We're leaving for a couple of hours!" the second black-haired girl yelled over to the bartender, who was replacing his sawed-off pool cue back under the bar.

"You boys go on in the back room and help yourselves to a free one." The old southern drawl echoed over from the bar. "And you girls git bac'ere before midnight! Paying your debts is one thing, and losing a whole night's profit is another!"

"Come on—what's your name?"

"Alex."

"Oh, I love that name!" The first girl took Alex's arm and tugged.

"Where are you girls taking him?" Luke couldn't believe what was happening.

"To our apartment."

"Where?"

"The King George Apartments, behind Bragg Boulevard."

"Alex, we'll meet you at the Shangri-la Lounge! Be there before two A.M." Luke shook his head. He had been trying to get a double from the twins since he had known them, but the five-hundred-dollar fee was too steep for his wallet and Alex had lucked out and was about to get a free round. "It's right across the boulevard from the King George Apartments."

"I don't know about this, girls." Alex walked between the two of them over to the Mercedes parked behind the building. "You look like you've done well for yourselves."

"We can pay our bills, if that's what you mean." The girls had mixed themselves up, and Alex couldn't tell which one was which. They dressed and talked alike.

"What are your names?" Alex tried thinking of something to say as he slipped over the front seat of the car between the girls.

"I'm Tommie and she's Tammie."

"Oh . . . ugh." Alex felt the girl's hand slip under the loose-fitting red sweatshirt he was wearing and start playing with the top of his trail-to-paradise under his belly button, down to the top metal button of his Levi's. He felt an instant response from his best friend, who was trying to break free of his denim bonds. "Maybe we should wait until we get there."

"Relax—this is just the prelude. Call it male foreplay." Tammie used her long fingernails to unbutton the top button on Alex's Levi's while her sister drove the car. She rubbed her palm over the bulge in his jeans and then leaned over and blew through the cloth where she felt the end of his pride.

"Aww . . . shit." Alex felt the warm air penetrate the denim. "It's been a while. I don't think I'm going to last long."

"We figured as much. That's why the foreplay before we get to our apartment." She stopped talking and finished unbuttoning his Levi's and then reached inside and helped his best friend break free and spring to attention in three heartbeats. "Mmmm . . ." Tammie ran her lips along the underside of Alex's erection and then without any notice she slipped her lips over the end of it and inhaled the whole thing down to his pubic hair.

Alex leaned forward to see if what he was feeling was true. He had never met a woman who could take all of him into her mouth. He was gifted not only in length but also in width.

Tammie gave a deep-throated growl that vibrated along the full length of his pride, and Alex felt the telltale tingling building up that he knew would turn into an emotional explosion in a very short time. He couldn't believe that he was going to come so soon, and fought to hold back.

"Is she good?" Tommie glanced over at Alex and looked back down the road.

"Very!" He ended the word with a guttural growl and knew that if he didn't do something quick he was going to embarrass himself. Dead puppies! Alex told himself to think about dead puppies in order to get his mind off what was happening below his waist. The thoughts worked for about a minute and then Tammie's talents won the battle. Alex groaned and started moving his hips. "Sorry . . ."

Tammie groaned along with Alex and continued earning her keep while her sister watched the pair ending the first round of their encounter. Tammie tucked Alex's pride back in his jeans and sat back up on the seat. She shook her head to fluff out her hair and smiled. "I won't have to eat for a week after that!"

"I'm jealous." Tommie patted Alex's leg and ended up by running her hand over the bulge still pressing against his Levi's. "I'm glad we're almost there." She removed her hand and put it back on the steering wheel to make the turn into the apartment complex. "You'd better button up until we get in the house."

Alex complied before getting out of the luxury car and following the girls into the apartment. He kept looking at Tammie's lips, still not believing that she could take all of him into her mouth.

"Well, I guess we can go right up to the bedroom, seeing that you're on a tight time schedule." Tommie led the way up the oak staircase. "But first we should take a shower." She turned to look at the handsome soldier, who was looking better and better to the professional call girl. "What's your favorite fruit?"

"Fruit?" Alex felt Tammie unbuttoning his Levi's again and Tommie sliding her cool hands under his sweatshirt and running her fingers along his back muscles. His voice became very husky. "Strawberries—I guess."

Tommie wrapped her arms around Alex's waist from behind and slid them along his hips until she could touch his tightly curled pubic hair, and then she slowly rolled small clumps of the hair between her thumbs and forefingers.

Alex took a deep breath when he felt Tammie's already respected tongue curling around his belly button. "Aren't we going to shower first?"

The two girls undressed Alex down to his military undershorts and then quickly slipped their own clothes off. Tammie spoke to her sister. "I hate those briefs on men!" She was referring to Alex's baggy olive-drab boxer shorts.

"Army issue, girls—what do you expect, bikini briefs?"

"Now, that would be nice," Tommie purred, and started leading Alex to the extra large shower in the bathroom. "Take those things off—please?"

Alex paused only long enough to shove his loose-fitting shorts down, and using a series of quick foot movements, he slipped out of his shorts and kicked them back to where the rest of his clothes were neatly folded.

Tommie paused inside the bathroom and took her time studying Alex's body. She could feel a warm glow starting to spread out from the ends of her nipples and end in tiny electrical flashes along the center of her back. That feeling rarely happened to her anymore, but Alex was turning her on just by the way he carried himself. "You've got one of those bodies that shouldn't ever be covered with clothes."

Alex smiled and enhanced the effect he was having on the professional girl. "I don't think they would like that back at Bragg, and besides"—Alex glanced down at his partial erection—"my best friend doesn't like the cold."

"Your *best friend*?" Tammie stopped sorting through their collection of different soaps and shampoos.

"Yeah, I grew up poor and he was the only toy I had to play with." Alex was trying to be funny, but the girls took him seriously.

"We grew up poor too—so we have something in common." Tommie turned on the multiple shower heads and tested the temperature of the water with her hand. "Time for our bath, Alex."

"Do these things come with the apartment?" Alex

stepped into the shower with the girls and felt the tiny jets of water attack his muscles.

"We paid extra for it. Now, just relax and enjoy." Tammie poured a strawberry-smelling shampoo on her hands and rubbed it into Alex's hair in such a way that his scalp tingled. The two girls took their time washing Alex's body as he stood in the center of the large shower, letting the multiple pulsating heads massage him. They were careful not to touch Alex's best friend. It was Tommie's turn and she wanted to save that part of his body for the bedroom.

Both girls dried Alex, using huge Turkish towels while he stood in the middle of the floor with his eyes closed. "I could get really used to this, girls."

"There's more to come." Tommie laid her towel down and gently took Alex's hand to lead him into the bedroom that had been set up for business. Her sister and she shared the ajoining bedroom for sleeping when they weren't working. "Lie down on your stomach so we can give you a massage."

Alex obeyed, and as soon as he lay down, he could feel the warmth coming up through the satin sheets from the heated water bed. Again the strong smell of strawberries filled the room. He closed his eyes and enjoyed the sensation as the girls rubbed the strawberry lotion into his muscles. Tammie and Tommie had divided his body exactly down the center and they had started with his head and worked their way down his body in perfect tandem. They paused when they reached his buttocks, and Tammie spoke for the first time since they had started the massage. "You've got a cute bubble-butt."

"That's what all you girls say." Alex's voice was muffled in the pillow.

They took their time working over their assigned cheeks and then slowly went down his legs and rubbed the strawberry lotion into each one of his toes.

"Roll over, big boy, and we'll work our way back

up." Tommie felt her skin burning. She was ready for her turn with Alex's best friend.

Alex hesitated for only a second and then turned over on his back. His pride was performing his best rendition of standing at attention. Alex laced his fingers behind his head and watched the girls work their way back up his legs. They paused when they reached the intersection of his legs and rubbed extra amounts of the edible lotion in the junction area of his body and then used their tongues and lips to remove the strawberry cream from his pubic hair. Alex felt as if every single nerve in his body had moved down to his crotch to enjoy the show. Without warning the twins moved their lips to each side of his best friend and slowly started working their way toward the nerve command center.

"We've got to be careful now, girls." Alex closed his eyes and let his body take over.

Just before they reached the critical area, Tammie backed away and Tommie took over completely. She slipped over Alex's narrow hips, and before he realized it, she slipped his pride into her protective sheath all the way down until their pubic hair rubbed against each other. Alex arched his back and then relaxed when she braced her arms against his shoulders and took him for a pony ride that got both of them sweating.

When Alex finally stepped out into the cool night air, his body muscles felt like overextended rubber bands and he was worried about being able to walk across the boulevard to catch his ride back to Fort Bragg. He glanced up at the bedroom window and saw both of the raven-haired girls smiling down at him. He waved and forced himself to start jogging down the row of tan brick apartments.

Bragg Boulevard had as many cars on it as it did during the daytime. Alex waited on the side of the road and oriented himself by using the familiar Martinizing Cleaners building.

A car full of GI's pulled over to the side of the road and one of the soldiers stuck his head out the window. "You need a ride back to post?"

"Thanks anyway—I've got a ride!" Alex waved the car off and jogged across the wide boulevard. He cut through a parking lot and saw Luke's convertible parked in back of the Shangri-la Lounge. They had been waiting for him and drinking from a case of beer.

"Well, looky who's back *already*!" The trainee saw Alex first from his cross-legged seat on the trunk of the car.

"Alex! You're alive!" Luke turned in his seat. "Did you escape or did the enemy release you?"

"If you ever get five hundred dollars together, they are definately worth it!" Alex reached for a beer.

"We all got laid too!" The trainee smiled around the end of his beer bottle. "What's that smell? Strawberries?"

Alex pulled his Levi's away from his waist and looked down. "I wore three inches off my best friend!"

The four Dog Lab trainees laughed into their beers.

A blaring car horn brought Alex's thoughts back to the park. A van had stopped next to the curb and was unloading a group of women dressed in long overcoats and warm wool caps. It looked as if they had planned on spending some time in the park. Alex watched closely as they unloaded picket signs and boxes of literature. They laughed and joked with each other. An early-morning driver passing by sounded his car horn while his passenger rolled down his window. "Get out of the park!"

One of the women flipped the driver the finger and yelled back, "Fuck you, asshole! We have our rights!"

Alex found a seat on a bench that allowed him to face the sun. The warm rays felt good on his face. He adjusted the CAR-15 under his long military overcoat so that it wouldn't show. He was sure that more than one carload of demonstrators would come, and a number of their supporters. It was going to be a very long day, waiting for the numbers to get just right.

One of the women looked up from the folding table she was setting up and noticed Alex sitting on the park bench across from them. "Will you look at that!" She pointed.

"What, dear?" One of the older women stopped stacking pamphlets on her table and reached for a thermos cup of steaming hot coffee.

"That's one of those Vietnam *murderers* over there!" Her voice carried over to where Alex was sitting. His eyes narrowed, but he didn't change his facial expression otherwise.

"Someone should tell him to leave!" The woman holding the coffee shook her head. "I don't want to share this park with a murderer!"

"I'll tell the son of a bitch to get out of here!" one of the women who was carrying three boxes all at one time volunteered. Her voice sounded like she had been eating sand.

Alex watched as the hefty woman strode toward him.

"Hey, fella!" she yelled from ten feet away.

Alex ignored her.

"Hey, you!" She pointed her finger at Alex. "I'm *talking* to you!"

Alex continued ignoring her. She looked back to see if her friends were watching and saw that all of them had stopped setting up their displays and stood facing them.

"Get your smelly ass out of this park. We're having a serious demonstration here today and the national press corps is going to be here." Just as she spoke, a news van with a special antenna attached to it pulled up and parked next to the curb. "See! They're already arriving! Now, get!"

Alex stretched out his legs in front of him and crossed his ankles. He continued ignoring the woman.

"Didn't you hear me? Are you a damned idiot too?" She was losing face with her friends and didn't know what to do. She couldn't return with the man still sitting on the bench. "Are you a Vietnam veteran?"

Alex slowly looked at the woman. He stared directly into her puffy eyes. "Yes."

"We can't have you here during our demonstration . . . none of us believed in that war!"

"Are you here demonstrating against the Vietnam War?" Alex's voice deepened.

"We're demonstrating for women's rights!"

"Rights? What right are you looking for on Christmas Day?"

"Yes, rights!"

"To do what?" Alex already knew the answer.

"For women to make the decision themselves if they wish to abort or keep a child."

"What about the child's rights?"

Her face flashed pure hate at the man. "Are you one of *those*?" She said the word like it tasted bitter crossing her tongue.

"What are *those*?"

"Male chauvinists, who don't believe in women's rights." She was on comfortable ground now. She had spent many years attacking *something*, especially men.

"Are you referring to a woman's *right* to *murder* her own baby? Because if you are, I find that disgusting!"

"You *bastard*!" She hissed the words. "A *Supreme Court justice* wrote the opinion that gave us that right!"

"I'm *sure* of one thing." Alex glared at the woman. "That *Supreme Court justice* will be standing in the line for hell, *ahead* of any man who served in Vietnam!"

"Get out of here!" She screamed the words.

Alex's hand shot up and grabbed her by the front of her wool coat. He squeezed her collar up against her fat chin and spoke softly but with extreme determination. "You get back there with your bitch girlfriends and leave this old Vietnam veteran alone." She felt the power of his hand through her coat, and fear entered her eyes for the first time in a very long time. Alex relaxed his grip on her collar. "I've known a lot of men who have killed in Vietnam, but I don't know a single man who's murdered his own kids!" He shoved her away from him. "Now, move it, bitch, and don't bother me anymore!"

"I'm . . . I'm going to have the police arrest you!" She obeyed him and walked back toward the security of her group.

Alex went back to looking up at the sun and enjoying the warmth against his face. He hoped she would stick around for a while.

CHAPTER SIX

✪✪✪✪✪✪✪✪✪✪✪✪✪✪✪

DEATH CLOUDS

Sash squeezed the foil the sandwich had been wrapped in and smashed it into a small ball. He sat looking through the windshield at the dark highway in front of the car's headlights. His thoughts were there, in the darkness where the unknown lived.

"Mom makes good sandwiches." Young Alex was driving. He glanced over at his father. "She made your favorite."

Sash nodded and sipped from the plastic cup of coffee. His wife did make good sandwiches. She was from the old school: she could cook from scratch and refused to use a microwave oven except to heat up something she had already made. When he had suggested that they hire a full-time cook, she nearly packed her bags and left him. It wasn't that she was so old-fashioned that she lived in another world; she just believed it was her right to provide and care for her family—a job she excelled at.

"You've got a good mother, Alex." Sash's thoughts had been the same as Alex's, and he was feeling guilty. Why had he been so damn lucky? He had survived the Vietnam War, not just physically, but mentally. He had been at the right time and at the right place with his father's meat business and had made millions of dollars. He had found the right woman after the war, and that was probably the real key to his success. She

151

had sensed his hurt when he returned from Vietnam and had gently guided him back to a normal life. Alex Jaxson hadn't been so lucky.

"Do you think we should call Mom?" Alex looked over at the car phone.

"It's still too early. If they need us, they know the number." Sash looked out his side window at the wall of black trees flashing by. "I'm sure she'll call when they get up and open their presents."

"You're right. . . . Dad?"

Sash knew from his son's voice that a painful question was going to follow.

"Yes, son."

"Do you think Uncle Alex will really do it? I mean, kill all those people?"

Sash paused before answering. A million thoughts flashed through his mind. "He's capable of it."

"I don't understand. Didn't you tell me that he was a medic in Vietnam?"

"The best."

"You'd think he would want to save lives, not take them." Alex eased off the gas pedal and tapped the brakes. The red lights on his radar detector flashed a warning. He had been cruising at ninety-five miles an hour. The big Rolls-Royce hugged the road well and the ride was very smooth. A Pennsylvania state trooper's cruiser flashed past, hidden in a turnaround in the median.

"I don't like this." Sash looked back over his shoulder to see if the trooper was going to follow them.

"Relax, Dad! You want to get there, don't you?"

"Yes, but alive!"

Alex changed the tape in the player and lowered the volume before the first song came on. He knew the rock group would bother his dad, but the music relaxed him when he drove. Sash didn't even show that he had noticed the music; he was slipping off in his own world of the past.

"Dad?"

"Huh?" Sash's tone said he didn't want to be disturbed.

"Do you think we should call the police?" Alex's voice carried the fear he was feeling.

"You know son, that's twice now in less than an hour that you're thinking the same thing I am!" He smiled at Alex. "This is getting scary. Damn! I might even start liking that execrable music!"

"I guess I've lived with you too long, Pops . . . you're starting to rub off."

Sash bit his lower lip and thought about Alex's question for a minute before answering. "No . . . no police yet. I owe your Uncle Alex too much."

"That must have been some really bad stuff over there." Alex checked the gas gauge. A roadside sign advertised a station in twelve miles. They had more than a half-tank.

Sash turned away from the side window and stared at his son. The young man had most of Mary's characteristics—blue eyes, wavy light brown hair, slender build—and when it was all put together, he was a very handsome youth.

Shock hit him and he sucked in a lungful of air. Alex turned to his father. "Something wrong, Dad?" His foot started reaching for the brake.

"Damn!" Sash leaned forward and stared harder at his son. Why hadn't he seen it before? "I just noticed."

"Noticed what, Dad?"

"Pay attention to the road." Sash leaned back in the seat. "If you had a little red in your hair and a slightly darker complexion . . . you'd look like your Uncle Alex."

Alex chuckled under his breath. "Who know, Pops . . . you spent a lot of time on the road getting the business going."

"Don't even joke about something like that!" Sash was instantly angry. "That's an insult to your mother!"

"Dad, I'm just kidding."

Sash closed his eyes. "Alex, are you afraid of dying?"

It was Alex's turn to pause and think before answering. "Dad, I've never really thought about it."

"Neither did we, son . . . neither did we." Sash lowered his seat back enough to relax in the soft leather, but still high enough to see the road. His mind slipped back to when he was eighteen years old and a war was going on halfway around the world from home.

"Maleko!"

Sash looked at his platoon sergeant.

"Maleko, take the right M-60 on the lead ACAV!"

Sash nodded and started walking up the line of M-113 armored personnel carriers, carrying his rucksack at his side. He stopped when he reached the first vehicle in line and threw his gear up on top.

"What the fuck are you doing, grunt!" One of the cavalry troops from the 11th Armored Cavalry looked down at Sash from where he was standing on top of the camouflage-painted fighting vehicle.

"My platoon sergeant told me to take over your right-side M-60." Maleko held up his own M-60 for the man to take.

"Bullshit! This is my fucking track and *my* men will man the guns!"

Maleko looked back over his shoulder and saw his platoon sergeant directing one of their M-113's back onto the road. He shook his head slowly from side to side. He really didn't need any crap right now from anyone. "Look, Sarge, why don't you take it up with my sergeant. I'm doing what I was told, and I don't need any shit!"

"You stay the fuck off my track or I'll kick your ass!" The sergeant stood with his hands on his hips.

Sash looked up at the soldier. He was one of the new breed of NCO's who were taking over Vietnam.

The soldier wasn't older than twenty and wore a woman's purple silk scarf around his forehead. He had probably been a private a couple of months earlier and had received rapid promotions in the field.

"Is there a problem here, Maleko?" Sash recognized his company commander's voice behind him.

"This cav sergeant doesn't want me on his track. Sergeant Meyers told me to take over the right gun position." Sash didn't turn to face his captain.

"Maleko is right, Sergeant. I gave the orders that I want some of my men on all of your tracks, especially the lead vehicle and the one bringing up the rear."

"You'd better talk with *my* captain then, *sir*, 'cause I ain't letting nobody ride my ACAV unless he's a member of my crew."

"Get him." The captain's voice was threatening. He was an old-school officer and didn't like the new breed of NCO that Vietman was producing in the line units. Fraggings were increasing all over Vietnam, and discipline was falling apart. That was the main reason he wanted some of his men on each of the tracks. He wanted to make sure that they were covered if they got in a firefight. The cav troop was detailed to haul them to their patrol area, but the infantry captain didn't trust them.

Sash watched his captain light a cigar and grind the match under his boot. The man was trying to control his anger.

"We have a problem here, Captain?" The cav commander's voice was condescending.

"Not really, *Captain*." The infantry commander grinned, holding the cigar in his teeth. "I've assigned men to each of your tracks for the ride out to our patrol area. Your sergeant here doesn't like that idea."

"Well . . . we have our own way of doing things, friend. That track is my sergeant's, and what he says goes." The cav captain grinned, using one side of his mouth. "Now, unless you want to *walk* up to Bo Tuc,

you'd better get used to *listening* to what you're told."
His voice lowered and he winked at the infantry officer. "Tell your men that they're riding *inside* the tracks.
I don't want any damn grunts riding on top where they
can get in our way."

The infantry captain turned and called over to his
first sergeant, "Top! Unload the tracks! We're walking!"

At first the cav captain thought his peer was joking
with him and leaned against the side of his track and
watched. After a couple of minutes it dawned on him
that the infantry captain was serious.

"Get good intervals!" The infantry captain signaled
with his hand for the company to move out up Highway 4. He didn't even glance at the cav captain when
he passed him.

"Hey! Asshole! We're supposed to take you there!
You can't walk!"

The infantry captain ignored his peer. He wasn't
going to transport his company in the belly of ACAV's,
especially when the road north of Nui Ba Den wasn't
secured. He had seen what happened to an M-113
when it was hit by B-40 and RPG-7 rockets.

Sash smiled and took a position right behind the
three-man point element with his M-60 machine gun.
If the point ran into any trouble, they were going to
need a lot of firepower—fast.

"Fire up! We're moving out!" The cav commander
ran down the line of fighting vehicles, yelling at each
of his track commanders. He knew he would be relieved of his command if he allowed the 1st Division
infantry company to walk all the way up to Bo Tuc,
near the Cambodian border. Three of the tracks
wouldn't start, and one of them threw a loose track in
the soft shoulder of the road. The cav captain threw
his helmet down on the asphalt highway and cursed. It
would be at least a couple of hours before he could
leave the site. If he took off without the four tracks,
he wouldn't be able to haul the infantry company once

he caught up to them, and if he called back to his battalion headquarters, he would be in very hot water because he had reported just that morning that all his tracks were operational, when in reality he had left five of them back in his base camp waiting for parts. He would be relieved of his command if the regimental commander found out he had been lying on his readiness reports. He slapped his leg and cursed again. That fucking infantry freak was screwing him over royally by taking off like that. He could have blamed the infantry for the delay, but now, with them gone, he was exposed.

The infantry company had gone a good ten clicks up the highway before they heard the tracks coming up behind them. The captain gave the signal for the men to break and then sent three of his people back down the road so that the ACAV scouts wouldn't open fire on them by mistake. The sergeant and his detail returned an hour later, guiding the first track up the road between the resting columns of infantry. The cav commander stopped his track when he saw the radio operator and the infantry captain.

"Hey. You guys ready to load up?" He smiled down at his peer.

"When you're ready to *listen*."

There was a long pause while the two officers waited each other out.

"All right. Your men can ride up top and you can have men on the lead and rear vehicles." The cav commander whispered the words.

"It's changed a little since back at the base of Nui Ba Den. I didn't realize just how dense the underbrush is next to the road. We're going to have to send out men on foot to prevent an ambush."

"Man! You are fucking crazy! It'll take forever to get up to your operations area if you walk! My tracks will run out of fuel if they have to idle all the way there!"

"*Forever*, friend, is when you're dead. Right now, my men are alive and I'm going to do my best to keep them that way."

"Your fucking troops will frag you if you make them walk when they can ride!"

Sash shifted his M-60 to the crook in his left arm and looked up at the captain on the track. He had heard enough of the officer's bullshit. "There aint going to be any fraggings on this patrol." He hefted his machine gun in a threatening manner.

"I'm going to report this to my regimental commander!"

Sash shook his head and walked away. He had heard enough. He wasn't looking forward to walking all of the way up to their AO, but he trusted his captain's instincts.

"What's going on back there, Maleko?" Sanchez called from the shade of a wild banana tree next to the highway.

"We'll be moving out soon."

"We walking?"

"Yeah, as flanks for the ACAV's."

"Shit, man!" Sanchez punched Costello's rucksack next to him. "That fucking guy has got to go. He's making us walk, when we can ride easy!"

"The captain's afraid of an ambush up ahead near the village. You can probably convince him that you're sick and get a ride inside one of the medic tracks." Sash zipped up his nylon flak jacket and started walking back to the front of the column. He could already feel the heat against his shoulders and stomach, but he had sworn to himself that he was going to wear chicken plate on every damn patrol.

Sanchez called out, "I ain't getting caught inside one of those damn death traps!"

Sash shrugged and kept on walking. He had been very upset when he had found out that Sanchez and his buddies had been assigned to his flight going to

Vietnam, and it had gotten worse when they were assigned to the same battalion and then company as replacements in the 1st Infantry Division. He had received a lot of dirty looks from them at first, but after a couple of months they started to ignore him and hang around with the company's heads. Sash was a loner when they were out of the field and spent most of his time writing letters home and working out to stay in prime shape.

The captain caught up to Maleko and told him that they would be moving out in ten minutes. He hadn't had time to take a rest, but that really didn't matter; at least the ACAV's were carrying plenty of water with them and they were walking on fairly level ground.

The village just north of Nui Ba Den was a well-known VC hamlet used to filter supplies to the units living in the nearby jungle in elaborate underground tunnels. The village was swept monthly by the local Vietnamese Regional Forces, but little was ever found. Sash and the infantry troops were very cautious as they walked through the village. They weren't expecting an ambush, but they were looking for timed satchel devices that could be thrown or attached to the tracks and would detonate once they had cleared the village. The VC used friendly little kids to beg for cigarettes and candy while one of the adults attached the explosives to the tracks.

The infantry captain called for a break once they had cleared the village. A large hill flanked the east side of the highway to the north and was making the infantry captain nervous. He called for his platoon leaders to meet with him behind the second track in the column. The cav commander had his tracks in a herringbone formation next to the road, with the engines idling. Sash could hear the conversation going on between the officers.

"I don't like the terrain, just from the way the map

shows it up ahead." The captain pointed to his field map. "Unless there has been some defoliation up ahead, that is prime ambush country until we cross the stream." He tapped his map.

"What do you think we should do, sir?" The first platoon leader bit his lower lip. The captain had been with the company for eight months, even refusing a staff job when his normal six months of field-command time was up. The lieutenant had learned to trust the captain's gut feelings.

"I'm going to send a ten-man point team a couple hundred meters ahead of the formation and see if they can flush out an ambush. Ten men just might make them jumpy enough to take the bait."

"Shit, sir . . ." The second platoon leader looked down at his boots.

The captain knew what the young officer was thinking. "Hey, Lieutenant, I don't like the idea of losing ten men either. If there's nothing out there, fine, but . . ."

The lieutenant nodded. It was better to risk ten men's lives than two whole companies. "I'd like to lead that patrol sir."

"It's yours. Pick who you want and move out."

Sash stood up from the overhang of bamboo he was using to rest under. "Lieutenant! I'd like to get away from the smell of diesel fuel for a while."

The lieutenant smiled and whispered affectionately under his breath, "Dumb-ass Russian!"

The infantry captain gave his lieutenant a half-hour to get organized and to get a lead on the column. Sash was the only M-60 machine-gunner with the advance patrol, and the lieutenant placed him near the center of the small unit so that he could move him to either end if they got hit. He could hear the tracks gun their engines and move back onto the road. They were still too close to the column. The lieutenant keyed his radio and called back to his captain to get permission to get a larger lead on the ACAV's so that they could hear better. The captain agreed to the request, knowing that he could get to them very quickly with the ACAV's in the event of trouble.

Sash kept his eyes on the jungle as they walked along the edge of the highway. They had made a gradual curve to the northeast around the large piece of high ground, and Sash could see why his captain had been nervous. It was a perfect place for an ambush. He didn't realize it, but the worst spot was just ahead of them on the road. The northern tip of the hill they had been paralleling curved slightly to the west and ended in two little pieces of high ground on the eastern side of the highway. On the west side were two almost identical jungle-covered hills with a narrow valley spreading out to their rear. It was a perfect ambush site.

Sash felt the sweat pouring off his face and wanted to reach back on his web gear for his canteen, but didn't want to take his hands off his M-60. He had felt very uneasy when they made the turn in the road and the sound of the tracks was almost muffled out. The closer they came to the slight rises in the ground that pinched the road from each side, the more he felt the hair on the back of his neck stand up.

The lieutenant sensed the same thing and signaled for the patrol to spread out on each side of the road and halt. Sash slid under some underbrush on the edge of the two-lane highway and felt his muscles thank him for the rest. He kept his eyes on the lieutenant and the men nearest his location. Everything was now being done by hand signals. The ten-man patrol had stopped playing at being infantry a couple thousand meters back down the road; they *were* infantry now, and everything they had been taught was coming into play. Something wasn't right. The jungle looked normal.

The birds acted normal. The air smelled normal. Something *wasn't* normal.

Sash flexed his shoulder to massage his muscles under his pack straps while he squatted there waiting for his lieutenant to give the word to move out. He glanced down at the dirt directly in front of him and saw an eight-inch centipede crawling toward him on its multiple pairs of legs. Sash could clearly see the huge pincers protruding from the sides of its mouth, and shivered. The creature was ugly. He leaned back against the short roadside elephant grass and poked at the poisonous insect. The iridescent centipede changed its course and started crawling across the road. Sash shuddered again: he could have been stung by that thing. He rested his rucksack on the ground and turned his head back over his shoulder to see if there were any other bugs on the elephant grass behind him. Sash's rucksack had pressed down the narrow strip of elephant grass that bordered the roadside, and he was looking directly down a fire lane.

Everything changed almost instantly. Birds screamed and flew away. The air smelled of burned gunpowder. The jungle didn't look normal anymore.

The first three rounds from the NVA soldier's RPD machine gun hit Sash's pack, tearing holes through it. One round burst open a can of frank and beans, another tore out the left side and bounced across the road, and the third round smacked against Sash's armored nylon vest, knocking the wind out of his lungs. He rolled to his right side, away from the fire lane that had been cut through the thick jungle floor. Sash's eyes flashed back and forth from clear vision to a blank grayness as he struggled for air. He felt like someone had hit him in the back with a ten-pound sledgehammer.

The lieutenant keyed his handset and yelled into the receiver, *"Ambush! Ambush!"*

The infantry commander didn't need to be told. He

could hear the small arms and RPG-7 grenades exploding ahead of them. He switched freqs over to the radio on the track the cav captain was riding on. "Let's move up there fast!"

The answer was almost immediate. "Fuck you! I ain't taking my tracks into a kill zone!"

"You son of a bitch!" The infantry commander grabbed his command radio's handset and spoke to the lieutenant leading the patrol. "Dogtrot Forward . . . what's your grid?" He didn't waste time waiting for identification.

The answer was immediate. "I can't get to my map. We had just made the turn in the road to the northeast and they nailed us. They were waiting, all right, Captain." The lieutenant's voice was filled with fear.

"Hang in there . . . I'm calling for a FAC and some artillery!"

The captain's radio operator had been working with him since his arrival in Vietnam, and the young soldier was good. He spun the dials to the air frequency and nodded for his captain to call. The infantry command section of the company functioned perfectly. A Forward Air Controller was already airborne above Tay Ninh and was due to arrive in minutes.

Sash felt the air rush back into his lungs. He rolled over and fired a long burst down the NVA's own fire lane. He kept moving, selecting targets and engaging them. The jungle was full of NVA soldiers who had started leaving their positions. The ambush had been sprung too early because of Sash's accidental discovery of the hidden fire lane, and the NVA knew that they had only a few minutes to get out of there before the Americans called in artillery and Cobra gunships. They would have stayed longer if they could have caught the whole column, but it wasn't worth it for a small patrol.

The lieutenant obeyed the FAC pilot and popped red smoke. Within a minute, the jungle erupted on both sides of the road in volleys of artillery fire. The artillery group responsible for that sector of III Corps had already preplanned artillery fires for that site along the road. The French had been ambushed in the exact spot five times during the French-Indochina War.

Sash pressed his face down in the loose soil next to the road and listened to the shrapnel whistle overhead. His thoughts were not on being hit by a stray hunk of steel, but on the whereabouts of the centipede.

The lieutenant held the handset pressed against his ear so tight that the pressure was causing severe pain. He pressed harder; it was a pain that he could control. Everything else around him was totally out of his control. He was alone in the grass bordering the road and didn't even know if the radio operator lying three feet away from him was still alive. The NVA had executed the ambush perfectly when it had been detected by Maleko. The fire lanes were cut out of the jungle with precision, and Chinese thirty-six-inch Claymore mines had been strategically placed to sweep the roadsides with thousands of ball-bearing-size projectiles.

Sash heard the distant sound of M-113 engines coming up the road and risked raising his head off the ground. The artillery fires were being adjusted by the FAC observer away from the highway and into blocking positions to the northwest and southeast. A soldier lay spread-eagled next to the road a dozen meters away from Sash. He could see that the man was dead. Another one of the ten-man patrol could be seen in the center of the highway, where the force from the Chinese Claymore had thrown the top half of his body.

Sash listened.

The sound of the tracks moved closer, but Sash could tell that the cavalry troops were being extremely cautious, and for good reason: the NVA could have left a number of suicide troops behind to take out their armored vehicles with RPG-7's.

Sash slipped deeper into the jungle bordering the road. The cav troopers would be trigger-happy. He figured they would stop when they saw the remains of the soldier in the road, and then his captain would start searching the brush for survivors of the ambush. It wouldn't be safe to move until then.

The lieutenant heard voices coming from down the road, but he couldn't make out the language. He prayed that they were Americans. He was terrified that the NVA would capture him.

The voices drew closer and he heard a heavily accented New York voice call out, "Hey! Any of you guys still out there!" Sanchez lowered himself into a combat crouch. The NVA was just as likely to answer his call as one of the patrol was.

"Over here!" The lieutenant waved from his hiding place.

"Step away from the jungle . . . slowly!" Sanchez waved for Martinez to cover him.

The lieutenant emerged from the edge of the jungle. Fear was still written all over his face. The infantry captain ran over to his officer and started talking to him in a very soft voice. He could see that the man was bordering on going into shock. "Lieutenant . . . everything is all right. We've driven off the NVA."

The lieutenant's eyes darted over the wall of green on each side of the road. He spoke in a voice that echoed. "Captain . . . they were all over the place. We didn't even have a chance to fire back."

"That's what happens in an ambush." The captain looked around the lieutenant, into the jungle. "Did you see anyone else back there?"

The lieutenant nodded slowly and then his eyes locked on the body of the soldier lying in the road. Flies had already found the man's internal organs and were buzzing around the body by the hundreds. The lieutenant swallowed a scream and then gagged.

"Cover that body!" The captain screamed the order to one of his medics.

The ACAV's slowly approached the NVA ambush

site behind the infantry company. The cav commander formed a perimeter around the site and kept artillery fire concentrated in the jungle around them. Sash and one other soldier had been found and were sitting inside the command track briefing the two captains when the first helicopter arrived and landed in the center of the circle. The cav squadron commander had arrived, followed by a Medevac ship to extract the dead. Seven soldiers had died, but the remaining three survivors were all capable of stying in the field.

"You can go back to the rear if you want to, Maleko—that bruise on your back is severe enough for a couple days off." The infantry captain pushed gently on the large bruise on Sash's back, which was rapidly getting darker. "You've made me a believer in chicken plate!"

Sash smiled. The bullet-proof nylon vest had stopped the round from going through his back and coming out his chest. "I think I'll be fine. I want to take part in the sweep."

"It's your call, soldier." The infantry captain nodded. He understood. Maleko couldn't go back to the rear right now. He had to ease away from the ambush slowly. "Third Platoon is getting ready to leave now."

Sash slipped his sweat-soaked fatigue jacket back on and pulled his web gear over it. A sharp pain shot across his shoulder blades. "Shit! I hope it works itself out quickly." He picked up his M-60 and checked it to make sure the ammo belt was feeding right before walking over to where he had discovered the NVA fire lane. He pointed out the camouflaged tunnel to his platoon sergeant and started crawling back up the straight fire lane until he reached the NVA machine-gun position. A pair of NVA soldiers lay dead in the shallow pit they had dug for the ambush. A new RPD light machine gun was still pointed down the fire lane with most of an ammo belt in it. A fresh groove had cut along the wooden stock where Sash's round had hit.

"You get them?" The platoon sergeant had followed Sash down the tunnel cut out of the jungle floor.

"Yeah . . . this started it all. I think they really wanted to let us pass and get the column, but . . ."

Sash felt the sergeant's hand on his shoulder. "That's what war's all about. A little bad luck and a little good luck. Bad for the patrol, but it would have been a hell of a lot worse if the column had stumbled into this shit!" The sergeant looked around the jungle where he was lying. The NVA had spent a lot of time and effort cutting interlocking trails between the fire positions. "Let's check it out." He pointed with his rifle barrel to the narrow trail that led into the NVA position.

Sash led the way. The next hour revealed an elaborate ambush that had a kill zone four hundred meters long. A reinforced company had been necessary to occupy the ambush site, and from the amount of construction around the positions, they had spent a couple of weeks in hiding, waiting for just the right target.

"Let's get back to the captain and report this. I think we'll be here a couple of days sweeping this complex."

The lieutenant colonel and the two captains were talking when Sash and his platoon sergeant returned. Sergeant Meyers briefed the officers on what they had found and recommended that a major sweep be made through the whole area and the NVA bunkers destroyed.

The cavalry squadron commander agreed. "I want your troop to stay here and support the infantry company's sweep of the area." The lieutenant colonel had recently been promoted and was getting ready to turn over his command to his replacement. "I don't know if I'll make it out to the field again before I take my new assignment . . ." He paused and stared out over the circle of ACAV's. "Captain, how many vehicles do you have out here in the field?"

The captain averted his eyes. "I had a few break down right before we left to pick up the infantry, sir."

"A *few*?" He took a step to the left so that he could see if he had missed a platoon. "It looks a hell of a lot like you're missing half your troop!"

"Ah . . . sir, I can explain—"

"You bet your ass you'll explain!" The officer had been in the cavalry too long not to know what was going on. The captain had been filing false reports on how many vehicles he actually had in the field. The results of that practice not only endangered the lives of the men but also could have made a major difference if they had been committed to a large battle. The senior staff would have thought they were committing a whole troop to the fight, when actually they would have been sending little more than a platoon. "I'm going to visit your rear area when I get back, Captain, and you'd better hope that I don't find any tracks back there!"

"Sir, I can explain!"

The infantry captain smiled. There was *some* justice in the world.

CHAPTER SEVEN

✪✪✪✪✪✪✪✪✪✪✪✪✪✪✪✪✪✪

WATER AND VENOM

"Do you want to stop for breakfast, Dad?"

"Ummm . . . pardon me, son?"

"Breakfast. Do you want to stop and get something to eat? I'm starving."

"What time is it?" Sash looked at his Rolex Presidental. "Six-thirty already. I must have dozed off."

"More like crashed!" Alex smiled and shook his head. "You should be thankful that I decided to come along."

"I am—in more ways than one." Sash remembered what he had been dreaming about. The image of the dead soldier's body lying in the center of Highway 4 appeared on the inside of the windshield. Sash could make out individual flies sucking the blood and other fluids from the top half of the soldier's body. He refused to look away from the image. If his mind wanted him to recall the ghastly war scene, he would go along with it. He had taught his children not to run away from problems, and he wasn't a hypocrite. Sash wondered why he was recalling the incident with more clarity than he had originally. He had barely glanced at the soldier's upper body after the Chinese Claymore had torn the man in two, yet twenty years later he could see everything in extreme detail.

"A penny for your thoughts."

Sash snapped his head around. "What?"

"Relax, Dad! Boy, are you jumpy!" Alex flashed a rare look of anger at his father. "I just said, a penny for your thoughts."

"Believe me, son, you don't want to buy them right now!" Sash hesitated, looking back at the windshield.

"Has all of this got to do with Uncle Alex calling?"

"You're a lot smarter than you look, son."

"Thanks a lot, Dad! I *am* eighteen, and that's not exactly a little boy anymore." Alex shook his head. "There's a set of Golden Arches . . . you want to stop?"

"McDonald's sounds good." Sash looked back at the windshield and the image was gone. He sighed his thanks.

"You know, Dad, I read in one of my psych books that sometimes it's good to remember bad things. It's like your brain is getting rid of stored thoughts it doesn't want to keep locked up anymore."

Sash smiled. The boy was sharp. He reached over and patted his son's knee. "I'm glad you came along, son."

Alex smiled. It felt good being with his father, knowing that he was doing something to help. He'd spent his whole life taking from his dad, and now he felt, for the first time, that he was giving something back. It was a good feeling, a man feeling.

"Order me a large black coffee and a . . . whatever they have to eat." Sash closed his eyes while his son ordered for the two of them over the drive-through speaker.

"We're lucky to find anything open this early on Christmas morning." Alex handed the wide-eyed girl the money and winked when he pulled away behind the wheel of the black Rolls-Royce.

Sash kept his eyes closed. "They usually keep places open on the main throughfares." He could smell the coffee and adjusted his seat back up straight. "Smells good."

"We're making good time." Alex unwrapped a bacon-and-egg muffin and laid it on an open napkin on his lap. "We should make it to Washington before noon."

Sash looked over at the speedometer and shook his head. "At least the engine is getting a workout. I'm afraid to see what our gas mileage is going to be!"

"Hey, old man! If you can afford one of these cars, you should be able to afford the gas!" Alex chuckled. His dad had told him the same thing when he had brought the Rolls home for the first time and Alex had told him that a Rolls got only eight to ten miles per gallon.

"Now, I really don't need any teenage back talk, son!" Sash punched Alex in the ribs.

"Dad! You're going to make me crash!" He started laughing.

"Do you want me to drive for a while?"

"Naw, I'm getting used to it. You can drive when we get to Washington, since you know the city."

"Fair deal." Sash looked out his side window at the snow-covered pine trees and a fast-running stream that hadn't frozen over.

Alex glanced over to where his dad was looking. "Now, that's a postcard scene!"

"Yes, it's breathtaking." Sash's eyes locked on the fast-running water and his nostrils smelled the scent coming from the soft leather seat, but his mind slipped back to another stream.

"I heard from the captain that one of the Special Forces CIDG companies west of here engaged a large NVA force right after we were ambushed." The lieutenant wouldn't look directly at Sash and kept his eyes moving over the jungle. Since the ambush, the lieutenent wouldn't look directly at anyone.

"Who won?" Sash kept rubbing the feeder tray on his M-60 with the oily cloth in his hand. He didn't look at the officer and kept his attention on his weapon.

"They reported finding fifty-six bodies after the fight, and a lot of weapons. Papers too, that confirm the NVA were with the 273rd North Vietnamese Regiment."

"Same unit that ambushed us." Sash hooked the carrying strap back on his machine gun and patted the foregrip.

"Yea . . . yeah . . ." The lieutenant's voice broke. "They built a new Special Forces camp over there called Prek Klok, and they're finishing one up near the border called Tong Le Chon. There's a rumor that we're going up there as soon as we finish here, and take some of the pressure off them."

"Which one?" Sash stood and looked down at the lieutenant.

"Tong Le Chon."

"Can't the Green Berets handle it?"

"They keep getting hit by the NVA and then the gooks slip back across the border. The camp is within mortar range of Cambodia."

"Why would they get that close?" Sash twisted his mouth in thought.

"I guess so they can observe the border."

Sash shrugged. "Mortars can be fired *both* ways, I guess." He looked over at the command track. "The captain said that we can go down to the stream and take baths. They've set up a couple ACAV's near the stream to cover us." Sash looked back over his shoulder at the young officer. "Are you coming?"

The lieutenant's eyes lost their focus. "Maybe later."

Sash stopped near the command track and waited until his captain got off the radio. "Captain, I don't think the lieutenant is going to make it."

"What's the problem?" The captain gave Maleko a hurried glance and returned his attention to writing his company's after-action report.

"I think the ambush has broken him." Sash tapped the side of his head with his index finger.

"Thanks, Maleko. I'll check him out later. I've been

172

watching him and have already decided on shipping him back to one of the field hospitals for observation."

The captain glanced back again at Maleko and noticed that he was carrying a soap case and a green camouflage towel. "You'd better hurry if you're going to wash. We're going to be moving out in two hours."

Sash nodded and started walking fast over to where a dozen troops were in different stages of undress around a natural depression in the stream. "Water warm?" Sash spoke to one of the cav troops standing up to his waist in the stream. The soldier shrugged and soaped down his chest.

"The water's great, Maleko!" one of the men from Sash's platoon answered, and flashed a threatening glance at the cav trooper. "Someone has told those assholes that they're better than the rest of the Army, and they believe it!"

Sash smiled. "If it makes them fight better, I couldn't care less." He sat down on a large smooth rock and pulled off his jungle boots and socks. The water felt cool. Sash hesitated and looked around the jungle before he unbuttoned his trousers. He didn't like the idea of being naked out in the open.

"I changed my mind. A bath sounds good."

Sash glanced behind him and saw the lieutenant taking off his fatigue jacket. "Yeah. It's a luxury, even though we'll be sweaty again in a half-hour." Sash picked up his bar of soap from the rock and waded into the clear pool until he was up to his waist before soaping down. He squatted until his head was underwater and then shampooed his hair with the bar of soap. It felt good once his body adjusted to the coolness of the mountain stream. Sash squatted again with his eyes closed and rubbed the soap out of his hair. He felt nervous being underwater with his eyes closed, and hurried to finish. When he broke the surface of the water, he heard men laughing at something. Sash wiped the water off his face with the palms of his hands and looked to see what was so funny. The lieutenant stood naked at the side of the pool staring at a dark brown spot that covered his left hip from his waist down to his knee. The officer was crying so hard that mucus covered his upper lip.

"Hey, Lieutenant! The water isn't *that* cold!" The ACAV sergeant who had nearly got in a fight with Sash earlier had made the comment, and all of the cav troopers around the pool started laughing.

Sash knew what the brown stain on the lieutenant's leg was. It was dried blood from the lieutenant's radio operator that had soaked through the lieutenant's fatigue pants. None of them had bathed since the ambush. The lieutenant must have missed the stain when he changed into his spare fatigues after the fight. Sash waded over to where the officer stood and reached over and took his arm. "Come on in and get wet, sir." He had to tug to get the lieutenant to move into the pool. Sash used his bar of soap to scrub the blood stain off the crying officer.

"That looks awful queer to me, grunt!" the ACAV sergeant yelled, loud enough for everyone to hear him, even the guards up on the two tracks.

"You've just got your noncommissioned-officer ass kicked, motherfucker!" One of the infantry NCO's at the pool started climbing over the rocks to reach the cav sergeant.

Sash ignored the trooper and finished scrubbing the stain off the young officer's body. Sash took his arm and guided him out in the pool until the water was deep enough to rinse off in, and splashed handfuls of water over the man. "Come on, sir, duck down and wash your face."

The officer shook his head from side to side.

"Hey, sir, you don't want all that dirt on your face when you fly back to the rear!" Sash tried speaking in a cheerful voice, but it was difficult. The radio operator's blood had affected him too.

The lieutenant slowly scooped up a double handful of water and splashed his face.

"Here, sir, use some soap." Sash laid his soap in the officer's hands.

Slowly the lieutenant started foaming the bar and washing his face.

"Stop right there!" The infantry captain's voice rolled over the pool and stopped his sergeant right before he reached the cav NCO. "Save it for the NVA." He glared at the cav trooper. "Not that you don't deserve an ass-kicking!" He had heard everything. The captain slowly shifted his gaze from the NCO back to Sash and the lieutenant. "I've got a chopper coming in right now to get you, Lieutenant. Put some clothes on."

The young officer nodded and started climbing out of the pool. Sash finished washing and rinsed off. He glanced at the cav NCO, who was sitting on a rock watching. The side of the pool all the cav troops were on was littered with different-size water-polished rocks that had been warmed by the sun. The cavalry had arrived at the water hole first and had picked the best site for themselves. The infantry had been given the shady side and had to wade out about ten feet before they were in the warm sun. The rocks went up the side of the steep hill for about fifty feet and then the jungle growth took over and covered them.

The lieutenant had gained some control over himself and looked shyly away as Sash approached. "Sorry."

"There's nothing to be sorry about, Lieutenant."

The lieutenant looked over at his fatigue pants and Sash could see his lower lip quiver. He read the officer's thoughts. "Here." Sash handed the lieutenant his clean pair of trousers. "They should fit you . . . might be a little big around the waist, but you can get a new pair back in the rear."

"I can't take your—"

Sash cut him off in mid-sentence. "Yes you can! I've got another set of fatigues in my pack."

175

"You sure?" The lieutenant thanked Sash with his eyes. He just couldn't bear to put his bloodstained trousers back on.

"Yeah, I'm sure." Sash wrapped his green towel around his waist and started gathering his gear for the short walk back to where their rucksacks were stored in the shade. He would have to put his old filthy pair of fatigues back on, but at least they weren't bloodstained.

The captain was sitting under a tall stand of mature bamboo when Sash returned. "Maleko, that was kind of you back there." The captain kept his eyes on his map.

Sash shrugged.

"He's been with me since I took command. He's a good officer, but everyone has his limit." The captain ground his teeth. He hated losing the lieutenant to a psych ward.

"Once he gets out of here for a while, he'll pull himself together."

"I hope so."

Sash knelt down and opened his pack. "Shit! I left my soap back there." He stuffed his toothbrush and paste in a side pocket and left his towel draped over his pack, but took his M-60 with him as he walked back over to the pool, wearing his dirty set of jungle fatigues. The sun had changed angles and Sash noticed as soon as he arrived at the pool that there was something lying halfway up the rocks on the side of the water the cav troops had picked as theirs. He went over and picked up his soap dish first and detoured around the edge of the water until he was close enough to make out what had caught his eye. It was a fairly large piece of snakeskin that had been shed by its owner.

The ACAV sergeant was still lying in the sun and had watched Sash walk around the pool. He was expecting trouble and thought that Sash was coming back to fight. "You have a problem, grunt?" The

NCO's voice rose as he adopted an effeminate tone. "Ain't nobody over here who wants you to wash their nuts for them."

Sash felt a warm sensation climbing up from his stomach. It was a feeling he had always experienced since he was a little kid when he knew he was going to fight someone. He didn't understand the NCO. There was no doubt that Sash could pound the skinny punk into the ground. The sergeant lifted the hand he had hidden behind a rock and Sash saw the reason for the man's bravado. The sergeant was holding the burning stub of a roach. "You smoke that shit in the field too?"

"It's better out here. Too much *fresh* air!"

The other cav members started laughing.

"Did you come over here looking for something?" The NCO's voice lowered.

Sash used the barrel of his M-60 to point at the snakeskin. "That caught my eye. Do you know what it is?"

The NCO twisted around and looked at the sun-dried white skin. He shrugged.

"It's a snakeskin."

"So . . ." He inhaled what was left of his joint and dropped the tiny butt down between the rocks at his feet.

"So? Where there's a snakeskin, you'll usually find a snake nearby, and these rocks look like a good place for one to burrow for the day."

"Fuck your snakes!" The NCO waved his hand at Sash. "Get the fuck out of here before we kick your ass!"

Sash stared at the stoned NCO for a couple of seconds and then turned and walked away. The man was a fool and not worth getting in trouble over. He bent down to get a closer look at the shed skin when he passed it. The layer of white skin was starting to deteriorate from being exposed to the weather. Sash scanned the rocks, pausing when his eyes detected movement in the shadows between the multicolored stones. He looked up in the sky and saw large white clouds rolling overhead. Streaks of sunlight between the clouds was causing the shadows to move between the rocks. Sash shrugged as he stood up again. The snakeskin was old and its owner had probably moved on.

The cav sergeant cupped his hands around his mouth and yelled over to where Sash was skirting the pool, "Watch out! Behind you!"

Sash flipped him the finger. He was more than tired of the man and would be glad to get rid of him when they reached Tong Le Chon in the morning.

The cav sergeant's track driver scooted up higher on the rocks back into the sunlight as the shadow crept up the side of the ravine. He held a fresh joint in his hand and inhaled deeply, holding the smoke in his lungs as he scurried over the larger rocks, which varied from basket size to small boulders.

"Get that smoke back down here, fucker!" the NCO yelled to his crew member.

"Man, those rocks are cold on my bare ass! Come up here where it's warmer!" The trooper stopped and sat down on a small seat formed by nature in the rock bed.

"Shit!" The NCO struggled to his feet and picked his way through the boulders and sharp-edged rocks until he reached his driver. He stretched out next to him and reached for the joint. The sun had warmed the rocks so they were comfortable to sit on. "It looks like you've found a natural bed!"

"Yeah, Sarge . . . I could almost take a nap."

"We're going to have to get dressed as soon as we finish smoking our little friend here." The NCO shook his head. "Damn! I hate those fucking line-infantry types!"

"Ouch!" The driver rolled over on his side. "Dammit!"

"What's wrong?" The sergeant watched Maleko walk around the pool and start up the trail to the command post.

"Motherfuck!" The driver tried standing up.

"What in the fuck is wrong with you!"

"Some fucking thing bit me!" He turned his ankle around so the sergeant could see the small puncture marks an inch below his ankle bone.

"Hold your leg up so I can get a better look." The sergeant was trying to focus his drug-controlled eyes. He turned halfway around to face his driver on the rock and unconsciously slipped one foot down between the rocks as his legs spread apart. "Ah!" The sergeant felt a slight sting and looked down. First his eyes focused on the tiny puncture marks on his right thigh, inches from his scrotum, and then he saw the black shadow between the rocks move. "What in the fuck is going on?" He tried standing.

"Oh, fuck! Sarge!" The driver saw them seconds before his sergeant realized what was going on. "Snakes! We're in the center of a nest of snakes!"

"Oh, God . . . we've been bitten . . . cobras . . . baby cobras." The sergeant saw a miniature cobra lift its head up between the rocks and spread its hood, probably the first time the snake had ever performed that act for another creature.

"Run!" The sergeant felt another sting on his left heel.

The driver struggled to his feet. He had been hit five times as he lay on the rocks naked. Baby cobras came complete with venom when they were born. "Sarge . . . I feel sick." He swayed and fell face-forward on the rocks, smashing his nose against his cheek.

"Oh, shit!" The NCO knew they both were dying and screamed at the top of his lungs in anguish, *"Snakes!"*

Sash stopped walking at the top of the trail and looked back to where the scream had come from. The cav NCO was standing on a large rock waving his arms and screaming something about snakes. Sash could see the driver lying facedown on the rocks with his legs turned at an unnatural angle. He looked over at the nearest track and called up to the guard, who was standing with his hand shielding his eyes and staring at the sergeant. "What's he yelling about?"

"Something about snakes."

The sergeant started running away from the nest and fell facefirst in the pool of water. The fast-acting toxic venom was interfering with his motor neurons and he was having a difficult time regaining his footing on the slippery bottom. The track driver had been mercifully knocked unconscious in his fall and didn't know he was still among the snakes, but the sergeant was experiencing all the terrifying effects of the venom.

"Call a medic and see if any of them are carrying antitoxin for cobra bites." Sash rushed his instructions to the track driver on guard and started jogging toward the struggling NCO in the water. All the other men washing in the pool eased over to the far side, away from the dying troopers, and grabbed their gear. Sash placed his M-60 on some nearby rocks and splashed into the water. "Hey! A couple of you guys—help me with him!" Sash grabbed the struggling sergeant by one arm and felt it slip through his hands. He reached again and this time grabbed the NCO by the hair and pulled him across the pool to the opposite bank. The man was going into convulsions and defecated in the shallow water. Sash struggled with his slippery burden and pulled the trooper up on the rocks. The NCO urinated involuntarily, spraying the dry rocks.

"Where's that medic?" Sash called back over his shoulder, and saw a pair of medics running toward him, carrying their aid kits.

"Shit! He looks bad off." One of the medics dropped down next to the sergeant.

"Do you have an antitoxin?"

"Yes, but . . ." The medic checked the NCO's eyes and saw that he was dying fast.

"Well, inject him!"

The medic obeyed.

Sash watched the other medic start going toward the ACAV driver lying in the rocks on the other side of the pool. "Hold up!" The medic didn't have to be told twice to stop. He didn't like the idea of crawling over rocks infested with cobras. He wasn't a coward and had performed a number of valorous acts during firefights, but hidden snakes, *lots* of hidden snakes, bothered him.

Sash beckoned for one of the infantrymen to come over to where they were standing. "Loan me your blooper and a couple fleshette rounds."

"What for?" The infantryman frowned at Sash.

"I'm going to go up there and get him."

"Fine . . . I'll go with you." The grunt smiled. "No one takes my main friend away from me."

"Sorry, I just thought that—"

"You thought wrong. Let's go, before he dies." The grunt switched rounds in his M-79 grenade launcher from high explosive to fleshette and took the lead of the three-man expeditionary force.

"Try to keep your feet on top of the larger rocks. I think they're all newborn cobras, and they shouldn't be able to strike higher than our boot tops." Sash was making sense, but the medic added a little wisdom of his own.

"Do cobras bear their young alive . . . or do they lay eggs?"

Sash frowned. "I don't know for sure, but I think they lay eggs."

"Fuck! That's all we need—their fucking mother up here baby-sitting!"

Sash rolled the driver over cautiously and looked underneath the man's body for snakes.

The sound of the M-79 going off startled both the

medic and Sash. The grunt had fired into the rocks above them and had reloaded the weapon in a fast fluid motion. "Fucking rocks up there are alive with snakes!" He fired again and reloaded. Sash watched where the soldier was firing and could see the shadows moving between the rocks.

"Let's get him out of here!" The medic reached down and grabbed the driver by the legs and felt a shiver ripple down his spine as he anticipated being bitten. Sash lifted the man under his arms and they rushed down the slope to the pool's edge. Sweat covered all three of their faces.

The grunt fired again and reloaded as he brought up the rear of the rescue party.

"Check his pulse." Sash reached for the vein next to the driver's ear. He could feel a slight pulse, but the man was still unconscious. "I think he's alive."

The medic checked the driver's wrist pulse and nodded. "I'll give him a shot of antivenin, but I don't think he's going to make it." The medic started counting the puncture marks that covered the trooper's body. He had been bitten at least ten times.

"Oh, my God!" the blooper operater whispered between his teeth.

Sash looked up from the dying trooper to where the grunt was pointing with the barrel of his launcher. She was coming out of the jungle at the upper edge of the rocks and the sun reflected off her shiny black skin. The female king cobra slowly lifted her body off the rocks and exposed her cream-colored underbelly and expanded her hood. She was regal, queen of the jungle, and angry.

"She's a mile long!" The medic's breath caught in his throat.

"No . . . two miles long!" The grunt forgot he was holding his M-79 with the breech open.

Sash looked up from the dying trooper. His eyes seemed to lock with the black orbs of the mother cobra, and they stared at each other for a year-long second before she flicked out her tongue and dropped down behind some rocks. The grunt snapped shut his blooper and took an involuntary step backward toward the water.

"Let's get him back to one of the ACAV's." The medic was making good sense.

Sash and the medic carried the trooper over to where the sergeant lay on the rocks. The other medic was administering what little first aid he could to the unconscious NCO. He looked up at their approach and slowly shook his head from side to side.

The M-60 machine gun on the left side of the ACAV that had been guarding the water hole opened fire, followed by the .50-caliber heavy machine gun on the vehicle. Sparks and chips of rock went flying in all directions, creating a larger danger to the men than the snakes. Sash shook his head. They would be lucky to hit even one of the baby cobras hiding between the boulders. It was a cheap way for the cav troops to see if their weapons were functioning properly, but that was about all that would come from the hail of fire.

Sash stood back and watched the cav troopers load the two snake-bitten men onto the top of one of their tracks. He looked over at the tranquil pool and at the vivid shades of green in the jungle wall that surrounded the water hole and smiled. This serenity could all change so damn fast—so damn fast.

"Maleko."

Sash turned to face his company commander. "Yes, sir?"

"The lieutenant is on his way back to our base camp. I had him scheduled for a night patrol, and it looks like you're going to have to take his place."

"Ambush or patrol, Captain?"

"Patrol. Do you think you can handle it?"

"I've done some night patrolling back in the States, sir—but never in the jungle." A hidden primeval fear started forming in the back of Sash's mind. He had never heard of an American unit pulling a night *patrol* in Vietnam. Normally, American units set out ambush parties at night, but even then, they went out in the daytime and set up the ambushes before dark. Americans just didn't move at night in the jungle. The NVA had exclusive rights to that tactic.

"We think the NVA have assigned a tag-along patrol to our column and we want to leave a stay-behind team near the road to watch for them and then catch up to us before daylight. I figured that you would be the best man for the job." The captain opened his 1:50,000-scale map and held it up against the side of the nearby ACAV. "We'll stop right about here by this stream junction for a break. The tracks will be left idling long enough for you and your patrol to slip into the jungle. We'll move about eight thousand meters down the road and set up a night laager site, where we'll wait for your team to link up with us in the morning."

"Eight thousand meters is a tough haul in the jungle, sir." Sash tapped the map with his finger.

"We figure the Vietcong are living in Bo Tuc, even though there's a Popular Forces company stationed in the village from the province. Hell, they could be PF's during the day and VC at night. It won't be the first fucking time that's happened during this war." The captain refolded his map and slipped it back into his side pocket. "You'll be traveling heavy tonight, with an extra M-60 assigned to your squad and two Starlight scopes. You won't be able to see shit until you get back on the road. If you hear *anyone* passing your position during the night before you move out, call me on the horn at once. I'll wait until they've passed you on the road and then call in artillery on them. It's important, Maleko, that you stay where we leave you until midnight. I'll know your *exact* location and you'll be protected from our own artillery. You're going to be hiding where Highway 4 and the northwest trail from Bo Tuc intersect. I'll need to know from which direction the enemy is coming if you hear them moving on the trail. Now, play it all back to me."

Sash thought for a couple of seconds and then repeated to his captain all of his instructions for the night patrol, and closed by adding, "Who's the extra machine-gunner going to be?"

"Taylor, from heavy-weapons platoon." The captain caught the look in Maleko's eyes. "It's his turn to pull patrol—is that going to be a problem?"

"I'd rather do this without Taylor. He's more of a problem than he's worth."

"Everybody says that, and Taylor is taking it easy because of it. If the motherfucker doesn't carry his share of the load or if he jeopardizes *anyone's* life, I want you to shoot the son of a bitch!"

Sash stared at his captain to see if the officer really meant what he was saying. The whole company knew that Taylor had been bragging about blowing the captain away because the officer had given him an Article 15 for smoking dope on guard duty.

"I need to get a decent night's sleep, Maleko, and since the cav troop is with us, tonight is going to be the night."

"Consider it done, Captain."

"I hate putting that racist bastard on your patrol, but there isn't too much trouble he can get into out there." The captain tried justifying what he had referred to earlier. "A fucking racist is a racist—black or white!"

Maleko assembled his squad after Taylor had reported to the track he was on. He briefed his men on their night mission and warned all of them to check their gear carefully to make sure that nothing would rattle. The cav troop commander gave the signal for the tracks to start their engines, and the roar of the huge diesels drowned out Maleko's voice. He yelled loud enough for his squad to hear his final instructions before they loaded up for the ride to their drop-off point. "Bring only ammo, Claymores, and bug juice!" He looked at his squad's radio operator. "Change batteries in the radio and check it to make sure they work. We'll carry nothing extra, and leave our rucksacks with the platoon sergeant."

Taylor glared at Maleko all the way down the road to where the captain was going to drop them off, but his animosity was having little effect.

Maleko checked the eight-by-twelve-inch piece of map he was carrying, which had their night-patrol site marked out in the center of it. He again ascertained that he was carrying a compass and then tried orienting himself on the moving ACAV. On the map he had determined where they were on the road, and guessed that it would be another fifteen minutes before they passed the abandoned Montagnard village that occupied the northwest quadrant of the highway-stream intersection where they were going to be dropped off. The captain had instructed him to set his squad up in the northeast quadrant so that they could observe the abandoned village from across the main road and still watch the smaller trail that went east back to the small village of Bo Tuc, where the company of PF's was stationed. The captain's instructions kept passing through his thoughts, especially his orders that *anything* going north on Highway 4 from the junction to where the two companies were going to laager would be the enemy—regardless of what uniforms they were wearing —and should be treated as NVA soldiers. All of the friendly forces had been warned about the two American units using the road, and the PF company commander had received a hand-delivered overlay of the operational area the Americans would be working. The patrols had been left off the overlays.

The column of tracks pulled off the road in a classic herringbone pattern. Maleko could see his captain pointing to the intersection about a hundred meters up the column from where they had stopped. He could see the old buildings and longhouses from the Montagnard village on the opposite side of the road as he jogged to join his captain.

"Set your squad up in there. Make sure your men enter at an angle, and I'll have some men rearrange the vegetation. Good luck, Maleko. I'll see you guys in the morning." The captain gave his Spec Four a loose salute.

Sash led his squad into the bamboo thicket and pointed out where he wanted each of the two-man teams to set up their weapons for the night. He selected a spot in the center of the circle and pointed for the RTO to stay there and dig a shallow foxhole before the sound of the idling tracks was gone and they would have to stop digging. The RTO attacked the clay soil, knowing that he had only a few minutes before he would have to stop digging, and he wanted to get deep enough to protect himself and Maleko from grazing fire.

Sash went to every position and checked that each man knew exactly what was expected of him. The squad would act as a listening post until midnight, and then they would leave the position and patrol back to the laager site, where the company would be waiting for them. It was a good eight-to-ten-hour patrol, and it would be daylight before they would link up.

The sound of the track drivers gunning their engines stopped the squad's digging in. Sash removed a small bottle of bug juice from his pocket and saturated his clothes with the liquid to keep the mosquitoes away. Slowly the sound of the ACAV's turned to a faint throb in the distance, and after a few minutes everything became quiet. The hum of the circling mosquitoes was the loudest sound they could hear until the rest of the jungle insects' mating calls declared the area safe again.

Sash signaled to the RTO that he was going to take a short nap and that he wanted to be woken in an hour. The RTO nodded and went back to monitoring the command frequency on the PRC-25 he was carrying. He had worked with Maleko for a long time and knew he would have his own chance to catch a few winks before dark. Sash used the stock of his M-60 as a headrest and stretched out under the bamboo branches in the muggy heat to sleep. He hooked his thumbs in his pistol belt to keep his hands from lying on the ground and hoped that the bug juice would keep all of the centipedes and scorpions away. He thought about the insects for a short while and then discarded his concerns about them. A man could worry himself sick in the jungle.

The RTO nudged him.

Maleko opened his eyes and listened without moving a muscle.

The RTO nudged him again and Maleko turned his head just enough to look at him. The soldier was pointing at his watch to tell him his time was up. It felt like only a couple of minutes since he had closed his eyes. Sash looked at his own watch and saw that he had been sleeping for two hours. He flashed an angry look at the RTO, but knew the man had given up some of his own nap time to allow Sash to rest. It had been a very generous thing to do.

Maleko sat up and instantly smelled the strong sweet odor. He looked at the RTO and pointed in the direction he thought the smell was coming from. The soldier's face turned red, and he shrugged. Maleko left his M-60 with the RTO and crawled quietly down the narrow matted-down trail that led to the position Taylor and a soldier from Alabama were occupying. The smell of marijuana was getting stronger. Taylor's position was only twenty feet from the CP.

Taylor saw Maleko coming and lifted the ivory pipe to his mouth and inhaled a deep lungful of smoke. He handed the pipe to his buddy, but the man knew better than to take it with Maleko watching.

"What the fuck do you think you're doing! You stupid son of a bitch!" Maleko kept his voice to a whisper, but even that sounded overloud.

Taylor answered by taking another toke from the pipe.

"There are only eight of us out here, and the company is fucking eight thousand meters away! The NVA can smell that shit for a mile in this jungle!" Sash snatched the pipe out of Taylor's hand and ground out the burning marijuana in the bowl before breaking the pipe in half and throwing it out into the bamboo thicket.

Taylor responded by smiling.

Sash grabbed Taylor's M-60 and removed the C-ration can that had been attached to the side of the machine gun under the ammunition tray to act as an additional support for the ammunition belt that fed into the weapon. The dinner-size C-ration can was a popular GI trick to assist the linked ammo going into the weapon, and helped prevent jamming. It was also a popular carrying case for a marijuana stash in the field because it kept the leaves dry. Sash saw the small indent where a fingernail could pull the lid back and opened the can. A plastic bag of marijuana had been stuffed inside.

"That's my shit, honky." Taylor reached for it and Sash wrapped his huge hand around the man's wrist to stop him.

"Not anymore! No dope in the field. You know the captain's rules."

"Fuck the captain!" Taylor flashed Sash his best hate look but it was ignored by his angry squad leader.

Sash looked at Taylor's buddy. "Do you have any shit?"

The man shook his head in the negative.

"If you're lying, I swear I'll see you court-martialed!"

"I'm not lying, Maleko."

Sash tore open the plastic bag and scattered the dope over the ground.

"You're *dead*, motherfucker!" Taylor tried standing, but Sash's hands were much quicker.

"If you ever threaten me again, it's *you* who'll be fucked up." Sash held Taylor so tightly by the front of his jacket that when Taylor tried jerking away, he tore his collar and lost three buttons. "I don't have time for your shit out here. We can settle this when we get back to the company." Sash dropped Taylor back down in the matted-down bamboo and left.

The whole conversation had taken place in whispers, but the men on either side of Taylor's position had heard most of what had gone on. None of the men in the squad had been pleased when they heard that Taylor was going out on patrol with them. He was known as a fuck-off, always going on sick call to the rear, making everyone else pull his field duty.

Sash could feel his heart pounding when he returned to the CP. He signaled for the RTO to catch some sleep before it got dark. The adrenaline from the incident kept Sash wide-awake until dark, and then the normal fear that came with an isolated night position kept him alert. He woke his RTO and had him make a radio check with the company CP in the laager area before total blackness settled in.

The muffled sound filtered through the bamboo thicket and brought Sash to full alert as he listened intently for anything that would identify the sound. A low voice came from the trail leading to the village of Bo Tuc. A large number of people was moving up the trail toward Highway 4. Sash turned his attention toward Taylor's position. If the man had some more marijuana stashed and started smoking it, they would all be dead.

It seemed to take an hour for the people on the trail to pass by, but Sash knew that a person's mind exaggerated anything that was affiliated with fear. He reached over in the dark and felt for his RTO. The man's leg shook under Sash's hand.

The soldier who had been on the corner of the intersection came crawling through the bamboo, followed closely by his teammate. He stopped often to hold up his Starlight scope so he could see where the trail went through the extremely thick bamboo. He spotted Maleko sitting next to the RTO and started crawling faster, until he touched Maleko's boot in the dark.

"Sash! There were fucking *hundreds* of them!"

"Shhh!" Maleko leaned forward in the dark and felt for the soldier's head and then located his ear so that he could whisper in it. "VC or PF's?"

"Fucking VC! Main-force VC! They were carrying RPG's, machine guns—fucking everything!"

"Did you get a head count with the Starlight scope?"

"I counted over two hundred of them before . . ." The soldier didn't want to tell his squad leader that he had lost his nerve and hidden back in the bamboo.

"This is important, so think before answering me. Which way did they turn on Highway 4?"

The soldier answered instantly. "North! Man they're going to hit the company!"

Sash felt the fear leaving him. It didn't make sense, but now that he could so something other than sit and listen, he felt better. He reached back in the dark and felt for his RTO. "Give me the handset." Sash felt the plastic touch his hand. He held the handset tightly against his ear and whispered after keying the radio, "Buckeye Six—Buckeye Double Deuce . . . over."

The reply came instantly. "Double Deuce—this is Six Romeo, over."

"Double Deuce—get Six on the horn, ASAP . . . over."

"Roger."

"Double Deuce—Six, over."

"Double Deuce—Victor Charlie Mike Foxtrot—two-hundred-plus—moving north on Highway Four. Time—present . . . over."

"Roger message, Double Deuce. What is your current situation? Over."

"Yellow—out." Sash told the captain that they were safe but in a dangerous situation by using the code word.

"What are we going to do?" The soldier was worried.

"First of all, we're all going to pull back and assemble here, and then we're going to move out."

"Where?"

"Up the road to link up with our company. We might be able to get the VC in a crossfire on the road."

"Are you fucking crazy! There were *hundreds* of them!"

"And we have two machine guns, and if we're *on* the road, we can use the highway as one hell of a wide fire lane!" Sash didn't add that the bamboo thicket was making him claustrophobic. "We'll have a better chance out on the road, and the VC don't know that we're going to be there. We'll have the advantage."

"Sash, let's think about this shit!"

"Assemble the squad." Sash took the Starlight scope from the soldier and crawled back down the trail to where the two-man outpost had been. It was much brighter on the trail, where the moonlight could filter down, and the road reflected enough light that made its dirt-and-gravel surface look like an illuminated strip in the jungle. He turned on the Starlight scope and looked down the road. Everything became bright green in the scope, and Sash could see both ways down the highway for a couple hundred meters before the roadway turned.

The soldier broke away from the jungle, but hesitated a couple of seconds, not knowing in which direction Maleko had gone until he heard a soft finger-snap.

He reached the spot on the highway where Maleko was using the Starlight scope and dropped down on one knee. "Bad shit!"

"What's going on?" Maleko kept the scope against his eye and focused the lens.

"Taylor's dead! His throat has been fucking cut!"

Maleko lowered the scope slowly and looked at the soldier in the dark. "VC?"

"Fuck no! It had to be someone on the patrol!"

Maleko inhaled deeply and exhaled slowly through his nose. There was a huge Vietcong unit somewhere between them and safety, and someone had actually murdered one of the patrol members. "Are you *sure* it wasn't a VC?" As soon as he had whispered the question, Maleko knew that it had to be one of their own men. A Vietcong scout would have alerted the larger unit to their presence in the bamboo thicket. "Fuck! As if two hundred VC aren't bad enough!"

"What do you want us to do?" The soldier's voice sounded scared.

Sash thought for a couple of seconds and then made his decision. "We're not going to leave his body here. We'll set up an ambush. Get the men together!"

The small patrol gathered tightly around Sash with their heads nearly touching, so he wouldn't have to speak above a soft whisper, and listened to his plan.

"If the Vietcong hit our company and the cav troop, they'll probably withdraw back down this highway to their village. If there was another way back to Bo Tuc, they would have used it earlier. If they break up into small units after the attack and try infiltrating back to their village, we'll have a contact-free night." Sash realized that he was taking too much time explaining why he wanted to set the ambush up at the highway and trail junction, but he also realized that being together was calming his small patrol and the men were regaining their confidence. What was becoming clear to him was that Americans were piss-poor night fighters. Maybe one in a hundred American soldiers had ever been alone at night in the woods—probably not even that many. The vast majority of the men fighting with him in Vietnam had been recruited off the streets of major metropolitan areas, where even in the worst neighborhoods there were streetlights. Sash forced himself to think about the ambush and began briefing again. "You five"—he tapped each of the men on the shoulder—"will set up all of our Claymore mines along the west side of the highway right before the intersection." Sash laid his hand on the shoulder of the soldier who had been teamed with Taylor during the day. "You'll use Taylor's M-60 and set up with me down the road." The soldier gave a curt nod in the dim light. He had already taken over the light machine gun. Sash continued his briefing, making up the plan as he talked. "The signal to blast the Claymores will be when I open fire with my M-60. I'll be watching the road with the Starlight scope. When I see the VC returning, we'll set up the two M-60's on the edges of the highway and put grazing fire along your front." He was speaking to the five men who would be working the sixteen Claymore antipersonnel mines.

"What if the VC come up the highway from the south?" The soldier's voice quavered in the dark.

"Then we let them pass through our ambush—I ain't fucking stupid, guys! Listen up! We have the advantage. They don't know we're here, and if they tangle with our guys up the road, they're going to return carrying a lot of wounded and dead."

"Let's try moving closer to our company." The low voice from the group in front of him angered Maleko.

"Listen, dammit! We've got Taylor's body—we can't carry it and I'm not going to leave it behind! That's one reason. The second reason is that the Vietcong might not be going to attack our company, but are setting up an ambush of their own for the cav troop

194

that they know will be returning down this highway."
Sash's words hit home. None of them wanted to spring
a Vietcong ambush—not with only seven of them.

"All right! It's settled, then. We stay here and set
up our own little ambush party. It's going to be a very
long night because we're going to have to spread out
and won't be able to double up." Sash knew that
having to spend the rest of the night alone at each
ambush position was going to be the hardest thing to
do for all of them, but it had to be done. "Let's go.
I'm going to position each of you myself."

Sash walked along the edge of the road, followed by
the four men he was going to place about forty feet
apart. The sixteen Claymores would cover a football
field, and he wasn't going to waste the effect because
the men were afraid to be separated. He helped each
one of the men set up his Claymores and then camouflaged the spot where the soldier slipped into the jungle to hide with the detonators. Sash gave each soldier
a short briefing to raise the man's confidence, closing
with the same statement to each of them: don't panic
and set off the Claymores prematurely. He returned to
where he had left Taylor's partner, who had been
covering them with Taylor's M-60 and was using the
second Starlight scope. "You turn around and cover
the highway to the south with your Starlight scope.
We're going to stay together on the same side of the
road." Sash knew he was taking a big risk, but it
would be impossible for them to communicate with
the road dividing them, and the RTO was a part of the
Claymore ambush. Sash had kept the PRC-25 radio so
he could call in air support and talk with the captain in
the morning—if they were still alive.

Sash checked his watch. He was having difficulty
staying awake. Taylor's partner moved next to him
and adjusted his Starlight scope. A series of muffled
sounds filtered down the highway from the north—too
far away to tell if it was a B-52 strike or a firefight.

Sash waited along with the rest of his patrol. He spent the time worst-casing what would happen if the patrol was overrun by Vietcong. He had already decided before first arriving in-country that he would not be taken prisoner. If he had to run, he wouldn't be able to carry both the radio and the M-60. He tried reasoning which item he should leave behind. Both machine guns had a thousand rounds of ammo apiece, but that would go fast if they had to execute an ambush. Fire superiority was the key to a successful ambush. Sash decided that he would stash the M-60 and rely on his pistol for protection. It was much more important to have a radio in the jungle so he could call for support and evacuation.

The sounds coming from the north increased, and a faint glow appeared in the sky from the flares being dropped. A flight of gunships coming up the road from Tay Ninh roared right over the ambush position and scared all of them.

Sash was sure that the large Vietcong unit had tried attacking the company's laager site. What he didn't know was that his early warning had given his captain time to plan a deadly surprise for the VC battalion. The enemy unit had sustained severe casualties and the Vietcong battalion commander had ordered an immediate withdrawal. Some of his men had been trapped on the north side of the American laager site and had slipped away into the jungle to use a secret trail to get back to the village, but the majority of his survivors, which was about half the men he had started out with, used the highway for a rapid retreat.

American military policy had made the VC commander's attack possible to begin with. He could never have moved his men so far through the jungle at night if it hadn't been for the standing orders that *both* sides in the war were so familiar with. Only small arms could be used on the highways that laced South Vietnam together, and even that required district-chief and province-chief approval. If an American aircraft spotted Vietcong troops using a highway at night, it took at least a half-hour to get clearance to open fire with small arms. Only a very stupid VC commander would keep his troops on a highway after hearing aircraft approaching. In effect, the American policy assured free access for VC and NVA forces during the hours of darkness on all of Vietnam's highways. The only thing they had to be careful about was night ambush patrols, and the Americans sent overlays to the districts every night. It was very rare that the VC didn't receive a copy also.

Maleko's tiny ambush was one of those rare occurrences, and the Vietcong battalion commander had his troops jogging along the sides of the highway in two columns, carrying their wounded in hasty stretchers made out of bamboo poles and lightweight American parachute cloth. He had hidden his dead after the fight and would return for them later.

Sash had been looking through the Starlight scope for more than five hours, and the green light was starting to affect his vision. He blinked rapidly and then actually took his eye away from the rubber cup on the scope to rub it before looking back again at the sight that had confused him. Four VC scouts were jogging toward him—two on each side of the road. He could see with the scope that a much larger force was following them about a hundred meters behind. Maleko nudged Taylor's partner to get him to turn around, and he heard the soldier's air catch in his throat when he saw the columns of jogging VC returning to their village. Sash held the Starlight scope in one hand and slipped the M-60's shoulder guard over his collarbone. He rested the scope over the top of the M-60 and wished that the device had been mounted on the weapon. Sash felt the large rock pressing against the barrel of his machine gun. He had placed a boulder next to each of the M-60's to keep them from going too far to the left and raking his own men.

The four scouts passed through the kill zone of the ambush and turned down the trail to the village of Bo Tuc. Sash thought that at least his captain could take pride in being right. The village was VC and the Popular Forces Company were government troops during the day and Vietcong at night. Sash wondered only for a second how the district chief was going to explain his losses the next day, but his attention was drawn to the first of the VC columns reaching the trail junction.

The sound of his M-60 was alone for only a second before Taylor's joined in. Sash couldn't see anything but the bright light coming from his flash suppressor. He moved the barrel of his machine gun to the right slowly and then back again until it touched the rock. He had practiced the slow movement a thousand times during the night in order to stay awake, and it was paying off handsomely as his grazing fire cut down the VC all the way to the rear of their columns.

"Fire the Claymores! *Fire the Claymores!*" Sash caught himself yelling over the roar of the twin machine guns. It seemed like hours since he had opened fire, but it had been only a few seconds. His M-60 clicked and stopped firing. Sash automatically went through the jammed-weapon sequence a couple of times before he realized that he had gone through the first belt of ammunition. He felt like a fool and actually felt his face getting red because he had missed the logical reason for his weapon to stop firing. He wasted a second to glance over at Taylor's partner, but could see only the muzzle flashes coming from the other machine gun.

The Claymores went off in a tremendous roar, and a couple seconds later, the second volley of the deadly antipersonnel mines went off. All of the patrol members had responded within twenty seconds of the M-60's firing, but to Sash it had seemed forever.

The Vietcong battalion commander didn't have time to score Sash's ambush as good or bad. He died being cut to ribbons by the Claymores, along with ninety percent of his men. The four scouts escaped by continuing to run down the trail to the village, where they quickly changed their uniforms and went to their PF bunkers. About a dozen stragglers also survived outside the deadly kill zone and slipped into the jungle to return to their village in the morning.

The two M-60's continued raking the jungle and the roadway until both of them were out of ammo. Sash listened to the sporadic M-16 rounds being fired, but there was nothing coming back at them from the jungle. The ambush had been a total success. There were no American casualties—except for Taylor.

Sash stood and slowly removed his pistol. He slipped one strap from the PRC-25 over his shoulder and walked down the center of the road. The first strong rays of daylight were breaking over the jungle trees. Sash heard a rooster crow when he reached the trail's junction with the highway. A light mist rolled along the surface of the road, making the bodies of the VC look as if they were floating on clouds.

Slowly the rest of the patrol emerged from the jungle, all of them wearing the shocked expressions of disbelief—disbelief that they had done what they were seeing and disbelief that they had actually survived the night.

The radio keyed and the captain's voice reached Sash's right ear from where he had hooked the handset to his web gear. "Buckeye Double Deuce—this is Buckeye Six, over."

Sash pressed the push-to-talk switch and felt his throat burn when he tried answering. "Double Deuce . . . over."

"Six—are you guys getting close to our location? Over."

"Negative, Six—we're still at our old site . . . over."

There was a long pause and then the captain came back on the air. "Six here—what's the problem, Double Deuce? Over."

"You'd better send us some support . . . over."

"Six—Have you made contact with Victor Charlie? Over."

"Double Deuce"—Sash looked in the faces of his patrol before answering—"roger your last transmission, Six."

The captain's voice rose a little over the radio. "Six—do you need gunship support? Over."

"Double Deuce—negative—just someone to count the bodies . . . out." Maleko hooked his handset back on his web gear and looked at the shocked faces of his patrol. "You guys did a good job. We lost only one man—right?" He looked deeply into the eyes of Taylor's partner.

The soldier from Alabama stared back at Maleko and then slowly reached up on his web gear and touched the handle of a hook-bladed linoleum knife that he carried taped to his left load-carrying strap. Sash's eyes followed the movement of the soldier's hand.

"There ain't no racist motherfuckers on this patrol —no mo'. It seems like the VC sought him out." The soldier looked down at the M-60 he was holding by its carrying handle. Smoke still came off the barrel.

Sash gave a curt nod. "We'll leave it at that." He looked at the rest of the patrol members' faces and they all nodded. They would all leave it at that.

CHAPTER EIGHT

✪✪✪✪✪✪✪✪✪✪✪✪✪✪✪✪

MUD!

The huge flag flying over the White House snapped
and cracked in the brisk wind. Alex watched the sym-
bol of American dreams dance for him in front of a
chorus line of billowing clouds. The storm the night
before had cleared the air of gasoline fumes and the
haze that normally hovered over Washington. It was a
brisk, crystal-clear country day in the nation's capital.

"Here, mister."

Alex turned to see who was talking to him. It was
one of the park bums he had given the reward money to.

"I thought you might be a little hungry." The white-
haired old man stroked his beard shyly.

"Thanks, but I'm not really very hungry." Alex
smiled.

"Well, you can eat it later." He lifted the lid off a
large Styrofoam cup of coffee. The fresh-brewed smell
floated through the odorless air.

"Now, that smells good." Alex reached for the coffee.

"It was free. The hotel has a courtesy table for its
guests where they serve free coffee and Danish." The
old man started chuckling to himself. "They sent us a
special cart to our room!" He slapped his leg and
laughed. "I don't think they wanted us wandering
around their lobby, even though we are paying guests."

Alex couldn't help grinning at the rheumy-eyed old
man. "What hotel are you guys staying at?"

"The Mayflower, up Connecticut Avenue."

"That's a very expensive place." Alex flashed a naughty look at the old man out of the corner of his eye.

"We're sharing one room, so's we can have a little money left over for . . . a few Christmas drinks."

"Go easy, old man, or they'll throw you guys out of there."

"Do you know they want seventy-five dollars for a fifth of cheap gin?" The old man nodded to accent his words. "I came back here to thank you, mister. I don't know why you gave us the money, but I want to tell you that this is the best Christmas any of us have had in a long, long time." The old man shifted his eyes down to the packed snow between his feet.

"I bet it was, old man." Alex shook his head. "You'd better get back there and enjoy it. . . . Merry Christmas."

"God bless you, son."

Alex nodded and went back to watching the flag dancing on the wind. The cup of hot coffee felt good in his hands. He looked at the Danish pastries wrapped in paper napkins on the bench next to him and opened one of the packages. The old man had wrapped each of the three pastries in its own napkin. Alex tasted the one he had opened, and as soon as his stomach felt the first bite of food reach it, he became famished and devoured the rest one after the other. He hadn't realized how hungry he was and how cold he had gotten after sitting out all night in the storm. The hot coffee hurt his teeth at first because they were so cold, and then the fluid warmed his whole body.

He took his time drinking the coffee and watched the women gather for their Christmas Day demonstration. The group was growing larger by the hour. Alex counted sixty-four women and five men working the tables and carrying picket signs. He figured that he had a couple more hours before it was his turn to demonstrate *his* rights.

The woman who had confronted Alex kept looking over at him sitting on the bench. She had watched the old man bring the coffee and rolls, and her anger was boiling under her skin. A large group of men singing Christmas carols as they walked toward the park drew her attention away from Alex. She waved and started smiling.

Alex saw the group of laughing men and made a quick head count before going back to watching the clouds. His moment might be sooner than he'd expected, if they kept arriving at that rate. The homemade belt of TNT chafed against his sides, forcing him to shift position on the bench. He reached under his loose overcoat and adjusted the belt and then unlatched the World War II Browning Automatic Rifle ammunition belt he was wearing over the TNT. He had filled the pouches of the BAR belt with ball bearings and nails.

Alex closed his eyes and lifted his chin until the warm sun was covering his face. The wind had calmed and it was turning into a beautiful day. The snow was already beginning to melt, but that was Washington. Weather with the wind. Alex smiled with his eyes still closed; that was Washington politics also.

"Excuse me." The voice was male but laced with a lisp.

Alex kept his eyes closed.

"I said, excuse me!"

Alex ignored the person standing near his bench.

"You are going to be difficult, I can see that Sheila was right."

Alex opened his eyes only enough to make out the three shadow figures standing in front of him. He had been listening to their approach and knew that none of them had come up behind him.

"I came over here to ask if you would like to join our demonstration for women's rights."

"No." Alex opened his eyes fully.

"We could use a Vietnam veteran in our ranks." The man smiled at Alex. "We'll pay you ten dollars."

"Fuck off."

One of the larger men in the group spoke. "You're being very rude."

Alex took his time looking at the man. He was obviously some kind of weight lifter, and was huge. "I just want to be left alone to sit here on this *public* bench and enjoy the sunshine."

"You've been bothering the ladies, and now you're insulting us." The big man spoke without concealing the threat in his voice. "I think it's about time you got your ass out of here."

Alex smiled and started lifting the barrel of his CAR-15. He hadn't wanted to start so early, but if he was forced to, he would.

The weight lifter took a step toward Alex but was stopped by the first man's arm. "We don't want any trouble right now, with the television cameras being set up." He nodded to the mobile van parked at the curb. "This is your last chance to join us."

"I don't take part in stuff like that. Personally, I don't believe in mothers murdering their own babies . . . someone else's—maybe I could support that—but not their own."

"You are one sick motherfucker!" The weight lifter shook his head.

Alex looked directly at the leader of the group. "Let me ask you a question. Do you think fourteen- and fifteen-year-old girls should have abortions if they get pregnant?"

"Absolutely!"

"Without exception?" Alex smiled but kept his lips closed tightly.

"Very few exceptions! It would ruin a young girl's life to have a baby at fourteen!"

"That's sad." Alex frowned. "I'm glad Mary, the Mother of God, didn't have to give birth to him today."

The man frowned and looked over at his friends for support and then back at Alex. "What has that got to do with this demonstration?"

"Oh . . . you didn't know?"

"Know what?"

"Mary was only fourteen . . . maybe fifteen years old when she bore Jesus."

"Bullshit!" The weight lifter balled his fist.

"Really, friend." Alex smiled. "I'm glad your group didn't exist in Christ's time or you would have murdered him."

"You son of a bitch!" The weight lifter started moving toward Alex.

The soft click of the selector switch on the CAR-15 was muffled by the heavy overcoat. Alex shifted slightly on his bench to place the barrel in line with the approaching man.

"Shit! The police!" The leader hissed the words.

"Is there a problem over here?"

Alex heard the police officer ask the question from behind his right shoulder.

"Officer, this bum is harassing the women over there." The leader spoke for the group.

"Have you been bothering those women over there?" The officer's voice dripped sarcasm.

Alex didn't look at the officer. "I've been sitting here on this public bench all morning, officer. I've been minding my own business, and they came over here to harass me."

"Well, it looks like we've got us a problem here." The police officer stepped around the park bench. "Two charges of harassment, and only one charge can stick. It looks like you'd better rejoin your demonstration or leave the park." The officer nodded back at the watching women. The group of men hesitated. "I said *now*."

Alex gave an exaggerated smile at the group and leaned back on the bench.

The police officer waited until the male demonstrators were out of hearing before he spoke. He placed one of his feet on the bench and rested his crossed arms on his leg. "Who did you serve with in Nam?" His voice had changed to a tone of respect.

"Special Forces. I was a medic."

"I'm impressed!"

Alex shrugged.

"I don't think there were any better medics in the Army, still aren't." The officer smiled. "I was the junior weapons man at Cai Cai."

Alex carefully removed his grip on the CAR-15 and pulled his hand free from his coat. He had torn the pocket out of the right-hand side so that he could have free access to his weapon. The police officer shook hands with Alex. "I was the medic at Tong Le Chon in sixty-seven."

"Isn't that when they got overrun?"

Alex nodded.

"Shit! Then you must be the medic who won the Distinguished Service Cross!" The officer squeezed Alex's hand harder. "Damn! I'm proud to meet you! That was one hell of a fight!"

Alex felt his cheeks redden in embarrassment. "A lot of the team fought well. We even had a couple of attached infantrymen who fought a lot harder than I did."

The officer smiled. "That fight was legendary, my friend."

Alex looked down at the snow and studied the numerous footprints in front of him. "Yeah, I guess it was."

"I've got to get over there and make sure those *ladies* don't get out of line." The policeman's voice was apologetic. "It was a real pleasure meeting you . . . ah . . . ?"

"Alex Jaxson."

"If any of those freaks screw with you again, just

give a nod and I'll run them off. I've got to stay out here all day until they leave."

"You're going to be in the park all day?"

"Yeah, a shit detail, especially on Christmas. My wife is pissed but the kids understand." The officer waved. "Gotta go earn my money. I'll try to stop by and chat a little later, if you're still here."

Alex inhaled a deep breath. He was having doubts for the first time since he had decided to take out the group of demonstrators. He would have to kill the cop first.

The police officer walked directly over to the woman who had the permit to demonstrate in the park. She flexed her jaws and waited until he was close enough to receive her full fury.

Alex watched the policeman's hands. He couldn't hear what was being said, but from the way the demonstrators were shaking their heads, it was something they didn't like hearing.

Alex had tried to block out Tong Le Chon from his mind, but mentioning it to the policeman had brought back many good and bad thoughts. He drifted in time; if his first memory of Tong Le Chon had been bad, he would have blocked it, but his first thought was good and he allowed the door to open.

Water poured off the vegetation and covered the ground in a sheet. Nothing remained dry unless it was wrapped in plastic. The ponchos the men wore had lost their effect and the soldiers wearing them kept them on only to retain some of their body heat. Water had found its way around the neck openings and slowly saturated the top half of the tiger suits the commandos and Special Forces men were wearing. It had been raining for so long that the insides of the ponchos had formed condensation and had slowly soaked the cloth that separated the rubber from the human skins.

Alex sat between two huge exposed roots of a giant

tree. The roots protected him on both sides and the spare poncho he had tied over the roots kept most of the rain out of his medical supplies. The tiny jungle aid station served its purpose and allowed him to treat the sick commandos. The CIDG company had been on patrol for eleven straight days and the men were starting to show the strain. They hadn't seen any signs of NVA activity in the area, and that had made it even worse. Small signs would have given the commandos some information as to the whereabouts of the enemy, such as direction of travel, numbers, types of units; even the NVA soldiers' morale could be detected from small signs left behind a traveling force. *No* sign made the Cambodian commandos very nervous, especially after they had heard about the American company ambushed on Highway 4 to the east of their camp.

Alex looked at the festering cut on the chest of the small Cambodian commando squatting down in front of him. The wound had been a minor cut, but because of all the rain and the high humidity, even small cuts became very painful and developed into what were called jungle ulcers. Alex rubbed an antibiotic ointment on the sore to control topical bacteria and spoke to the commando through the Cambodian interpreter, who was squatting in a corner of the small field dispensary. One of the courses in the Special Forces training group had been how to effectively use an interpreter, and now Alex understood how important the class was for effective communication between two people who spoke different languages. One of the prime lessons in the course was never to look at the interpreter, but at the person you were talking to when you spoke; even if the person didn't understand what you were saying, it was important that eye contact be maintained throughout the conversation. Alex spoke to the commando and at the same time read the man's facial expressions.

"How's it going in here?" The executive officer stuck his head under the poncho flap.

"Good. We've got a lot of jungle ulcers and malaria starting to pop up."

"We should be heading back to the camp in the morning." The lieutenant used his index finger and his thumb to squeeze the edge of his camouflage tiger cap. The act stopped the water from dripping in front of his eyes for only a second or two and then the mini-waterfalls started up again. He wanted to get out of the rain as much as the commandos did. "The captain says that the 1st Division has sent us an infantry company for a couple of weeks."

"One?"

"Hell, Jaxson! You know that *one* American company is worth ten companies of these little people!" The lieutenant tried to be sarcastic but failed. It would be good to have an American unit patrolling the jungle around the camp, mostly because the company would have a lot of on-call support backing it up.

"Something is wrong out here. We should have seen some sign of the NVA—old bunkers or something." Alex zipped up his medical kit.

"I agree. That ambush on the infantry has all of us worried. It looks like the NVA are starting to mass, and that means they're going to hit some American base camp."

"At least we've got our bunkers finished and the berm built up high enough to protect us from grazing fire." Alex had spent only a dozen nights inside of Tong Le Chon since he had arrived in Vietnam, and that had been almost three months ago. Medics were constantly required to go out with the patrols, and one of them was always in the field, except for very short periods of overlap. He had been very happy to hear that Sergeant First Class Billy Mills was going to be his senior medic in the camp, but was disappointed when he found out that Mills was the one person in the camp that he would see the least of; when Mills was back in the base camp, he was out in the field, and vice versa.

"Be packed and ready to go at first light." The lieutenant disappeared back into the rain.

Alex leaned against the wet root and closed his eyes. He was exhausted from the long patrol and knew that if he didn't get any sleep now, he wouldn't get any until they reached the A camp the next day. He dozed.

A soft popping sound reached Alex's poncho hutch from out on the perimeter. The sound was joined by another, and then the dull thud of a grenade exploding reached him around the millions of raindrops falling out of the sky. Alex woke instantly and reached for his Swedish K 9mm submachine gun. He stuck his head out from under the poncho and listened. It was quiet.

A shape emerged from the rain and dropped down next to Alex. It was the other American from the A Team. "Alex, bring your kit. One of our outposts surprised two NVA. One's dead and the other one's seriously wounded."

Alex grabbed his battle kit and sprang out into the monsoon. He kept the sergeant's shape in front of him as he followed the NCO back out to the nearby perimeter. The Cambodians had dragged the NVA bodies back to their first position. Alex dropped down on one knee and checked the NVA soldier's pulse.

"He still alive?" The lieutenant had joined their small group.

"Yes. Let's take him back to my aid station, where I can take a closer look at him." Alex motioned for two of the commandos to carry the wounded NVA soldier.

"I'm going back to my sector in case these two were just a probe." The lieutenant disappeared in the sheet of water.

"Watch him, Alex." The weapons sergeant nodded at the NVA soldier. "He might try to pull some fast shit on you, and I don't want an NVA loose inside our perimeter."

Alex nodded.

The NVA was already placed under the poncho when Alex caught up to the commandos. There wasn't much room for him to work, but he knew he would have to hurry or the man would go into shock and die on him. The interpreter held the neon lantern above the prone body while Alex unbuttoned the soldier's shirt. He had been hit once in the shoulder and again in the lower side by a carbine. It had been the NVA's lucky day— if he had received those wounds from an M-16, he would have already been dead from the shock of the rounds.

The NVA soldier opened his eyes and watched Alex. He spoke very softly between short breaths, but Alex couldn't understand what he was saying.

"Phap . . ." The Cambodian interpreter answered Alex's question: "He speak French."

Alex took a closer look at the North Vietnamese soldier and saw that he wasn't much older than he himself, and the young man's features were not Vietnamese. "He *Phap*?" Alex pointed at the wounded North Vietnamese soldier.

The interpreter shook his head and spat out a small piece of fish bone that had almost stuck in his throat. He looked down in the narrow plastic package of indigenous rations he was eating from and frowned. "He have French father and North Vietnamese mother." The interpreter shook his head and made an ugly face. "He no good—let die." The little Cambodian spat red juice on the ground.

"Do you speak French?" Alex glared over the body of the wounded NVA soldier at the Cambodian mercenary.

The man shrugged and picked at the food he was holding with his chopsticks. "I speak Cambodian, English, Vietnamese . . ." He glaced up and saw the firm look on Alex's face and added, ". . . little bit French."

"Good! Tell me what he's saying." Alex reached for the PRC-77 radio in his rucksack. The three Americans on patrol took turns carrying the heavy communications gear, and it was his turn. He looked at the frequency setting and then keyed the set. It took a couple of seconds before he was answered.

"Mud Nine . . . this is . . . Mud Seven, over." The call signs were appropriate for the weather conditions.

"This is Mud Nine, would you get Mud Eight on the line for me, it's an emergency."

"Roger, Nine . . . wait . . . out."

Alex used a metal probe to check the path of the bullets in the wounded NVA soldier while he waited for Sergeant Mills to get over to the team communications bunker back at Tong Le Chon. He saw that a large vein had been clipped when the bullet had gone through the soldier's shoulder. Blood seeped from the wound and had formed a small puddle on the sheet of plastic Alex had laid under him. He removed a small package of blood expander from his first-aid kit and shoved his Randall fighting knife in the tree root over the soldier so that he could hang the package up over the man's arm. Alex injected the needle and felt the NVA soldier tighten his arm slightly in response.

"Him bad. No French, no Vietnamese, same-same dog." The interpreter curled his upper lip off his teeth. "Him die."

"Thanks for your astute opinion, but I'll make the medical decisions for this patrol." Alex glanced up at the Cambodian. "There's an extra five thousand piasters in it for you if you interpret exactly what he's saying in French for me."

The Cambodian nodded. He wasn't going to turn down a bonus, even for a half-breed. If the dumb American wanted the dog to live, he could accept that for five thousand P's.

The NVA soldier mumbled something under his breath and groaned. Alex looked at the interpreter, who was casually eating again. "Well? What did he say?"

"No make sense . . . he talk to his father."

"What did he say?"

"He say father ashamed because he been shot on first recon patrol."

Alex looked back down at the young soldier. It had been bad luck for him but good for the patrol.

The radio keyed and Mills came on the line. "Mud Nine . . . this is Mud Eight . . . over."

Alex picked up the handset. "Eight . . . Nine . . . I have a wounded NVA soldier here and I'm going to need a patch through to a surgeon back at the hospital . . . over."

Mills dropped the call signs. "What kind of wounds?"

"He took a carbine hit in the side and that one looks like it will hold with a pressure bandage, but he took another hit in the shoulder and he's got a bleeding main vein that I'm going to have to patch or he'll bleed to death before we can get him out of here . . . over."

"Roger, Nine . . . I'll have a radio linkup for you in two minutes—stand by."

The soldier had been mumbling the whole time Alex had been on the radio. "What's he talking about?"

"He talking to father. Me think he *dicky dau*!" The Cambodian made the universal crazy sign by twirling his finger at the side of his head.

"He father is dead. He say that soon he join he father. I think that a good idea!"

"Finish!" Alex opened his medical kit's surgical pouch and removed a scalpel and some extra-fine thread with a stitching needle already attached.

"He father was a French colonel, name LaTruseau. I know this man."

"You know of the colonel?"

'Yes. I was a KKK warrior before Green Berets hire me. CIA tell KKK that they pay *beaucoup* gold for the head of LaTruseau. This his son! Maybe much gold for him!" The interpreter was now becoming very interested in the young North Vietnamese soldier.

213

Alex tried reading behind the Cambodian interpreter's eyes but failed. He knew that the KKK were a very heinous gang of bandits that had preyed on the French and Vietminh alike during that war, and for centuries they had been the perfect mercenaries. The KKK had the same initals as the American Ku Klux Klan, but the Cambodian version made their American cousins look like choir boys. The Cambodian KKK still used human slaves, and there were rumors that they still had quite a few French soldiers hidden in their jungle camps as slaves to the KKK warlords.

Alex put that information about the interpreter in the back of his mind for future reference. "Continue!"

"He talk to mother now. She live in Hanoi. He now talk to father again!" The interpreter threw up his hands in confusion.

Alex realized that the soldier was delirious and was in great danger of going into shock. "I want you to talk to him in French. If he talks to his father . . . you answer him."

"That crazy man!" The interperter didn't understand what Alex wanted from him. The idea was to keep the delirious soldier talking. "Just do it!"

The interpreter looked around to see if any of his peers were near the aid station before he answered the NVA soldier. Five thousand P's was a lot of money.

"Mud Nine . . . Eight . . . over."

"Mud Nine . . . over." Alex keyed his set.

"I have your patch set up on this freq for you. Dr. Kemp will guide you through your operation . . . over."

"Thanks, Eight . . . over."

There were a couple of seconds of static, and a deep voice came over the air. Alex could tell that the doctor was not familiar with using a radio. "Ugh, Nine . . . this is Dr. Kemp . . . please describe the wounds for me . . ." There was a slight break in the transmission and then the doctor came back on the line: ". . . ugh . . . over."

Alex smiled. "Roger, Dr. Kemp. My patient is suffering from two gunshot wounds; one to his right side and a more serious wound through his upper-right shoulder. It looks as if the round passed under his collarbone but clipped one of the main veins on its way out. He's bleeding badly from that wound . . . over."

"Do you have any clamps with you?" The doctor started talking like he was on a telephone.

"Yes, I do . . . over."

"Good . . . isolate the damaged vein and clamp it off."

Alex followed the doctor's instructions. He had handed the radio's handset to the interpreter and worked with both his hands. The operation took almost two hours using the radio, but when Alex closed the wound, the NVA soldier was still alive. He replaced the packet of blood expander with a fresh one and bandaged the wounds. The doctor remained on the radio until Alex had finished.

"Thanks, Doc . . . he just might make it now."

"I'll be waiting for your arrival in emergency receiving when you get out of that jungle, young man. I'm looking forward to meeting you."

"Roger that, Doc. . . . Mud Eight? Have you been monitoring? Over."

"Roger, Nine . . . I'm here . . . over."

"Nine . . . I think we should have some intelligence people standing by also. Our interpreter thinks this NVA soldier is the son of a French turncoat named LaTruseau . . . over."

There was a long pause and Alex keyed his set again. "Eight . . . did you receive my transmission? Over."

The pause continued for another couple of seconds and Mills came back on the line. "Nine . . . are you using the PRC-77? Over."

"This is Nine. Of course . . . over." Alex was pissed.

Mills should know that he wouldn't have used any other radio for such a long, detailed broadcast. The PRC-77 was a secure voice set.

"Thank God! . . . Listen, Alex . . ." Mills dropped all call signs. "You personally stay with that NVA soldier. I don't want anyone else but round-eyes near him . . . understand?"

"Roger . . . but why?"

"Just do as you're told and brief the lieutenant. We'll have choppers out there as soon as it stops raining to pick him up, and that'll be during hours of darkness if we can break through the clouds . . . over."

"Fine . . . I think he's stable enough to be moved . . . over."

"Keep him alive, Alex!"

"I'll do my best, boss!"

"Thanks, old man . . ." Mills chuckled and looked over at the team captain, who had been standing behind him.

"What a fucking find! The son of that Communist bastard!" The captain smiled for the first time since he had been assigned to Tong Le Chon.

There was a break in the cloud cover a little after two o'clock in the morning and a flight of Air Force recovery helicopters with Cobra gunships as escorts dropped down through the hole in the black cloud mass. The crew wasn't on the ground for more than five minutes to extract the NVA soldier and Alex. The surgeon wanted Alex to brief him on what he had done and what the wound had looked like. It was a smart move and would prevent them from having to open the wounds again if Alex had done his job. They weren't expecting too much from him because he was only a sergeant and not a medical doctor.

Alex was surprised to find that a doctor instead of the normal medic was on board the rescue chopper. He had also been surprised to find out that there had been a flight of choppers standing by ever since he had made his radio call. It was obvious that the young NVA soldier was important to someone.

Dr. Kemp and a special surgical crew were standing in the hallway when the chopper landed. Alex followed the stretcher-bearers into the hospital.

"Are you Sergeant Jaxson?" A medic dressed in an immaculate white uniform grabbed Alex by the arm.

"Yes."

"Please come with me, Sarge, and get prepped for the operating room." The medic led the way to a large dressing room. "You can throw your old clothes in that bin over there and shower quickly while I lay out your surgical clothes." The medic looked over at Alex and saw that he hadn't moved. "Please hurry, everyone is waiting for you!"

Alex looked down at his mud-covered clothes and was shocked by the contrast between him and the scrubbed contents of the room. He caught his reflection in a mirror on the wall and couldn't believe how dirty he was. Out in the field he looked like everybody else, but in the hospital he was a shocker. He thought of the NVA soldier he had operated on in a totally muddy environment. The man couldn't survive such filth without contracting some kind of a deadly disease.

"*Please* hurry, Sarge!" The medic was begging.

Alex leapt into action. He tore the clothes off his body and dropped them on the floor. His boots slipped off easily; he had combat-laced them. The shower felt good, but didn't last very long; just long enough to soap down with a disinfectant, and then he suited up for the operating room. He slipped his feet into the soft slippers and followed the impatient medic down the corridor to a double door that had a military policeman standing at either side of it, armed with a submachine gun.

Dr. Kemp looked up from the man on the operating table when he heard the doors open. "Ahhh . . . Sergeant Jaxson?"

"Yes, sir." Alex paused. The room was filled with doctors and nurses. There must have been at least fifteen people surrounding the operating table. Alex looked at the patient under the bright operating lights. It was quite different from the dim light he had used under the poncho hutch. Under the bright lights the NVA soldier looked much younger. He had also been cleaned up.

"Your closing looks remarkably well done."

"Thanks, sir. You can thank a dog named Cowboy."

"What's really important is what you did inside."

'I did what you instructed over the radio." Alex looked at the eyes peering at him above the surgical masks.

"Come over here and show me what you did." Kemp beckoned for Alex to join him next to the operating table.

Alex pointed at the sutured flesh on the soldier. "I placed a clamp here . . . and here . . ." He pointed, using a sterilized steel probe that he had picked up off one of the trays. One of the doctors across from where Alex was standing caught his eye and Alex could see that the man was struggling to hold back the contempt he was feeling for the sergeant. Alex felt the anger boiling inside of his stomach. He had met pompous asses like him before—they were always too valuable to go out in the field, where they could get their precious asses shot off, but sergeants were expendable! Alex lost all of his fear and started rattling off the exact procedures he had used during his operation. If they didn't like what he had done, they could do it themselves next time. "There was a small hole in the vein and I closed it with five sutures. It closed nicely and there was no bleeding. I ensured that he was moved carefully, and I'm convinced the vein hasn't opened—"

"Convinced?" The doctor who had been watching him with contempt in his eyes asked the question.

Alex didn't honor him with a dirty look. "Yes, convinced." He looked over at Dr. Kemp. "May I continue briefing you, sir, without any further interruptions from your staff?"

The old surgeon smiled underneath his surgical mask. It was about time that someone put that hotshot doctor from New York in his place. "Please do, *Sergeant*."

"I also put sutures in his pectoralis major. The bullet missed his deltoid." Alex used the tip of the probe to mark the path of the vein. "I'm sure it was the subclavian vein that was damaged, not the artery."

"Very good, Sergeant Jaxson." The surgeon was rubbing it in for the recently assigned doctor who had been glaring at the young Special Forces medic. "What about the wound in his side?"

"I made a cursory inspection of the wound and placed a pressure bandage over it. I didn't see much exterior bleeding, so I assumed there was no damage internally—"

The new doctor interrupted Alex again. "You *assumed*?"

Alex flashed a threatening glare at the man. "Yes, *doctor*, I assumed! One assumes on a *battlefield*, doctor." Alex returned his attention back to the surgeon but fired a verbal Parthian shot over his shoulder. "You're welcome to come along the next time we go on patrol, doctor."

"You smart-ass!"

The senior surgeon broke up the confrontation. "Enough! We've got work to do on this young solder." He looked at Alex. "You've done a fine job, young man, and if you wanted to, you could make a great surgeon."

"Thank you, sir."

"Why don't you go get something to eat or drink, and I'll get back with you when we've finished here."

Alex started to leave the operating room, but paused to listen to the young doctor's question.

"Sir, are we going to open his shoulder?"

The surgeon continued inspecting the side wound on the NVA soldier as he answered, "No—I haven't seen a better closing since I've been practicing, and if the boy was as good inside, I couldn't do any better myself."

Alex watched the portion of the young doctor's face above the mask turn bright red. The doctor looked over at Alex and felt his throat tighten and burn when Alex winked at him and left through the swinging doors.

The special operating team had worked on the NVA soldier for more than three hours. They had opened the young man up and had checked all of his vital organs for damage before closing him. Alex had been right: there was no internal bleeding from the bullet that had entered his side, and the incision the surgeon had made would leave a larger scar than the bullet's entry had made. It was very late afternoon when the surgeon appeared in the mess hall where Alex had been waiting, accompanied by a distinguished-looking gentlemen wearing a civilian walking suit.

"Sergeant Jaxson, I'd like for you to meet Mr. LeBlond. He is with the CIA."

"It's a pleasure meeting you, Alex." The agent held out his hand and Alex shook it. "I would like to thank you for your help in saving young LaTruseau's life. He is quite a prize."

"How's that, Mr. LeBlond?" Alex was feeling the effects of the coffee he had drunk while waiting, and felt jittery.

"His father was a famous French colonel who changed sides after the Indochina War and worked for the North Vietnamese Army. He has caused us a great deal of grief, and recently he was killed. A lot of high-level intelligence was lost. His son . . ." LeBlond looked around to see who was listening. The tables were almost empty except for one in the far corner of the large room. He lowered his voice as a precaution. ". . . was one of a special North Vietnamese unit that was made up entirely of Eurasian children. You see, Sergeant Jaxson, the Vietnamese don't believe in mixed races, and the children who were the results of a Vietnamese-French union were looked down upon after the French defeat. The children couldn't go to school, hold good jobs, or for that matter partake in any social or even religious events. They were the Vietnamese version of the Indian untouchables. That was until a North Vietnamese officer named Ngo came up with a very bright idea: why not train the Eurasians as agents and suicide soldiers for attacks against American bases in the south?"

"He's one of them?" Alex nodded in the direction of the operating room where the NVA soldier had been.

"Yes, he's not only one of them but also one of the first ones to finish the training and be sent south. We're going to be able to gain a great deal of information from him."

"What if he doesn't cooperate?"

"He will, Alex . . . believe me, he will."

"I didn't save his life, Mr. LeBlond, to have the CIA torture him." Alex locked eyes with the agent.

LeBlond broke the stare with a chuckle. "We've gone beyond those tactics, Alex. You see, the Eurasians have been told by the North Vietnamese that their fathers abandoned them, and for the most part, that's true. Their French daddies didn't want them knocking at their doors back in France and expose their infidelities to their wives, now, would they?"

"It sounds like the Eurasian kids were victims of a shitty world."

"Bingo! Alex, you are one sharp guy!"

Alex flashed the CIA agent a look that told him to stop the bullshit. "Can I see him before I go back to my camp?"

The surgeon looked over at the agent in charge.

"I don't see why not." LeBlond grabbed Alex's arm. "I can speak French fluently, so we won't need to wait for an interpreter."

Alex shook his head and smiled. "Right, sir."

"Yes, you *are* a sharp young man, Alex. You're probably going to go far in this world."

Alex felt like screwing with the special agent. "Not this kid. I was born poor in New York and I've got only a ghetto waiting for me when I get back there, unless . . ."

"Unless what, Alex?" LeBlond pushed open one of the swinging doors to the ward the NVA soldier was being kept in.

"Really, how important is this NVA guy?"

"Very."

"Important enough to reward me with a full-ride scholarship to a med school when I get discharged from the Army?"

"Alex! I don't have that kind of money or influence!" LeBlond lowered his voice. "If I did, of course I'd try to help you."

"You might not have the money, but the CIA does." Alex smiled at the agent with his lips pressed together and wiggled his eyebrows.

LeBlond laughed and threw his arm over Alex's shoulder. "Yes! You are a very sharp young man. . . . We'll see what we can do for you, Alex . . . we'll see!"

His laughter echoed all the way down the hallway to the nurse's station.

CHAPTER NINE

✪✪✪✪✪✪✪✪✪✪✪✪✪✪✪✪✪

FRIENDS AND ENEMIES

A loud scream broke through Alex's wall of thoughts. He looked over to where the Women's Rights League had set up their folding tables and saw an old bag lady hitting one of the demonstrators with a garbage bag partially filled with street pickings.

"You fucking bitch! How can you hand out stuff like that on Christmas Day!" The old lady spat a glob of brown tobacco juice on the front of the demonstrator's coat. "What are you afraid of? Getting laid?" She slapped her leg and roared a harsh laugh over vocal cords that had known too much whiskey and cigar smoke. She turned her attention to the police officer who was watching. "Teddy, I'm really ashamed of you! How can you let these bitches hand out literature like this on Christmas?"

"Maud . . . take it easy, girl." The officer reached up and played with the open collar of his overcoat. "They have a legal permit, Maud." He sounded apologetic.

"Hot damn! What is this country coming to?" She shook her head and spat a brown streak out into the street. "The next time I talk to young Ronnie, I'm going to get this shit straightened out!" She picked up her garbage bags and started shuffling away from the group.

"Aren't you going to arrest her?" Sheila recovered

223

from the shock of the old woman's physical attack. "Look at what she did to my coat!" The large woman stood with her arms held out from her sides and was leaning forward so that the excess spit would drip down to the ground.

"Lady, if there is *one* person in Washington that I'll never arrest, it's Maud." The police officer watched the old woman cross the street with the light. "She's probably the most famous bag lady in Washington. Did you know she had an hour's conversation with President Reagan right here in this park?" The officer pointed with his thumb over his shoulder. "Right over there on that bench. Lady! She's the queen of this city as far as I'm concerned. Without her, my rear end wouldn't be worth a plugged nickel. Her friends keep me informed as to what's going on, and they've saved this officer's life more than once."

"I don't give a damn how you feel about her! She assaulted me!" Sheila screamed at the police officer.

"Ma'am . . ." He glared at the demonstrator. "That's not the way I saw it. You grabbed her by the arm as she was trying to walk past you and she spat in self-defense."

"She was ignoring me!"

"There are no laws saying that a person has to pay attention to a demonstrator, ma'am." The policeman turned around and walked away.

Alex watched the bag lady disappear down the street. He found it a little ironic that the rejects of American society were defending the lives of America's children and the crème de la crème of the sixties were the ones advocating their deaths. He had hoped that one of the religious groups would have set up a counterdemonstration against the advocates of abortion, but the park was empty except for him and the pro-abortion demonstrators.

Alex looked out over the virgin snow that covered the grass behind the bench facing him and stood up.

He stretched and walked over to the blanket of white. Rays from the warm sun had started to melt the sparkling blanket. Alex took a large step onto one of nature's blackboards and started marking out a message with his feet. He wrote the bottom line first and walked back along the sidewalk to where it intersected with another concrete walkway. The grass area was rectangular and formed an almost perfect billboard-size message pad. Alex spaced out the letters in his mind before he stepped back onto the snow again, and using very small steps, stomped out the message: "ISRAEL MURDERED HER PROPHETS—AMERICA MURDERS HER HEROES."

He hopped up on the park bench and looked down, pleased with his handiwork. It was nearing the time for him to begin his real work. Alex looked over at the group of demonstrators and took a quick head count. The group had picked up a few more members but was still short forty-two people of what he had wanted. He smiled to himself; there were no children in the demonstration. He would be able to keep his word to his war buddy.

Alex took a deep breath and stepped down from the bench. He started to walk slowly toward the folding tables, which were stacked high with anti-everything literature.

A caravan of five cars pulled over to the curb on the far side of the street and stopped.

Alex stopped walking.

The car doors facing the sidewalk all opened simultaneously and from each one a teenage boy holding a small jar in each hand appeared. Alex watched closely. He could see that they had practiced the maneuver before coming to the park; it was too precise to be a fluke. The boys all cocked their right arms and threw their first jars together, then started throwing jars at their own speed. There were other kids inside the cars, handing bottles to the launchers. It took only a minute before the teenagers hopped back in the vehicles and the caravan roared away down the street. The rear window in the last car was rolled down and Alex could clearly hear a teenage girl's voice yell out: *"Baby killers!"*

One of the jars had overshot the demonstration area and landed a couple of feet in front of Alex. He looked down and saw the shattered Gerber's baby-food jar. The picture of a chubby-faced baby could still be identified. The jars had been filled with some kind of animal blood and chicken embryos.

Alex looked around the park and saw the splotches of blood against the snow. He closed his eyes. He still saw the blood. He squeezed his eyes tighter. He still saw the blood.

Blood . . . blood . . . blood . . .

The helicopter banked and touched down just long enough on the pad for Alex to jump out before the pilot gunned the turbine engine and left the helipad at Tong Le Chon. The camp was too hot to spend much time on the ground. The pilot's intuition had served him well. The chopper was still in sight when four mortar rounds landed within fifty feet of the pad. Alex had heard them whistling in and dived for the closest ditch.

Sergeant Mills counted the rounds and then casually stepped out of the command bunker's entrance. "Welcome home, Jaxson. Did you get some sleep while you were screwing around back at the hospital?"

Alex stood and looked down at the layer of mud covering the front of his clean uniform. "Shit!"

"Now, Jaxson! You didn't expect to stay clean for very long, did you?"

"It sure felt good for as long as it lasted!" Alex shook hands with the team's senior medic.

"Are you ready to get back to work?" Mills gave Alex a lopsided grin.

"Fuck! Those two days off felt like an hour!" Alex hefted the rucksack he was carrying. "I brought back some hard-to-get medical supplies. One of the doctors assured me that this stuff is the best on the market for jungle ulcers and dysentery. There's one glitch, though."

"What's that?"

"Only a doctor can administer either of the medicines."

"Well, Dr. Jaxson, how are you feeling today?"

"Fine, Dr. Mills, just fine!" Alex laughed and slapped Mills on the shoulder.

The team captain was waiting inside the command bunker for Alex to enter. He sat in the center of the complex, across the operations table from an infantry captain. Alex took a deep lungful of the humid bunker air and thought to himself: Welcome home. The structure was unique and well-built to withstand even 122mm rockets. The team of engineers had lined up two rows of five steel Conex containers each, face-to-face, twenty feet apart. They had left a space between each of the Conex containers, exactly one sandbag length, and then airlifted in fourteen forty-foot-long squared logs and placed them on the containers to support the roof of steel planking and layers of sandbags. The ends of the command bunker were finished off with a pair of Conex containers with enough room in between them for entrances and exits. The bunker had been prepackaged by the B Team and had been airlifted out to the Tong Le Chon site in exactly the order required for assembly. It had taken the team of engineers two days to bulldoze and Rome plow the campsite, but once that task was accomplished, the command bunker went up in a half-day and the initial perimeter bunkers were operational by nightfall. Once the steel Conex containers were in place, the engineers bulldozed huge piles of dirt up around them. Since they had already been packed with supplies and equipment, it was only a matter of opening the container doors and beginning operations. The spaces in between the steel containers were filled with dirt by hand, and three rows of prefilled sandbags were stacked on the inside to hold back the dirt.

The team leader glanced up at Alex and grinned. "That was an excellent mission, Jaxson. You did a super job keeping that NVA alive."

"Thanks, sir." Alex started walking toward the Conex that he shared with Mills and the camp's medical supplies.

"You kept an NVA soldier alive?" The infantry captain frowned.

"This one was a special case. The intelligence people came in their pants when they heard about him." The captain nodded at Alex. "Why don't you get your stuff ready? You're scheduled for tomorrow's patrol."

Alex had expected as much.

"I let a friend of yours borrow your cot for a couple hours' sleep," Mills told Alex.

Alex glanced over at their Conex, which had one of its steel doors partially closed to keep out the light. "A friend?"

"That's what he said he was. He came in with the infantry captain." Mills shrugged. "Maybe he was bullshiting to get a dry place to lie down for a while."

Alex opened the Conex door slowly and looked in. "*Sash!*" He started to reach over and shake the sleeping soldier, then stopped. Sash looked exhausted, and Alex decided that as much as he would like to talk to him, he would let him sleep.

"Aren't you going to wake him?" Mills smiled.

Alex spoke to the infantry officer. "Sir, when are you leaving to go back to your bivouac site?"

The captain looked at his watch. "Maybe three or four more hours."

Alex nodded. "I'll let the weak dick sleep."

The infantry captain looked up at the Green Beret commander and winked. Alex had performed a very unselfish act that he knew Maleko would appreciate.

None of the infantry company had slept on a dry bed in three weeks.

Alex pulled his camouflage poncho liner out of the wooden ammunition box he used for storage and draped it over Sash. The huge machine-gunner shifted slightly on the canvas folding cot and slipped back into an exhausted stupor. Alex stepped out of the Conex and placed his rucksack full of medical supplies on one of the cots they had lined up at their end of the command bunker for emergency wounded during a major attack from the NVA. Mills joined him and they sorted through the packages of hard-to-get items.

Maleko groaned and then stretched his muscles before opening his eyes. He felt stiff after having slept for six hours without shifting his position on the cot. He listened to the voices coming from the operations area.

The door opened all the way and a man's head slipped into the dark container. "You awake yet?"

"Alex!" Sash threw his legs off the cot and sat up.

"Yeah! How you doing?" Alex shook hands with his buddy from basic training. "Darn! It seems like just yesterday!"

"Over a year." Sash noticed the staff-sergeant stripes on Alex's sleeves. "You borrowing someone's shirt?"

Alex chuckled. "Nope. You like that?" He rubbed his hand over the four stripes.

"That's fantastic! Four stripes in two years!"

"Well, don't give me that much credit. Special Forces back in the States were getting a lot of promotion allocations. All you had to do was meet the minimum waiver criteria and they would slap another stripe on your arm! I mean, I didn't even have time to have buck-sergeant stripes sewn on my AG-44's before I was promoted to E6."

"I thought making Speck Four was a big deal!" Sash shook his head.

"It is! Don't forget, Sash, Special Forces units don't

have a slot for anything lower than an E5 on their A teams."

Mills leaned against the steel Conex container door and added, "Being the honor graduate in Dog Lab helped."

"Did you make honor graduate in Special Forces?" Sash shook his head in disbelief and spoke to Mills. "He made honor graduate in basic training too!"

Alex blushed. "Ease off, guys."

"You deserved your accelerated promotions, and there's nothing to be ashamed about." Mills held out his hand to Sash. "Billy Mills."

Sash shook hands and nodded over at Alex. "I hope you're taking good care of my partner."

"That's a given, Maleko." Mills nodded at the captains standing in front of a battle map of the area. "Your C.O. wanted me to tell you that he's leaving in fifteen minutes."

"Shit, so soon!" Sash slapped Alex's leg. "How long have you been back here?"

"A few hours."

"You should have woken me!"

"Bullshit! I could hear you snoring all the way out on the helipad!" Alex laughed. "You would have kicked my ass if I woke you up!"

"I was tired, that's for sure. We haven't been getting much sleep, ever since the NVA ambushed us on Highway 4."

"That was your company?" Mills's voice lowered.

"Well, the whole company wasn't caught in the kill zone. We sent a ten-man team up ahead of the column and they sprang the ambush. Only three of us survived."

Mills pointed at a map of their operations area on the wall of the Conex container. The map had all of the local villages marked on it, where they conducted medical patrols for the inhabitants. Maleko oriented himself on the 1:50,000-scale map and tapped the spot on Highway 4. "Right there is where the NVA had set up their kill zone."

"I told you! Didn't I tell you?" Mills looked over at Alex. "I told you that damn place bothered me! Didn't I?"

Alex nodded. Every time they flew over or patrolled that area, Mills would mention that it was a perfect ambush location. "We should have the captain call in a B-52 Arc Light mission on that grid."

"Good idea!" Mills started walking away to tell the captain. "Damn good idea!"

Alex shook his head. "He's a good man."

"Sounds like it." Sash leaned forward on the cot so that he could see what his captain was doing. "By the way, who do you think is assigned to my company?"

Alex shrugged.

"Sanchez!" Sash shook his head in disbelief. "Would you believe that shit! And talk about bad luck! His three buddies are there too!"

"Martinez, Lopez, and Costello?"

"Bingo! They came into the Army under the buddy system and all of their assignments up to their field unit were guaranteed." Maleko stood and reached for the low ceiling and pushed against it to work his tight muscles. "Can you imagine how I felt in the Oakland Depot when those four assholes walked in and I found out that they were *all* on the same flight as mine to Vietnam!"

"Have they caused you any trouble?" Alex's voice reflected his worry. Everyone had heard about the fraggings that were going on in the troop units, and Sanchez was fully capable of conducting one.

"At first it was a little tight, but they've mellowed a little since basic training. But don't get me wrong— they'd love to kick my ass!"

"Watch your six o'clock, partner!" Alex made a pistol-firing motion with his finger and thumb.

"Always do!" Sash reached down and hefted his

M-60. He had tucked it close to him under the cot while he slept. "My captain is calling. We've got to walk back out to the bivouac site before it gets dark."

"Where are you guys located?"

"About four hundred meters north of your camp. We're going to be moving out in the morning to make a sweep along the border."

Alex felt his stomach tighten. It was a premonition. "How long are you guys going to be out there?"

"We've been assigned to protect your campsite until you've got yourselves established—I guess a couple of weeks."

"How many men in your company?" Alex was getting worried.

Sash frowned. "I heard the captain mention something like sixty-one this morning, but we've got four men due in on the next chopper from R&R, and a couple going back to the rear for sick call. It's normally somewhere around sixty or seventy men in the field."

"That's an infantry company?" Alex twisted his lip. "Shit, we field a hundred and twenty at least with a company!"

"Your guys live here. Ours aren't as used to the jungle. Besides, most of our *senior* NCO's can't hump the hills. When they reach one of the line units, their profile sheets are usually the first thing they hand the captain." Sash shook his head in disgust. "There are a few stateside E7's and 8's in the field, but *damn* few!"

"That's one thing I can say about Special Forces, the senior NCO's partake in the fucking war!" Alex threw a box of high-potency vitamins at Sash. "Roll up your sleeve before you go and I'll hit you with a B_{12} shot."

"You shitting me?" Sash looked at Alex.

"No, I'm serious—B_{12} will help you fight all of that nasty crap out there in the jungle."

Sash obeyed and set his M-60 on the cot. The infantry captain stuck his head in the Conex entrance. "You ready, Maleko?"

"Yes, sir."

"What's that?" The captain nodded at the needle about to enter Sash's arm.

"B_{12} . . . want some, sir?" Alex injected the vitamin into Sash's arm.

"I'll pass." The captain adjusted his web gear. "Do you have something good for the shits?"

"Sure do, Captain." Alex removed a large bottle of tiny white pills from the rack on the wall and emptied a couple dozen of the powerful tablets into a small pill vial. "Here you go, sir." Alex handed the vial to the officer. "Take two with every meal until your bowels tighten up."

"Thanks." The captain nodded toward the exit.

"See you later, partner." Sash punched Alex lightly on the shoulder.

"Keep your powder dry." Alex winked.

"Always do!"

Alex watched the pair of infantrymen exit the bunker from his Conex container. He could see Mills standing in front of the team's battle map and walked over to join him. A large blue square had been marked on the map in grease pencil and coded with the infantry company's identification and call signs. Alex stared at the box and felt his stomach tighten again. He flexed his jaws and tried shaking off the feeling of dread.

"You'll be with the ready-reaction company, Jaxson." The team commander spoke up from the large bank of radios he was sitting in front of. The static nearly drowned out his voice.

Alex nodded.

"It'll be the Second Company and the team sergeant will be in command."

Alex nodded again. He liked the idea of going out in the field with the Second Company, because they were all Chinese Nungs who had been fighting together as a company for ten years. Their leadership was superb, and a Nung company had never been known to abandon an American in the field.

Sash followed his captain along the trail back to their bivouac site. They had picked up their escort squad just outside the camp's gate. The jungle smelled fresh after having been in the underground bunker for so long. He enjoyed the smell of fresh air, but missed the security of the bunker. The best that he would have for the next couple of weeks would be a foxhole, and he would have to dig one every damn night.

The infantry company moved out of their overnight position at first light, when there was still a lot of fog on the ground. Sash didn't like moving so soon, but their lieutenant had explained that it would be better to take the risk early in the day and not get caught short of their objective and have to travel in the dark. Sash had never understood the idea of damned objectives in the jungle. It really didn't matter where you were, because if the NVA wanted to find you, they would, and if they were in fortified bunkers, they would draw you into their position by using small NVA units as bait. None of the infantrymen liked the idea of patrolling so close to the Cambodian border. The NVA could hit them and quickly withdraw into their "neutral" sanctuaries, and if a small company was unlucky enough to stumble over the border and run into one of the NVA's forward supply areas, the NVA would attack them like hornets protecting their hives.

The rain had stopped the fourth day the infantry company was on patrol. The company commander gave his men the day off from patrolling to dry out their gear. The company had taken up a defensive position in the fork of a large stream that had flooded because of the rain. They had patrolled the border area and were slowly working their way back to Tong Le Chon, using a platoon checkerboard technique. The trend was continuing and there hadn't been any sightings of NVA movement in the jungle, not even along well-defined trails. It was eerie.

Sash removed everything from his rucksack and spread the items out over the warm rocks to dry. He desperately wanted to bathe in the stream, but he knew it was too dangerous and he was not going to risk it, even though there were two squads posted as outposts on the far side. He was satisfied with being dry for the first time in weeks. Steam was coming off his M-60 from the hot rays of the sun, which instantly started the evaporation process once the thick clouds had left.

"I don't know what's fucking worse—raining all the fucking time or the humidity when the sun takes over!" The platoon sergeant was bitching.

"Sarge! I didn't know you knew how to bitch!" Sash winked over at the senior NCO. He was one of the rare ones who had demanded a field assignment from a training committee back in the States.

The NCO flashed a glare at Maleko and fought a smile. "Every fucking once-in-a-while, soldier!"

"Just checking, Sarge."

"Maleko! How would you like your ass out there on a night ambush?"

"Would it make a difference if I said no?"

The sergeant first class shook his head. "Tonight, in the northern sector, and guess who's going to be with you."

"Who, Sarge?" Sash didn't care, and knew that the senior NCO wasn't really screwing with him. The sergeant was meticulous in ensuring that the dangerous details were rotated fairly and that all the men had their turns.

"Our Puerto Rican contingency." The platoon sergeant looked at Maleko. "You're the senior man in charge."

"Shit! What happened to their squad leader?"

"Rotated for R&R."

"Their fire-team leader?"

"Sick." The sergeant slapped his notebook against his leg to seal the order. "You're the man tonight . . . What's wrong? Are you prejudiced?"

"Hell, Sarge!" Sash flashed a warning to the NCO. "I was raised in Hamtramck, Michigan. If you were prejudiced there, man, you didn't live long. Naw . . . I just had some problems with that group way back in basic training. As far as fighting goes, those guys have been fighting together as a team since kindergarten!"

"Well, then, I can sleep good tonight, knowing that the five of you will be out there protecting me."

"Do that, Sarge . . . you do that!" Sash repacked his gear and started walking over to where Sanchez and his gang were sleeping in the sun.

"Sanchez!" Sash cradled his machine gun.

"Yeah." He kept his eyes closed and his face aimed toward the sun.

"We're on night outpost together."

Sanchez raised his body up on one elbow. "Together, *señor?*"

Cut the bullshit, Sanchez. We're on tonight as a team, and I'm the senior man."

"*We've* always been a team, *señor*, but I don't know about your white Polish ass."

"Russian, *hombre* . . . that's 'white Russian ass.' "

"Hey! He speaks Spanish, man!" Costello entered the conversation.

"We move out in an hour."

"Man! That's three o'clock! Why so early, man?" Lopez opened his eyes and spat at the end of the sentence.

"Because, *man*, I want to have our positions dug in before dark and conduct a little close-in recon of the area around us."

"You're some kind of gung-ho motherfucker!" Costello squeaked in his bit.

"You really don't need to get involved in this, Costello . . . except to pack your entrenching tool to dig with."

Sanchez shook his right hand with his fingers loose. "Ow! Some hot words there, *amigo mio!*"

Sash glanced at his watch before leaving the four soldiers. "Fifty-five minutes and we *di-di*."

"Ai! He speaks Vietnamese too!" Sanchez started laughing.

Maleko found a flat rock near his rucksack and sat down to inspect his M-60 and the belts of ammunition he was taking with him. He inspected each link to make sure there would be no misfeeding of the weapon if he had to fire it during the night. The other machine-gunners thought Maleko was crazy because of the elaborate precautions he always took, no matter how tired he was, but Sash had noticed that more and more of the other men had started quietly following suit.

Sash changed positions on the rock. He felt his stomach tighten for no reason at all, and a brassy taste covered his tongue. He always had that taste in his mouth right before something big happened in his life.

The jungle roared with sounds during the night. It was as if all the insects and jungle creatures where celebrating the break in the monsoons. Sash had set up his outpost early, and the men had a chance to rest before night had fallen. He had positioned the team in three foxholes—Sanchez and Costello to his right, and Lopez and Martinez to his left. He had taken a position slightly behind the slanted foxholes the other four men occupied so that he could cover either or both of them with automatic fire.

Sash felt a long-legged insect walk across his neck and gingerly reached back to brush it off. Tree frogs called to each other above his position, keeping watch from above. The insects made an excellent early-warning system. There was no moon and the night was totally black under the huge trees and triple-canopy jungle. Sash caught himself dozing off and took two amphetamine tablets to stay awake.

A bright blue bird landed on the branch of the tree directly above Sash's camouflaged foxhole and looked down at the foxhole Sanchez was snoring in. The bird didn't know what was making the noise down below, but she knew that she was safe on her branch from whatever it was.

Sash chucked a rock and hit Costello's helmet. He signaled for him to wake Sanchez.

The sound of something coming through the jungle drew Sash's attention away from the foxhole. Another sound joined the first one, further to his left side. Sash pushed the safety off his weapon and waited. The bamboo rustled and clicked ten meters in front of Lopez. Sash listened intently for any other sounds that would identify the creatures moving through the jungle. A grunt was what Sash wanted to hear, signaling a herd of pigs, but instead he got a soft whisper in Vietnamese floating over to his position.

Sash clicked the handset of his radio three times. He listened for an answer but didn't hear one. He repeated the signal and felt the sweat break out on his forehead. He whispered in his mind for the captain's radio operator to answer his alert signal.

The jungle came alive with movement on both of their flanks. A large force was moving through the jungle toward the company. The initial sounds had been the point elements for the two NVA companies passing them, and now the advancing columns were passing less than fifty feet on either side of Sash's outpost positions. Sash got a quick glimpse of Sanchez's face and could see that the soldier was pleading with his eyes for Sash to let the huge enemy force pass by them. It would be suicidal for them to open fire.

Sash keyed the handset again three times and waited. The company had to be alerted or there would be a slaughter. There was no answer. Sash removed a pin from one of his hand grenades and took a deep breath before he threw it. They had set two Claymore mines out in front of each flanking foxhole, but Sanchez had control of two of them and Lopez controlled the firing devices for the other two. Sash knew that neither of them was going to fire the Claymores unless forced to.

The grenade went off in a muffled explosion.

The captain jerked awake in his foxhole and heard the radio being keyed. His radio operator was sound asleep. "Wake up! What was that?"

Sanchez and Lopez fired their Claymores so fast that they sounded like a single explosion.

"It's coming from our outpost." The first platoon sergeant tried getting the sleep out of his eyes. The whole company had fallen asleep because of the false security the singing insects had given them.

The northern section of the company's perimeter opened fire. At first it was a single M-16, and then another one joined it, followed by Claymores going off all along the line. The roar of American weapons became almost deafening and the captain picked up his handset to call his platoon leaders to shut down the platoons. He figured a jumpy guard out at the outpost had detonated his Claymore by accident and the sleeping perimeter guards had panicked and opened fire. He thought that thought for about two seconds, until the first RPG-7 grenade landed three feet in front of his foxhole. "Fuck!"

The single expressive word was not descriptive enough for what followed, but it was a good start.

The NVA engaged the perimeter from yards and then feet away. Hand-to-hand fighting occurred almost immediately along the whole northern perimeter. If Maleko had waited just one more minute before throwing his hand grenade, the whole company would have been overrun. The grenade had alerted the front line just in time to catch the initial wave of Sappers before they had reached the sleeping soldiers.

The infantry captain switched frequencies and called back to the A camp. "Black Boots Six . . . Cougar Lover Six. . . . Emergency! We're being overrun by a large NVA force. . . . Fire our defensive concentrations and get me some air support . . . over."

"Cougar Lover Six . . . Black Boots Five . . . wilco . . . over."

There was no reply from the infantry captain. The company was fighting for its life in small groups.

The team leader alerted the ready-reaction company of Nungs. Alex had his rucksack placed next to his Conex container door and his Swedish K loaded and ready. He slipped on his boots and web gear and rushed to meet up with the Second Company as it started leaving through the camp's temporary gate. The next few minutes would be extremely dangerous for the company until they could reach the tree line of the jungle. Alex caught up with the command element that was traveling with the second platoon. The Nungs were so competent as leaders that the only reason they needed an American with them was for air and artillery support. Alex could smell the burning incense sticks tied to some of the barrels of the Nung soldiers' rifles. They always burned incense just before they went into battle.

Sash waited behind the sights of his M-60 for a target to appear in the target-rich jungle. The NVA had them completely circled and would have wiped out the small patrol if it hadn't been for their total commitment to their attack on the American infantry company they had discovered late the day before. Sash's move to set up early had placed them in position before the NVA scouts had reconnoitered the company perimeter. Sash's patrol had all been resting when the NVA passed their positions the day before, and that small maneuver had saved their lives, because the NVA commander had not committed any troops to them. The patrol was safe until the NVA withdrew, and then they would be wiped out in a matter of minutes.

The team sergeant from Alex's Special Forces unit beckoned for Alex to join him. The point element from the Nung company was reinforced with a light machine gun and two M-79 grenade launchers. They would be the first ones to make contact with the enemy and they would need a lot of firepower immediately available. Alex felt his throat turn dry. It wasn't like going out on a normal patrol, where the chances of not making contact with the NVA were much greater; he *knew* they were going to make contact, and his body was preparing him for it.

The sound of the fighting grew louder. When they reached the protection of the jungle, Alex felt a slight sense of relief, which turned quickly into acute awareness of the surrounding vegetation. His eyes swept the green-and-tan wall for any signs that something was out of place. He shifted his medical-aid kit more to the center of his back and squeezed the handgrip on his Swedish K. The whole Second Company had left their rucksacks behind in the compound. They carried only ammo and fighting gear.

The relief column stopped moving forward. The Nung commander signaled for the team sergeant to move forward, and the two of them conferred for a couple of minutes and then the company changed direction and moved down the prearranged access lane to the besieged American company. The small-arms firing had died down since the inital barrage, but there was still a lot of fighting going on around the American unit's perimeter. Alex knew that they would have to hit the American perimeter *exactly* along the access lane or the Americans would mistake them for NVA. That was always the major risk of a Vietnamese or Chinese relief force for an American unit—being mistaken for NVA.

Contact was made with the NVA by the point element, and a violent but brief encounter ensued. The lead element of the Nung company linked up with the American perimeter at the same time volleys of artillery fire started falling to the east and west of the perimeter. A couple of the rounds came a little too close for comfort, but the majority of them landed on target. The artillery brigade responsible for the area had an airborne forward observer flying above the fight, directing extremely accurate artillery fires by using the new A camp as a surveyed reference point to shift from.

Alex ran across the semicleared inner perimeter over to the company's command post and dropped down on one knee. "Where's Maleko's foxhole?"

The captain's radio operator glanced up. "He was on the northern outpost. Man, they're all dead for sure!"

"Where is it? How far out?" Alex grabbed the soldier's shoulder and turned him around.

"North . . . maybe a hundred meters from the perimeter." The soldier pointed to a barely visible path leading into the jungle between two foxholes that were littered with dead and dying men.

Alex waved over at the Nung commander and yelled, "Hatchet Force!" He pointed to the jungle and started running in that direction. The Nung commander didn't hesitate, but screamed orders for his company's elite force to join the American sergeant. The special Hatchet Force was normally a platoon composed of the best fighters in the company. During peacetime, its members would probably be murderers and the dregs of society, but in war they were a valued commodity.

Sash heard the NVA returning down their marked lanes in the jungle. There were some strays from the attacking force who had become disoriented and were crashing through the jungle to meet at their assembly areas. Sash saw the first NVA soldier break out of the jungle less than ten feet in front of his foxhole. He fired a short burst, trying to control his rounds because he was firing toward the company perimeter. Another NVA soldier broke out of the jungle and Costello opened up with his M-16.

The NVA commander heard the American weapons firing and ordered one of his platoons to destroy the nearby American outpost. He smiled to himself because now he knew why the Americans had fired no artillery to the northern side of their perimeter. He had expected severe casualties withdrawing through an American artillery and air barrage, but the attack had not come. He knew that until the Americans were sure the outpost was destroyed, they would not fire on that position.

Alex didn't hesitate. He led the Hatchet Force through the jungle toward the outpost. The Nungs were the first ones to spot the NVA platoon, and opened fire. The Nungs chanted old war songs and closed in for hand-to-hand combat, using pistols and fighting knives. The fighting was violent. Alex saw the NVA command element for the platoon and took them out with a long burst from his 9mm Swedish K.

The NVA platoon started withdrawing to the protection of their own bunker line, but the Nungs refused to allow them to disengage.

Alex searched the jungle for any signs of an American outpost and then became frustrated and yelled out, *"Sash!"*

Maleko heard his name called above the sounds of the battle raging to their eastern perimeter. He had been confused over who would be fighting so close to their outpost and so far away from the company's perimeter. Sash had instructed his men to remain hidden and fire only when they were forced to. Sanchez and Lopez were both wounded. Costello had dragged Sanchez over to where Sash was, and Martinez had helped Lopez get over to the consolidated position. Sash put both of the wounded men in his foxhole and then set up a hasty perimeter around them.

"Did you hear that shit?" Martinez kicked Sash's boot. "Those fucking gooks know your name!"

"It's a friend!" Sash kept his right hand on the trigger of his M-60 and cupped the side of his mouth with his left-hand. *"Alex! Over here!"*

Alex made a fist and pointed in the direction Sash had called from. The Nung squad acting as his personal bodyguard obeyed the command and started toward Sash's voice. *"Sash! Hold your fire . . . I've got little people with me!"*

Maleko turned to his men and whispered, "You guys hear?"

Martinez and Costello nodded and lowered their bodies against the ground to wait.

Sash saw Alex first. "Over here!" he whispered. Fighting was sporadic, but the NVA were still a powerful fighting force, far from being whipped.

"Do you have any wounded?" Alex dropped down next to his buddy.

"Two." Sash pointed to the foxhole.

Alex hesitated for only a second when he saw who was in the hole, then started performing emergency medical treatment on Sanchez, who was the more seriously wounded. He stabilized him and then slapped a hasty bandage on Lopez's calf where a bullet had gone through.

The Nung guards waited in combat crouches for Alex to finish the first aid. None of them looked concerned that the NVA might be coming back in force. They were members of the Second Company's elite Hatchet Force and knew that if they survived the fight, they would be heroes back in camp, which was what they lived for.

"Look at those gooks!" Lopez gestured at the Nungs on guard. "Motherfuckers think they're bad!"

Alex ignored Lopez and finished a morphine injection on Sanchez. "We're going to have to carry him out of here."

Sash said, "Fine, I'll do it." He was the strongest man there.

"No . . . we're going to need your machine gun to get back to the camp." Alex flipped his Swedish K over his shoulder and pulled Sanchez up to his feet. "Lopez! You're going to have to walk on your own. Use your M-16 for a crutch." Alex adjusted Sanchez's limp body over his shoulder and started moving back to the rest of the Hatchet Force. Sash and the others of his outpost brought up the rear.

The NVA commander realized that he could counterattack now and probably achieve a major victory. The American company had been severely mauled and wouldn't be expecting another attack. He gave the order for his unit to engage and stay in close to the Americans and their relief force. If they could push the Americans back to the clearing that surrounded the new A camp, they would be easy targets. The camp would not open fire, afraid of hitting their own men, and the artillery would be useless so close to the main camp.

Sash brought up the rear of the Hatchet Force platoon. One of the Nungs smiled at him and patted his shoulder, then said something to Sash in Chinese. Sash smiled back and then shifted his attention to his surroundings. The jungle was littered with bodies as the NVA fought a rear-action battle back to the American company's perimeter.

Alex noticed that there weren't any American or Nung dead mixed in with the NVA. The Nungs were policing the battlefield as they withdrew to the Americans.

The American captain sighed when he saw Maleko and the outpost patrol emerge from the jungle. He looked over at the Special Forces team sergeant and smiled. "We can close up our remaining perimeter and hold out now until reinforcements arrive."

The Nung commander spoke broken English. "We go! NVA come back . . . too many fight."

The American captain looked at the team sergeant. "We can hold them now with your company."

"Sir, I'd listen to him." The team sergeant nodded at the small Chinese warrior. "He's been around, and believe me, if he says go . . . we should go."

The captain thought for a second and gave the signal to police up their wounded and start withdrawing back to the A camp. He radioed back that they were coming and then he directed the artillery observer to provide blocking fires to cover their withdrawal.

Alex stayed back with Sash to support the rearguard action. They would give the rest of the unit a couple hundred meters' head start and then start pulling back themselves. Alex hoped that the NVA would have had enough by now and leave them alone. It was too much to hope for. The combined companies had left the old perimeter, and the rear guard was just slipping back into the jungle when a barrage of mortar rounds landed inside the American perimeter. If they had stayed there and tried to hold out until replacements arrived, they would have suffered severe casualties in just that single mortar attack.

The NVA troops poured out of the jungle and found the American foxholes empty. They rushed across the open area and picked up the trail of the withdrawing soldiers.

Sash let loose a long burst and dropped down on the ground. The NVA force had found them. The Nungs answered the NVA with a volley of hand grenades. The big Nung who had fought beside Sash at the outpost grabbed his shoulder and pulled him back up on his feet. He motioned violently with his head back toward the A camp. Sash understood; they could not stop, but had to fight a delaying action.

The wounded and those men carrying them reached the main gate and could hear the heavy fighting going on in the jungle behind them. The Nungs paused at the gates and then went back inside the camp to man some of the bunkers. The rear guard was the only element left outside the berm.

Mills sat behind the .50-caliber and wiped his sweaty palms on his jacket. "Come on, Jaxson . . . get your ass back here, boy!"

The jungle parted and the backs of three men appeared. Two wore the camouflage uniforms of commandos and the third man wore dark sweat-stained jungle fatigues and carried an M-60 machine gun. Mills saw the NVA moving along the edge of the jungle and opened fire with the heavy weapon. The perimeter erupted, giving covering fire to the last of the rescue force.

Alex stumbled through the gate, followed by Sash. The big Nung paused in the center of the open gate and screamed something at the NVA and then casually flipped the finger at the jungle.

Alex dropped back against the muddy bank of the berm, and Sash followed suit next to him.

"Shit! Unbelievable *shit*!"

"Amen!" Sash looked straight up into the robin's-egg-blue sky and sighed softly. "Amen."

CHAPTER TEN

✖✖✖✖✖✖✖✖✖✖✖✖✖✖✖✖✖✖✖✖✖✖✖

165th NVA REGIMENT

The vision refused to leave. Alex blinked his eyes rapidly, trying to disengage, but the secret door in his mind had been opened and wasn't going to be locked again just because Alex wanted it. The soft white snow worked like a movie screen set up for Cinemascope.

The black Rolls-Royce circled the park twice before pulling up next to the curb and stopping in a no-parking zone.

"Is that Uncle Alex over there, Dad?" Young Alex pointed through the dirty window.

"Could be. He's the only person wearing a military coat, but I can't tell from way over here."

"I don't think it would be a good idea to park by those demonstrators." Young Alex pushed the button that lowered his window so that he could see better. "What's the red stuff all over the snow?"

Sash leaned back in his seat so that he could see better out of Alex's open window. "Probably blood of some kind, or food dye." He opened his door. "I've got to walk over there and make sure. From here it's too hard to tell if that's Alex."

"I'm going with you."

"Why don't you wait here with the car in case a police officer decides to give us a ticket." Sash stepped out of the Rolls and felt the slush cover his Gucci loafer and soak through his sock.

Alex remained sitting on the passenger's side with his window down. Sash looked back at him from the sidewalk and nodded for his son to join him. A police officer would have to be a hard-core case to give him a ticket on Christmas, and even then, it didn't matter. If the man sitting on the park bench was Alex, there was a lot more at stake than a ten-dollar parking ticket.

Alex didn't see Sash approaching his park bench. He was lost in his daytime nightmare.

Sanchez groaned when Alex dropped him against the soft mud on the berm. Small-arms rounds whistled over their heads from the NVA gunners hiding in the jungle. The fire was answered from the perimeter guards.

"Is everyone back inside?" The team captain leaned over and asked the team sergeant the question. He nodded and struggled to regain normal breathing. "Good! We can use our mortars now!" The captain signaled the weapons team that had been standing by in the mortar pit. The first round slipped down the tube, followed by five more, before the first one landed in the jungle. They were firing high-angle defensive concentrations with preplanned locations. The cheese on the 4.2-inch mortar had already been cut and the team was systematically setting deflections and charges for the targets. Every possible stream junction, dip in the ground, observation point, or assembly area for six thousand meters around the camp was being hit by the 4.2-inch mortar and its two sister 81's positioned and manned at opposite ends of the camp.

Sanchez opened his eyes. "Thanks, man . . . I owe you a big one." He tried smiling at Alex.

"First, we've got to get you patched up properly." Alex nodded for Sash to take Sanchez's feet and help him get him on a stretcher. "I don't think we're going to be able to call a Medevac in here for a while." Alex used his eyes to reflect his concern to Sash. "We've got a lot of wounded to take care of, and I'd better get my ass moving over to the medical center or Mills will shit all over himself." Alex struggled to get to his feet. He hadn't realized how tired he was.

Mills had left his position on the .50-caliber machine gun as soon as the first of the wounded started coming into camp. The eight stretchers they had set up in the command bunker had filled up almost instantly with wounded. He was on his fifth patient when Alex entered the bunker.

"Where have you been, partner?"

"Fucking off, boss!" Alex dropped his Swedish K on the floor; both of the cots in their Conex were occupied by wounded commandos. "Where do you want me to start?"

"We've got a couple that are in bad shape." Mills continued bandaging the leg of a wounded American. He patted the man's shoulder when he finished. "Let me hit you with a shot of antibiotics, and you can get back out there for the second round."

"Shit, thanks a lot, Doc!" The soldier shook his head and slipped down off the stretcher that had been placed on two sawhorses. "I thought wounds like this were the kind that got a guy out of the field."

"They are! The bus will be out in front of the main gate at five . . . if you'd like to go out there and wait for it, be my guest."

"I think I'll find me a nice bunker to wait in." The soldier grinned.

"Smart kid!" Mills patted his shoulder again and looked over at the next wounded man. "Next! The doctor is *in*!" Mills hummed popular country-and-western songs as he worked rapidly to stop the bleeding of the numerous wounded men in the bunker.

Alex looked over at Sash. "I could use your help."

"Sure . . . what do you want me to do?" Sash set his M-60 on the floor next to the wall and rolled up his sleeves. "Is there somewhere I can wash up a little?"

"Yes . . . over there." Alex nodded; both his hands were working on the severely wounded Nung. He clamped off a bleeder while Sash washed quickly in a basin and slipped on a pair of rubber gloves. The whole operating area was far from sanitary, but the equipment was good and the men were safe under the layers of steel and sandbags. Sash could hear muffled explosions outside the bunker and wondered if he should try to find his platoon sergeant. He shrugged and decided that Alex needed his help more right now.

"How many medics do you have in your company?" Alex talked as he operated on the Nung.

"Should be six, right now."

"Where are they?" Alex started closing the wound.

"Probably out there with the company. I don't think they know this place exists."

"We need to get them in here to help us." Alex didn't lift his head from the man. The Nung lay on the stretcher with his eyes wide open. He tried to lift his head and watch what Alex was doing, but was too weak from the tremendous amount of blood he had lost. Alex had given the man only a local anesthetic because he didn't have the equipment or the time to administer anything stronger. Most men would be groaning in pain, but the Nung only watched. Alex smiled at the middle-aged warrior and patted his thigh. "Good! You'll heal fine!"

The Nung thanked him in Chinese and tried getting up off the cot. Alex had to gently push him back down so that the IV wouldn't get torn out of his arm. "You're going to be all right, but first you must rest for a couple of days." The interpreter rattled off the translation and the Nung answered with a curt sentence. The interpreter shook his head. "Him say, he must join squad and fight NVA!"

"Not with that IV hanging above him! Have him put in one of the perimeter bunkers where he can lie down." Alex started working on the next man as he spoke.

It was starting to get dark when Alex and Mills finally finished with the last of the wounded. A half-dozen times the division tried sending in Medevacs to extract the American and Nung wounded, and each time the Medevac choppers were forced to turn back because of heavy antiaircraft fire. The last run tried to low-level into the camp, but two of the escort Cobras had been shot down as they tried suppressing the NVA gunners, and the mission was aborted.

Alex lay back on the sloping sandbags that coated the command bunker and rested his eyes. Sash took a seat next to him and followed suit. They were lying stretched out next to the entrance and could scurry undercover in seconds if they heard incoming rockets or mortars.

"Do you think they'll attack us tonight?" Sash kept his hand on his M-60.

"Probably. They have to do something soon, because by tomorrow your division will be airlifting in a couple of battalions and the Air Force will have all kinds of fast-movers fucking with them all the way back to Cambodia." Alex felt his arms trying to float up off the sandbags. He was extremely tired. "I need some sleep."

"Why don't you catch a couple of hours and I'll play bodyguard." Sash pulled his legs up and wrapped his arms around his knees. The position felt good and relaxed his back muscles.

Alex kept his eyes closed. "You did really well in there. I didn't expect you to handle all the blood and stuff."

"I don't want to be crude, but I told you back in basic that we own a meat market. Blood is something I got used to when I was a baby."

"You did a damn good job and I appreciate it."

"Thanks. You weren't so bad yourself. I don't think a medical doctor could have done much better."

"Well, you can give the credit to a dog named Cowboy."

Sash was a little confused. "Explain."

"Cowboy was a dog assigned to me during my Special Forces Dog Lab—that was the hardest part of our training. We operated on dogs to give us the confidence to operate on humans, and believe me, it works!" Alex smiled with his eyes closed. "Of course, every damn hippie and cruelty-to-animals society in the States picketed the base, because they said we were torturing animals. Shit! If it wasn't for the animals, half of these men today would have bled to death. Mills and I performed a lot of serious medical operations in there today. I'm not bragging, but you didn't see any doctors out here today either!"

"I've heard about a couple doctors down at Fort Sam Houston who refused to train Green Beret medics because you guys were enlisted."

"Yeah, that went on all the time. Our fucking country is falling apart back there. You'd think that they'd realize it."

"What?"

"When a country's men lose the will to fight . . . it's all over. Just a matter of time before someone else takes over what they had. Shit, look at the Japanese, they're better capitalists than we are, and just about anybody can kick our Army's ass. The Chinese did it in Korea and the North Vietnamese are doing it right now. If we took away our artillery and air superiority . . . who do you think would win out there in the jungle?"

Sash thought about what Alex was saying. There was a lot of truth in it. It wasn't because the American soldier lacked guts, it was a matter of sending a high-school team up against a professional football team and expecting them to win. The NVA had senior officers and noncommissioned officers *with* their troops in the jungle, not riding around in helicopters trying to direct a battle from five thousand feet away over the radio. The smart battalion and brigade commanders would allow for the commander on the ground to control the fight, and that was just about as bad. The NVA company commander averaged forty years old; the American company commander was in his mid-twenties. The NVA commander had been fighting a jungle war for at least fifteen years; the American commander was lucky to have a couple of months under his belt in Vietnam before he met his first NVA.

"We're doing pretty good so far." Sash had to say something in defense of his division.

"Yup." Alex took a deep breath. "If they're going to hit us tonight, it'll be before two in the morning so they'll have the cover of darkness to slip back into Cambodia. You should try to get some sleep."

"Mind if I join you guys?" Mills squatted down on the sandbag incline next to Alex. "I checked our patients. You did some really good work in there. We might lose a couple of them during the night, but they would have probably died anyway even if we had Medevacked them." Mills handed the open bottle he was holding to Alex.

Alex could feel the square bottle in his hand and rose up on one elbow. He took a swig and rinsed his mouth out before swallowing a mouthful. "Hmmm, good stuff!"

"Jack Daniel's! Nothing but the best for my friends." He handed the bottle over to Sash, who took a long pull and handed it back. "Your captain wants you to set your M-60 up on top of the command bunker to supply supporting fire in case the NVA attack and break through the perimeter." Mills smiled. "It's easy duty and will give you a chance to sleep."

Sash nodded. "That was thoughtful."

"All of the Americans have been put in positions in the inner perimeter—we've got our fighting bunkers full already." Mills looked over at Alex, who was still lying with his eyes closed. "The captain wants you to man bunker seven over by the main gate and take care of any wounded along that whole side of the camp."

Alex nodded and remained lying on the sun-heated sandbags for another minute before he sat up. "I've got to restock my aid kit before I go out there."

"Relax . . . you've got plenty of time." Mills looked at the luminous dial on his watch. "It's only eight . . . he wants you out there before midnight."

"Good. I think I'll stay right here and get some sleep." Alex dropped back on the sandbags.

"Well, I've got to do some cleaning up inside." Mills handed Sash the bottle again, but Sash shook his head.

"Thanks anyway, but another shot would knock me out."

Sash sat on the incline in a Vietnamese squat and watched and listened to the A camp settle in for the night. He was glad they had the eight-foot-high earthen berm surrounding the camp to stop any grazing fire. The NVA would have to get inside the camp for their small arms to be effective, or use mortars, which would work only if they caught someone going between the bunkers. Every one of the men inside the A camp had some type of overhead cover. He had listened to the officers talking at the other end of the command bunker, and there was a lot of artillery and air support on call, including Puff-the-Magic-Dragon, an AC-47 gunship that had tremendous firepower and two flare ships to light up the night. He almost hoped the NVA would attack; at least they would have fighting positions that were a hell of a lot better than the jungle offered.

The camp settled down and slowly the men started falling asleep from sheer exhaustion. The jungle surrounding the partially completed camp was quiet. The two captains stepped out of the command bunker and stood in the dark. A sliver of a moon lit the sky, but it wasn't strong enough to send shadows out over the ground.

"What do you think? Will they attack tonight or pass up the opportunity?" The infantry captain looked over at the Green Beret officer, even though he couldn't see his face in the dark.

"Who knows what the NVA will do? I know that this camp is a thorn in their side. We straddle one of their main infiltration routes south to Tay Ninh and Saigon. We knew they would be pissed off when we planned this camp and Prek Klok southwest of here."

"How long has the camp been here?"

"A month . . . maybe a little less as a camp, but they think we're building this camp under the old schedule. I don't think the NVA realize that all of those Conex containers were full of supplies and ammunition. They might attack, thinking that we've depleted our reserve ammunition supply. It's obvious that we haven't had any resupply choppers land here today."

"I checked on our wounded." The infantry captain's voice filled with respect. "Your medics are really good. You wouldn't want to lend me one of them for a couple of weeks, would you?"

The Green Beret captain chuckled. "Now you know why we get so damned pissed off when the line units steal them from us when they in process through Camp Alpha in Saigon."

"I won't bullshit you. After seeing them work on my wounded men, I would steal them myself!"

"The solution isn't to steal our medics; it's to upgrade the rest of the Army's training."

"How long does it take to train one of your medics?" The infantry captain lit a cigarette and his face glowed from the light. He had one of his eyes shut to retain his night vision.

"Over a year, and that's if the man is lucky enough to catch all of his classes in sequence."

The infantry captain looked out over the perimeter wire. "What was that?" He reached back for his M-16 at the same time.

The Beret officer turned his head to one side to listen. He heard a soft popping sound in the distance and recognized it instantly. *"Incoming! . . ."* He ran back to the entrance of the bunker and cupped his hands around his mouth. *"Incoming!"*

The first volley landed seconds after the officers had taken cover. Five of the mortar rounds landed on the roof of the command bunker. Sash was lying flat on the roof, and the three rows of sandbags surrounding his observation post had protected his body from the explosions. The only damage done to him was that his ears were ringing.

The camp took more than five hundred mortar rounds during the next hour, and then there was an eerie silence. All of the men manning the weapons in the perimeter bunkers were waiting behind their weapons. Either they would be attacked within the next couple of minutes by the NVA or they would be spared until the next day, and then the chances of the NVA remaining in the area were small.

A mortar inside the perimeter popped and an illumination round lit up the camp in a dull orange light. The first parachute flare burned out at exactly the same time a second flare ignited. The guards searched the jungle for any sign of movement. The inside of the camp was quiet as the men waited. The Americans were all awake and manning their weapons. One of the men broke away from his bunker and ran for the shitter.

A bugle sounded back in the jungle and all hell broke loose. Waves of NVA soldiers poured out from behind practically every bush. Sash had never seen so many NVA in his life. The whole North Vietnamese

Army must have decided on attacking them all at the same time. Sash was watching the elite 165th NVA Regiment assault. The enemy unit had never failed to take an objective since it was formed to fight against the French outside of Hanoi. This was the very first time that they were being committed as a regiment to a battle, and the regimental commander had instructed that his regimental flag be brought along to the fight. He was sure that they would overrun the irritating Green Beret outpost with very few casualties. The NVA unit that had gotten its nose bloodied earlier that day was from the 273rd VC Regiment, which had been recently equipped with NVA uniforms and weapons. His unit was fresh from the north and wouldn't take a beating from a bunch of Chinese misfits and American drug users. He was sure of a quick victory.

The Nung soldiers manning the bunkers went automatically to their final protective fires when they saw the horde of NVA attacking. Instead of selecting individual targets, the machine-gunners placed the barrels of their weapons against their FPL stakes and started firing interlocking bursts. The mortar crews fired their FPL rounds and filled the depressions surrounding the camp with shrapnel. The NVA had nowhere to hide; they were forced either to increase their assualt or to retreat. The NVA regimental commander committed his reserve. The large number of assaulting infantrymen pressed over the barbed wire and rushed up the slopes of the berm. Nungs left their fighting bunkers so they wouldn't get trapped inside, and engaged the NVA in individual fights.

Sash saw a large number of NVA rush the main gate carrying a bangalore torpedo, and opened fire. He kept his eye on the bunker Alex was in and surrounded it with machine-gun fire until he saw Alex look out and then leap from the entrance carrying his medical-aid kit. Alex pulled a wounded Nung behind his bunker for protection and administered first aid.

He ran out again and carried another wounded man back to the rear of his bunker and stopped the bleeding of his wound before repeating the act.

Sash kept a watch on Alex's position and covered him from the command bunker. Alex was oblivious of the fighting going on around him as he ran from bunker to bunker taking care of the wounded the best that he could. He had reached the end of his bunker line and turned around to work his way back when an NVA soldier blocked his way. Alex used his right fist to punch the soldier in the mouth and then kneed him. The NVA went down on his knees and Alex dodged past him. Sash realized that Alex was not carrying a weapon. He fired a short burst and ended the NVA soldier's concern over his busted lip.

Alex reached his bunker by the main gate only seconds before the NVA bangalore torpedo exploded. The steel frame of the gate cartwheeled through the air and landed against the sandbag wall surrounding the mortar pit fifty meters away. A special NVA sapper team sprang up from their hiding place in the jungle and rushed through the open gate. Their mission was to destroy the bunkers inside the camp with the satchel charges they carried in special pouches around their waists. Alex ignored the first squad of sappers that entered the camp through the gate. He was concentrating on stopping the blood from running into a wounded Nung's eyes and didn't see the NVA approaching him from behind.

"Die, American pig!" The NVA soldier spoke the sentence in perfect English. He should have just bayoneted Alex and kept his mouth shut. Alex twisted to his left and the bayonet slid up to the rifle barrel in the soft berm mud. Alex kicked out sideways from his knees and caught the NVA soldier's ankles. The enemy tripped and fell over on his side. Alex sprang up and saw a machete sticking out of the mud next to the bunker and instinctively reached for it. The portion of the blade that had been in the muddy clay still had a large hunk of sticky red laterite clinging to it as he swung. The weight on the end of the blade increased the force of the swing, and when the sharp blade contacted the NVA's neck, the soldier's head fell sideways off his shoulders. Sash watched the headless man remain standing for a couple of seconds, and then the body collapsed in a bloody pile at Alex's feet.

Five NVA sappers filled the entranceway to the camp, carrying their satchel charges at the ready as they selected individual targets. Alex didn't hesitate, and charged them with only the machete for a weapon. He surprised the squad and had closed with them so fast that they couldn't draw their pistols. Alex swung the blade wild, but every time he stroked the machete, he hit some flesh. Blood sprayed everywhere.

Sash saw what was happening at the main gate and knew that as soon as the last of the five NVA fell, the NVA covering the gate would take out Alex with small-arms fire. He ran down the sloping side of the bunker and engaged a sapper who was about to toss a satchel charge into the command bunker. The soldier fell backward and his fused explosive dropped down at his feet. Sash ran as hard as he could toward the main gate, where Alex was hacking away with the machete, and felt the force of the charge going off behind him. He staggered and then regained his balance.

Alex sensed his approach and whirled around to engage the figure rushing toward him.

"Alex! It's me! Sash!"

Alex lowered the machete slightly and tried refocusing his eyes. He had been fighting on pure instinct. Under the mortar flare that was lighting up the camp, Sash saw the bloody machete in Alex's hand and the red-gold glow of blood covering his right arm up to his shoulder. Large splotches of blood marked his face and the front of his tiger suit. Sash was stopped in his tracks, looking at the macabre scene under the glimmering manmade light.

Movement behind Alex at the edge of the jungle brought Sash back to life. He sidestepped Alex and opened fire with his M-60. "Alex! Get back behind the bunker!"

Alex didn't move.

"Alex! Take care of the wounded!"

Alex responded and dived behind the bunker where he had carried his wounded men for protection.

The M-60 machine gun Sash was holding flipped up in the air and caught Sash across the forehead. Blood burst out almost instantly. Sash looked down, surprised at his weapon, and saw the groove across the upper hand guard where an NVA bullet had hit it. He re-cocked the charging handle and pointed the weapon down again at the jungle. It still worked. Sash sidestepped until he was behind the bunker and then turned around to challenge any NVA who might have slipped up on them from the rear. He saw a team of Nungs running between the ammo bunker and the command post. They stopped to mop up a small group of NVA hiding against the wall of the 4.2-inch mortar pit they had taken out. Both of the American Green Berets operating the tube had been shot without even realizing that the NVA had breached the perimeter. They had been so busy firing their weapon and breaking out ammo that the sappers had had an easy target.

A trumpet blew again somewhere just inside the wall of green surrounding the camp. A few NVA survivors tried making it back across the open clearing surrounding the camp but were hit by heavy cross fire. The attack was a failure, but the NVA regiment had succeeded in breaching the perimeter and had destroyed six of the perimeter bunkers and three of the supply bunkers inside the camp. The ammunition bunker was saved, along with the command bunker.

"Are they withdrawing?" Alex had dropped down on his knees and was resting his forehead against the hilt of the machete he was holding upright with his left hand in the mud, the palm of his right hand capped over that. There wasn't anything left in Alex. He was completely exhausted.

"It's over . . . for now." Sash leaned back against the side of the fighting bunker and looked out over the carnage. The sun was breaking and a soft gray light illuminated the battlefield. Sash hadn't realized what a huge loss the NVA had suffered trying to cut through the camp's final protective fires until the rays of the sun removed the black cover that hid the dead. Hundreds of NVA laid scattered over the open clearing and piled up in places where they had tried to breach the defensive wire. The inside of the camp was littered with mixed dead. The Nungs had taken severe losses when they tried to defend the ammunition bunker and the mortar pits, but the American infantry company had suffered few losses fighting from their inner-perimeter positions and had actually surprised the NVA sappers, who thought that once they were inside the perimeter, the pickings would be easy.

Alex tried struggling to his feet and dropped back in the mud. "Wounded . . . I've got to get to the wounded."

"Relax, Alex . . . our medics have everything under control. You did a good job patching them up during the attack. It's only a matter now of getting some Medevacs in here." Sash had barely spoken the word when they heard helicopters approaching the camp from the southeast. At first it was a pass by a flight of Cobra gunships that fired up the jungle surrounding the camp, and then eight slicks appeared out of nowhere and unloaded American infantry troops in the clearing to the south of the camp. The men instantly disappeared in the jungle, and another lift of eight choppers landed to their west side and unloaded their cargo of fighting men. The maneuver was repeated until the camp was surrounded by a fresh infantry battalion. The division had committed an entire brigade to the Battle of Tong Le Chon.

Alex looked up and watched the chopper spiral down out of the sky. He could see that it had huge red crosses painted on either side door. The Medevac landed on top of the command bunker and was loaded up with wounded Nungs and Americans almost instantly. The chopper left and was replaced by another one and another one, until all of the wounded were extracted, and then the slicks started landing to pick up the body bags holding the dead. Alex looked away.

"Here come the brass." Sash spoke the word with such a neutral tone that he sounded like an electronic voice that you would hear coming from a spaceship.

Alex didn't look up, but sat down, holding the machete between his legs as he leaned forward against it. The blood had dried on the blade, turning it a rosy-black color. He heard people walking toward him in the sucking mud, but didn't look up. He was hoping they would just walk on past his position.

"You men did a great job! Well done!" The voice was deep.

Sash answered, "Thank you, General."

"I brought in some food on the chopper for you men." The division commander's voice dropped even lower. "Merry Christmas!"

Alex looked up, and his eyes automatically focused and locked with the general's. The two men stared at each other for what seemed like hours before the general spoke. "Son, there's Christmas dinner in those Mermite cans for you."

"Christmas? Today is Christmas?" Alex had completely forgotten Christmas.

"Sure is, soldier!" The general's aide-de-camp tried sounding cheerful. "There should be enough food for all of the Americans here in camp to have a little turkey and mashed potatoes—"

"Thanks, sir," Sash interrupted.

The general stepped around the edge of the fighting bunker and saw the carnage that had been caused by the machete. Decapitated and hacked-apart NVA bodies filled the gap where the gate had been torn from its hinges. "My God . . . my dear, dear God!"

The aide stepped around the edge of the bunker to see what his general was talking about, and stopped with his eyes popping wide open. "Oh . . . ugh!" He vomited against the side of the bunker.

Sash looked over at Alex and realized that he wasn't tuned in to what was going on around him, so he spoke to the general. "They didn't get to his wounded." Sash nodded down at the bloodstained ground behind the bunker where the wounded soldiers had been only a few minutes earlier.

The general looked back at Alex and then down at the machete he was holding between his legs, and put the whole story together quickly. Now he understood why the Green Beret had so much blood covering him.

One of the gunners who was on the general's chopper came running over to where he stood, carrying four paper plates piled high with Christmas food. "Anyone hungry?" He tried acting cheerful but couldn't take his eyes off the NVA dead.

"Sure . . ." Sash took a plate for himself and one for Alex. "Do you have something to eat with?"

"Uh . . . sure!" The gunner tore his eyes away from the NVA dead and reached down in the side pocket of his trousers and handed Sash two packages of plastic flatware.

"Thanks." Sash handed Alex a plate of the fantastic-smelling hot food and sat down next to him. "Let's eat something, buddy."

Alex nodded and took the plate and plastic fork Sash handed him.

The sight of blood and bodies lying all around the area didn't bother Sash as much as it did the other Americans. It wasn't because he was some kind of murderer who enjoyed the sight of blood, but because he had become conditioned to seeing blood and cut flesh by working in his father's butcher shop. There was a difference between freshly butchered animals and hacked-apart humans, but not much.

Alex started eating automatically. His body was famished and demanded food.

A soldier from the division staff ran at a hobble toward where they were sitting. From a position up on the berm, the general and his aide were still looking out over the battlefield that surrounded the camp. The soldier stopped in front of Alex and Sash and opened the Mermite container he was carrying. The smell was the first thing to reach Alex and Sash. A smell that could be recognized instantly as sugar cookies. "Help yourselves, guys." The soldier looked away sheepishly. He felt like an ass offering Christmas cookies to these guys who had just finished fighting a battle for their lives, but the general had personally flown the cookies and other food into the camp and had ordered that it be distributed while he was there.

Alex closed his eyes and breathed in the smell of Christmas. He opened them and looked down into the shipping container that had hundreds of cookie Santa Clauses stacked on top of each other. He saw that one of them was broken in half and reached for it. Blood covered most of his exposed skin and Alex pulled his hand back and tried rubbing the dried blood off on his pant leg. It wouldn't come off.

Sash could see that Alex was becoming frantic trying to wipe the dried blood off his hand before reaching into the container for the Christmas cookie, and did it for him.

"Here, Alex." He handed him an unbroken cookie.

Alex shook his head. "That one . . . the broken one."

Sash picked out the pieces and handed them to Alex.

"Thanks." Alex laid the two pieces down on a nearby

sandbag and finished eating his food with his eyes locked on the two halves of Santa Claus.

"That was good!" Sash shoveled the last of his mashed potatoes into his mouth and talked around the food as he swallowed it. "I could use seconds." He glanced over at Alex and stood up. "Do you want me to bring you some more back if there's any left?"

Alex didn't answer.

Sash used the carrying strap to hold his M-60, which freed both his hands to carry back the heaping plates of food. He could see Alex on his knees next to the fighting bunker and it looked like he was pounding something with the flat edge of the machete. Sash started running toward his war buddy. He sensed that something was wrong.

The general stepped down from the berm just as Sash arrived back at the bunker. Alex had pounded the Christmas cookie into an unrecognizable blob on the sandbag. Sash set the plates down on a nearby ammo crate and grabbed Alex by the shoulders. "Stop it!" Alex looked up at his friend. Tears had washed two trails down his cheeks.

What Alex always remembered from that incident was the container of Christmas cookies, but Sash remembered a completely different thing. Not the blood, nor the battle that had raged throughout the night. Sash remembered those emerald-green eyes that reflected his friend's soul. A soul that had seen and been scorched by the pits of hell.

CHAPTER ELEVEN

✪✪✪✪✪✪✪✪✪✪✪✪✪✪✪✪✪✪✪✪✪✪

CHRISTMAS COOKIES REVISITED

Sash adjusted the collar on his black cashmere topcoat and paused to survey the occupants of the park. The women's-rights group were concentrating on waving down passing cars along their side of the park. Sash saw the police officer standing next to a lamppost watching the demonstrators and the television crewmen who were assembling a camera and preparing for a live broadcast.

"That has to be him over there, Dad." Young Alex nodded at the bum on the park bench.

"Probably." Sash remembered the telephone incident, hearing the police officer refer to Alex as a bum. Sash reached out and touched his son's arm. He couldn't help showing the worry on his face. "Alex, I don't think he would hurt you for anything in the world, but he might be a little sick . . ."

"I understand, Dad. If things start looking bad, I'll go back to the car . . . I promise."

Sash started walking toward the park bum. He stared hard as he drew near, and tried identifying his old war buddy underneath the full beard and loose-fitting Army overcoat. It was just too hard to tell after twenty years. Sash stopped in front of the bench and looked down.

The bum opened his eyes, and Sash knew instantly that he was looking at Alex. The emerald-green eyes still sparkled.

"Hello, Alex."

"Sash . . . I should have known you'd do something foolish and come here." He patted the bench and looked around the immediate area. "How did you get here?"

Sash sat down next to Alex.

"Is this my godson?" Alex grinned under his beard at the teenager.

"Hello, Uncle Alex." The young man leaned over and hugged the park bum and kissed him on the cheek.

Sash saw that what his son had done pleased his old war buddy. "That's part of having a Russian godson— you get kissed a lot, especially if you're loved."

"It looks like you've done a respectable job raising him, Sash." Alex coughed to cover the emotion welling up inside him. "So! What brings you to Washington, D.C., on Christmas Day?"

"You."

Alex shrugged. "I wish you hadn't come. You know that you're making this much harder for me."

"That's exactly why I came." Sash crossed his legs in front of him and glanced over at the police officer, who was watching them.

"I was just sitting here thinking about Tong Le Chon." Alex closed his eyes again.

Young Alex tapped his father's shoulder and pointed at the message written in the snow.

"Yes, it's been twenty years. God, how fast time slips by!" Sash looked at his watch. "In fact, it's almost the exact hour."

"What hour?" Alex asked the question with his eyes still closed. He lifted his face so that the sun's rays could touch it.

"You and I were sitting on the berm eating Christmas dinner together."

"I was just thinking about that, old buddy!" Alex looked over at Sash and patted his leg. "Really! Just before you arrived, I was thinking about that damned dinner and those Christmas cookies."

"You know, there are two ways of looking at it. Personally, I remember it was the best Christmas dinner I've ever eaten."

"I wish I could." The words sounded like a desperate man's prayer.

"Here, Uncle Alex." Young Alex held out the small gift, which had been rewrapped. "Your Christmas present. I've already told you what it is over the telephone, but my sister wouldn't let us go until she wrapped it again."

"You've got a thoughtful family, Sash." A moist film spread over the emerald-green eyes, making them sparkle in the bright sunlight.

Sash played one of his trump cards. "Why don't you get in my car and come back to Michigan with us? I promise you'll love it there."

"I know I would." Alex opened the package and stared down at the Gucci watch. "Thanks again, Godson. It's a great gift. I'll be the only park bum in Washington with my own designer watch!"

"You don't have to be a bum, Alex! I'll hire you and put you in a three-piece suit!" Sash's voice was becoming desperate.

Alex smiled and placed his hand on his old friend's shoulder. "I have a job, buddy. Would you believe me if I told you I was a medical doctor?"

"An M.D.?" Young Alex was shocked.

"The top of my class!" Alex leaned back against the bench. "When I left Nam, I only had a year left to serve on my enlistment, but that didn't matter anyway. I was selected to attend the Army's Bootstrap Program and got my undergraduate degree. Then this guy I met in Vietnam named LeBlond appeared out of nowhere and reminded me of a deal we had made, and handed me a full-ride scholarship to one of the best medical schools in the country."

"LeBlond?" Sash was curious. "You never mentioned that name before."

"He was a CIA man assigned to some superspook operation over there, and I accidentally did him what he considered a very big favor. I jokingly told him that the Agency could send me to med school as a reward."

"So you're a doctor?" Sash asked the question with a slight tinge of doubt in his voice.

"Sash! I didn't say *witch* doctor! I'm still a practicing *surgeon*." Alex smiled. "You know me! I always end up grabbing more that I set out to do!"

"You were probably the honor graduate of that too!" Sash shook his head and explained his comment to his son. "Your uncle was the honor graduate in our basic-training company and he liked the feeling so well that he became the honor graduate in every other phase of training throughout his military career."

Alex rubbed his beard and winked at his godson.

"So! Do you have a medical practice somewhere?" Sash pointed at the clothes Alex was wearing. "And why the getup?"

"For the first couple of years out of medical school, I worked with a group of doctors. We formed our own clinic." Alex frowned. He had forgotten to do something. "Sash, do you have a piece of scrap paper and a pen with you?"

"Sure." Sash removed his notepad from his jacket and handed the leather-bound pocket secretary to Alex.

"Nice." Alex held up the pen. "Real gold?"

"Give me a break, Alex!" Sash was becoming annoyed at the teasing.

Alex wrote the name of a banking firm on the pad and a couple of telephone numbers under it. "This is the name of my New York bank and the telephone numbers where you can reach one of my sisters. Keena is the oldest and will handle all of my financial accounts."

"Dammit, Alex! Don't talk like that!" Sash leaned forward on the park bench. "Alex . . . I don't want to lose you like this. You mean too much to me."

Alex smiled and patted Sash's knee the way an old man would comfort a small boy. "Buddy . . ." Alex's eyes lost their focus. "Do you know how many lives I've saved?"

Sash didn't answer.

"Thousands! Thousands and thousands of lives, and I cannot forgive myself for the butchering I did at Tong Le Chon!"

"Alex, dammit! If you hadn't killed those NVA, they would have murdered our wounded. You know that!" Sash didn't know how to get the point across to his friend. Alex had had a difficult choice to make, and he had been forced to take human life in order to save human life; someone had to die that day.

"You know, Sash, I've told myself that a million times. I've told myself that I am a highly intelligent human being and should be able to rationalize it just as you've done." Alex looked at his friend and tears rolled out of his eyes. "But late at night when everything is quiet, it always comes back."

"What comes back?"

"You and me sitting on that damn berm eating Christmas dinner, surrounded by that horrible saturnalia of blood." A sly grin formed on Alex's face before he continued, "And then the worst part happens. A Merminte can opens and a chorus line of singing Santa Claus cookies pops out and dances over the hacked-apart bodies." Alex looked up at his godson. "Sick, isn't it?"

Young Alex didn't know how to reply, but he felt the man's grief and started crying.

Alex looked back at Sash. "See . . . I know the kid twenty minutes and I've got him crying!"

"Alex, my friend, the boy was raised loving you—you're his godfather, and that's a special person in our family. He sees that you're hurting, so he's hurting."

"I thought handling the guilt would be easy. Hell, I've got some of the best psychiatrists in New York for friends, but I never once mentioned it to them."

"Why not?" Sash noticed that the police officer was slowly walking over to where they were sitting.

"Friends . . . they were just that, my friends, and if I dumped on them, all of that would change and I would become another one of their fucked-up patients." Alex saw the officer approaching and buttoned up the front of his Army overcoat, using his left hand. "I know this cop. He was in Nam."

"Is that your Rolls-Royce parked over there?" The police officer nodded toward Sash's car.

"Yes, it is, officer."

"You're in a no-parking zone."

"I'll have my son move it."

"What's going on here?" The policeman nodded at Alex.

"Friends of mine, officer. Sash was in Nam with me."

"Really, now?" The officer smiled. "You've come a long way from Vietnam." He glanced over at the road-grime-covered car.

"A little luck and a lot of hard work."

"Michigan license plates."

"My son and I drove down here for the day."

"Oh?"

"Yes . . . to visit Alex." Sash nodded at the bearded man on the bench.

"You drove down here from Michigan to visit a park bum on Christmas Day."

"Yes, we did, officer."

"Oh." The policeman rubbed the side of his neck

and twisted his mouth as he thought. "Makes sense." He winked and started walking back toward the demonstrators. "Try to stay away from that group over there. I just received a call from the station that a large group of people from a local Christian league is going to be arriving in a few minutes. It should get pretty hot around here soon." He adjusted his holster belt. "Forget about moving your car. I don't think it will block traffic today, as long as you don't plan on staying too long."

"We'll be leaving soon, officer. Thanks."

Alex placed his left hand on his knee and stood up. "Well, good friend, I think I'd better get moving before those other people arrive. They'll probably have kids with them."

"Alex . . ." Sash tried standing, but Alex gently pushed him back down on the bench.

"I know what I'm doing, Sash. This is the only way left for me."

"Alex, I don't know if any of those people out there demonstrating for their rights to kill their own babies are innocent. Some of them might just be out there because they have nothing better to do, but one of them, just *one* . . . might be worth saving."

Alex looked at the group of demonstrators and then back at Sash. He smiled. "You don't think it's a good idea, taking out a bunch of hippies?"

"No, I don't, Alex. No matter how much pain they've caused us Vietnam veterans . . . no matter how much pain."

"You're not going to try to stop me, are you?" Alex stared directly into his war buddy's eyes, looking for deception.

"If I was going to do that, I'd have brought the police with me. I wish you would change your mind, Alex . . . but I won't try to stop you."

"Good." Alex started down the sidewalk. The sun had melted the snow off the concrete.

Sash and his son watched Alex leave.

"Dad . . ." Young Alex took a step toward his godfather and looked back at his father. "Dad, I can't just let him go kill himself."

Sash nodded, giving his permission for his son to follow after his war buddy.

Young Alex ran to catch up. He reached up and touched his godfather's shoulder. The older man kept walking without turning around.

"Uncle Alex?" The teenager felt the man's muscles tighten under his hand.

Alex slowly turned around. He glanced back at Sash standing in the distance and then looked down at his godson. "Yes?"

The boy didn't know how to begin saying what he felt, and then suddenly the verbal dam burst. "Uncle Alex, please . . . don't do it . Please . . . for me?"

The old Vietnam veteran looked deep into his namesake's eyes. He looked past the surface handsomeness and into the teenager's hidden soul. Normally, if someone stared that hard at him, young Alex would look away or feel embarrassed, but this stare from his godfather wasn't threatening. The two of them stood there looking at each other for a couple of minutes. A flicker of a smile caught the corner of the older man's mouth and disappeared. He gave his godson a curt nod and turned to finish his walk.

Sash had been watching the encounter, but they were too far away for him to hear what was being said. His eyes wandered over to the message printed in the snow: "ISRAEL MURDERED HER PROPHETS—AMERICA MURDERS HER HEROES." The edges around the footprints had started melting, but the message was still easy to read. The words made a lot of sense; America always seemed to attack her heroes and nag them until they committed suicide or just gave up and dropped out of society. He looked back toward the demonstration and saw Alex walking from his son toward the women's-rights group. A part of him wanted to call the police to stop his friend from committing a horrible crime, but a strong part of him that was based on a loyalty cemented with blood told him to leave it alone.

Young Alex reached his father and smiled. "I don't think he's going to do it."

"Good." Sash sat back down on the bench and watched his war buddy approach the women.

Sheila saw the park bum approaching her row of folding tables. So far there hadn't been that many people driving by the park, and her group wasn't drawing the attention that she wanted. The bum dressed in the military overcoat would be a good way to draw the attention of the media van's television cameras. So far the reporter and his crew had stayed inside the van and drunk hot coffee. She needed something to get her people excited about. What she didn't know was that Alex was seeking her.

The policeman watched Alex approach and smiled when he waved at him. The officer sensed that something was going on, but he couldn't quite place what it was. He watched Alex reach down and pick up some literature that showed the different stages of the human fetus.

A church bus pulled up to the curb on the opposite side of the park and unloaded a large group of adults and a couple dozen small children. The adults were carrying large full-color picket signs that graphically showed the torn-apart bodies of tiny babies. Young Alex noticed that the children did not look up at the posters their parents were carrying, but formed into a choir and started singing Christmas songs.

The television crew left the van and started preparing to film the Christian group. Sheila's face got red from anger. "Those bastards are going to film over there!"

Alex looked up from the pamphlet he was reading and smiled at the radical leader.

Sheila saw the look on the war veteran's face and broke. "What in the hell do you think is so damn funny!"

Alex kept smiling.

"She asked you what's so damn funny?" The weight lifter had stepped behind Alex.

"I've had about enough of you, fella." Alex kept the smile on his face.

"And what do you plan on doing about it, soldier boy?"

Alex's overcoat flew open and the barrel of his CAR-15 stopped against the side of the weight lifter's throat. The move was so fast that it caught the strongman completely off-guard. "I might just blow your head off for starters." Alex pushed up under the man's jaw until the weight lifter gagged.

Sheila had been watching the church group organizing on the far side of the park and had missed the event. One of the other demonstrators gasped. "He has a gun!"

Alex pushed with the barrel. "Get over there and be a good boy, will you?"

The weight lifter obeyed without saying a word.

"What in the hell do you think you're doing!" Sheila still hadn't realized the danger she was in.

Alex quickly slipped off his overcoat, and the homemade bomb around his waist came into plain view.

"Oh! My God, he has a bomb!" another demonstrator cried.

"You're a nut! A fucking nut!" Sheila started screaming.

The police officer had been watching the opposition group unload from the bus and had wandered halfway down the sidewalk toward them. He was closer to Sash and his son on the park bench than he was to Alex when he turned around to see what the woman was screaming about. He saw Alex and the dark red sticks of dynamite around his waist. Then he saw Alex raise his arm, holding the very familiar CAR-15 sub-machine gun. The officer reached for his pistol and murmured under his breath, "Oh, shit!"

Sash grabbed the police officer by the shoulder. "Officer . . . give it a little time. I don't think he's going to do anything."

"What are you talking about, man! Can't you see the bomb and that damn machine gun!" The officer reached back on his belt for his hand-held radio transmitter. "Station Four. I have a suspect here at my location with a submachine gun and explosives. Request assistance. Please approach my location from the south without lights or sirens, over."

The reply was almost instantaneous. "Roger, Station Four. Backup unit is on the way."

Sash leaned back against the park bench and watched what was going on with Alex. He knew that the police would kill him if he resisted arrest. He was hoping that Alex would surrender to the police after scaring the pro-abortion demonstrators. Sash had already made up his mind that he would hire the best law firm in Washington to represent his war buddy.

Alex held the CAR-15 pointed directly at the demonstrators and slowly made eye contact with each one of them. Alex could see most of the spectrum of human emotion in their eyes.

Alex looked quickly over at his godson and then back at the group of social misfits standing in front of him. He would be doing the world a favor by taking all of them out with him. He need only to flip the switch on the timer attached to his belt. He looked back at his godson and took a deep breath. "Are any of you people mothers or fathers?" Alex swept the crowd with the barrel of his weapon.

A woman standing near the center of the gathering slowly raised her hand.

"Have you ever had an abortion?"

She shook her head left and right.

"Where's your child?"

"My husband stole him from me." The woman was terrified.

Alex noticed the woman standing next to her reach over and hold the mother's hand and squeeze gently.

"You people condemn us Vietnam veterans for killing enemies of our nation. You've spat on us and harassed us when we returned home from that rotten war. You elected into office those politicians"—Alex used the barrel of his CAR-15 to point over at the Capitol— "who sent us over there, but none of *their* sons fought in that war! You stand here today on Christmas and exercise your right to assemble, a right the soldiers of this nation have given to you and paid for with their lives!" Alex looked over at Sheila. "You call me a murderer, yet you are here on a day that celebrates *birth* . . . and you advocate the worst crime that can be committed on this earth—maternal infanticide." Alex saw the dark blue police van pull up at the far end of the park. "Watch my lips! I'm going to tell you this only one time, in case none of our politicians, priests, social workers, and educators have told you: *killing your own babies is wrong!*" Alex spaced each of the words. "Now you can't say you haven't been told." He smiled and waved at the crowd. "You're on your own."

The television crew had quietly been filming the whole scene, zooming in on the expressions of the demonstrators as Alex talked to them.

Alex used his free hand to unlatch the BAR belt around his waist. He threw the heavy pouched belt containing the ball bearings and nails down at his feet. He glanced over at the van and saw that there were men peering around the back corners. He had a little difficulty unhooking the pistol belt the sticks of dynamite were attached to, and the weight lifter tried moving forward in the crowd. Alex lowered the barrel of his CAR-15 and smiled at the huge man. "Sure . . .

come on ahead if you want to be the first one." The man stopped.

Sash tried leaning forward on the bench to get a better view at what was going on. He saw Alex drop something and then point his weapon at another one of the men. "I wish we could hear what was being said."

"I think we'll have that chance, Dad." Young Alex pointed at the television crew. "It'll be on the five-o'clock news."

Alex used the couple of seconds when everyone was watching the weight lifter to unhook his pistol belt. "Sheila? It is Sheila, isn't it?"

The lead demonstrator swallowed and nodded.

"Well, Sheila"—Alex winked—"here's a little present for you." He handed the well-rigged bomb to the large woman. "Go ahead and take it . . . it's not set to go off."

She felt the belt in her hand. The fear that had been boiling down in her stomach erupted, and she vomited.

"A touch of the flu, Sheila?" Alex's voice was extremely patronizing. "You should see a doctor . . . you might even be suffering from morning sickness, girl!"

The front of a Washington police car pulled forward too much and could be seen sticking out from the edge of a building down the street. Alex knew that he would have to move quickly or they would have him completely surrounded, if they didn't already. He paused only for a second to wave good-bye to his godson, and then, without warning, he sprinted across the street and scaled the wrought-iron fence that surrounded the White House grounds.

The massed police force was caught by surprise. No one had expected him to make such a foolish move. The White House grounds were patrolled constantly by the Secret Service.

Sash closed his eyes. He knew what Alex was doing.

He had promised not to kill the demonstrators, and he was keeping his word.

The instant Alex had crossed over the fence, a series of silent alarms went off in the security control room. The Secret Service detail had already been alerted by the local police about a possible bomb threat and were standing by.

Alex ran over the unblemished layer of snow that covered the perfectly maintained lawn. An elaborate ground sensor system sent signals back to the control room.

"He's in sector ten, heading across the lawn toward gate five. He's not coming toward the White House." The sensor operator monitored his equipment and gave a silent sigh of relief. A suicidal bomber could cause a lot of damage to the old building, and they were at the basement level.

Alex ran around a large stand of leafless flowering ground shrubs and saw the first pair of Secret Service guards running toward him. He looked back the way he had come and saw another set of submachine-gun-carrying men following his tracks through the snow. Alex stopped running and held his CAR-15 up over his head. He had only the one magazine of ammunition that was already in the weapon with him. The Secret Service men who had been approaching him from the direction of the White House dropped down into combat crouches.

"Drop your weapon!" the agent closest to Alex commanded.

Alex smiled and pulled the trigger.

Sash heard the CAR-15 going off in a long burst. He remained sitting on the park bench holding his head in his hands with his eyes closed. It seemed a very long time before the answer to Alex's challenge reached him, but it had actually been only a matter of seconds.

"Excuse me, sir." The voice came from directly in front of Sash.

Sash opened his eyes and looked up. He was surrounded by at least a dozen armored-vest-clad SWAT team members, standing with their weapons ready to fire.

"Sir . . . the police officer told us that you knew the man. I would like for you to come with us." The voice was polite but firm.

"Sure." Sash started to stand, and the police officers reacted as if that were a threat. They threw him down on the concrete sidewalk.

"What in the hell are you doing to my dad!" Young Alex tried reaching his father and was thrown down on the ground next to him.

Sash felt the cold wet pavement pressing against his cheek and just lay there waiting until the SWAT team had frisked him. He could hear his son yelling at the police officers going through his pockets.

"We came here to *stop* him!"

"I would keep my mouth shut if I were you, *boy*, until you've been read your rights!" The voice was gruff, but Sash could tell that the police officer was speaking tough to hide his own fear.

Sash spoke from his prone position in the cold slush on the sidewalk. "Son, let them go through their police procedures and we'll have a chance to tell our story when they're satisfied." Sash's calm voice after having been treated so roughly by the SWAT team shamed the officer in charge.

"Get him on his feet!" The police lieutenant was wearing mirrored sunglasses.

"Thanks, officer." Sash tried brushing the frozen chunks of snow and ice off the front of his topcoat. "Would you mind letting my son get up?" He nodded at Alex, who was a lot worse off than he had been. They had him down on his stomach, and an officer had his knee rammed in the boy's lower back.

The lieutenant nodded and they dragged Alex to his feet.

Sash handed the lieutenant his car keys. "Would you have someone drive my car to wherever you're taking us?" He nodded at the parked Rolls-Royce.

The lieutenant looked worried for the first time since they had arrived at the park bench.

"Sir!" The patrolman ran over to where the SWAT lieutenant was standing. "Sir, this man wasn't a part of what happened. I think he's telling the truth when he said he came here with his son to stop the Vietnam vet."

"Thanks, officer." Sash removed his topcoat and tried squeezing some of the water out of it.

"Let's go over to the station and sort this out." The lieutenant took the safest way out. He would turn the whole thing over to his captain.

"Good idea." Sash winked at the officers. "Are you ready, son?"

Young Alex glared at the SWAT team.

"Come on, son. They were only doing their jobs." Sash put his hand over his son's shoulder and followed the SWAT lieutenant over to the step-van.

CHAPTER TWELVE

✪✪✪✪✪✪✪✪✪✪✪✪✪✪✪✪✪✪✪✪✪✪✪✪

A CIRCLE OF
WARRIORS

The television announcer looked down at the script in front of him and shook his head. He had served in Vietnam and didn't like what was written on the paper. He looked up at the teleprompter and saw the same words appear on the screen. The red light under the center camera flashed on.

"Good morning. . . . We've been showing the extraordinary footage of the incident that took place in Lafayette Park for the last few days and there have been a number of unusual twists since our station broke the story to you on Christmas Day. . . . We have a special report for you from our New York affiliate."

The broadcast was switched to a woman standing out in front of New York's Bellevue Hospital.

She stood holding a microphone in one hand and her coat collar shut in her other hand. A strong winter wind was making a rushing sound, but instead of distracting from her broadcast, it added a touch of suffering. "The Alex Jaxson story has gained a new series of twists since that tragic moment when he was gunned down on the White House grounds by Secret Service men who were assigned to protect the President. . . . It seems that Alex Jaxson was not what was formerly believed. He was dressed like one of Washington's familiar park bums when he was filmed by our affiliate station, but in actuality he was a very highly thought-of practicing emergency-room surgeon here at New York's famous Bellevue Hospital!"

The camera cut to the reporter standing inside the hospital with the emergency-room doors directly behind her. "*Dr.* Jaxson worked in this emergency room for over five years, but the interesting twist to this story is that he also worked in a Harlem clinic that performed emergency services." The camera cut to the front of the clinic. "The story of Dr. Jaxson takes on a bizarre character now. We have discovered that during this entire five-year period, Dr. Jaxson never occupied an apartment or a private residence. He normally worked a twelve-hour shift at Bellevue and then he would catch a taxi here"—the camera swept the front of the clinic—"to work another very long shift. He kept a change of clothes at both locations and for the most part slept on couches at both locations and ate hospital meals and wore hospital garb." The camera returned to the reporter at Bellevue. She was smiling. "Dr. Alex Jaxson was a unique and eccentric man. We have an eyewitness taxicab driver who told us that one day Dr. Jaxson ran out the front door of Bellevue and told him to take him to the Harlem clinic, where he had him wait out front for over an hour while he operated on a gunshot victim and then returned to the cab covered with blood and ordered the driver to take him back to Bellevue. Dr. Jaxson tipped the driver a hundred dollars, and the patient states the doctor never sent him a bill! . . . Yes, folks, Dr. Jaxson's story is unfolding before your very eyes. Was he an American hero . . . or a guilt-ridden Vietnam butcher? . . ." The camera cut to the message Alex had written in the snow: "ISRAEL MURDERED HER PROPHETS—AMERICA MURDERS HER HEROES."

The snow message had become the media slogan for the Alex Jaxson story, which was sweeping international news.

Sash got up and walked across the room. The announcer came back on the screen and spoke. "Alex Jaxson will be buried today at one o'clock in Arlington National Cemetery. The President himself had to intercede on behalf of Jaxson's family for the interment to take place . . ."

Sash turned off the television and walked over to the windows to look down at the entrance of the hotel from his suite. A row of flags flew along the entrance walkway to the Washington Sheraton, where he was staying with his family.

"Dear, was that on the news again?" his wife called to him from the bathroom the women were using.

"Yes, Mary . . . it was on the news again." Sash poured himself a double shot of vodka from the stocked bar and carried it back over to the window.

"You would think they would leave the poor man alone!" The sentence varied in volume when she turned to face the mirror.

"Dad! Alex said my tie is tied wrong!" Bobby came out of the bedroom door opposite the girls' bedroom.

Sash glanced at his youngest son. "It looks fine to me. Alex doesn't have much experience with ties." Sash set his drink down on the windowsill and adjusted the knot the boy had tied until it was presentable. Alex appeared in the doorway smiling. Sash winked at him and smiled back. "Alex, give your little brother a break—this tie is tied just fine."

Bobby's face lit up. He had insisted on getting dressed in the black suit in the men's bedroom instead of going with his mother and sister.

Sash patted the little boy's bottom. "Now, get your pants on and don't ruin the crease. We've got to look very sharp for Uncle Alex's funeral."

"Do you think the television cameras will be there, Dad?" Bobby took the glass from the windowsill and sniffed the contents. He wrinkled his nose and set the glass back down.

'There's some juice in the refrigerator behind the bar." Sash took his drink and drained it. He looked over at the bar, trying to decide if he should have a refill, and decided not to. He would like to get very drunk and miss the funeral, but he knew that could never happen.

"Sash! Don't let him have too much juice or he'll have to go to the bathroom during the ceremony!' Mary called from her bedroom.

Bobby rolled his eyes and stopped pouring orange juice into the tall glass.

Alex stepped out of the bedroom carrying his black topcoat in the crook of his arm. Sash smiled at his son and nodded at the bar. "How about a beer before we go?"

Alex laid his coat over the back of a chair and went to the bar. "I think I'll hold it down to a Mountain Dew."

A soft knock on the door distracted Bobby from his orange juice. "I'll get it, Dad!" He was up and over to the door before Sash could stop him.

A man wearing a dark-brown-and-tan National Park Service uniform was standing there looking very nervous.

"May I help you?" Sash was wary because of all the news coverage Alex's death had gained. A park-service guard had been killed, and Sash was worried that there might be some repercussions.

"Are you Mr. Maleko?" The guard looked both ways down the hall.

"Yes, I am." Sash walked over to the open door and eased Bobby over to one side.

"Please excuse me." The guard fumbled for something in his jacket pocket. "I saw the television coverage on Jaxson. I was the guard who told him that my coworker was an ex-hippie . . ." Guilt spread over the man's face.

"Would you like to step inside for a few minutes?

We're just about ready to leave for the funeral, but can I offer you a drink or something?"

"Thank you, I've only got a minute, but . . ." The guard stepped into the room.

Sash searched the man with his eyes, looking for a weapon, and saw none. "Alex, fix our friend here a drink."

"What would you like, sir?" Alex sipped from his Mountain Dew behind the bar.

"A Coke. I'm on duty . . ." The guard felt his hands shaking, "Make that a double Scotch on the rocks! Mr. Maleko, I'm sorry . . . very sorry for what happened to your friend."

"Thank you." Sash waited. There was more the man had to say.

"It wasn't really your friend's fault. My coworker was stoned when he approached him in the park. The autopsy report showed that he was so far gone that it was a wonder he could walk from his truck over to where your friend was sitting."

"I heard rumors to that effect." Sash's lawyers had told him that there had been a confidential investigation, and because of the results, charges had been dropped against Sash for aiding and abetting a murderer. The government's case against him had been very sketchy to begin with, but they were trying to find someone to prosecute, because even though the original story that broke against Alex had been against the veteran, popular opinion had turned Jaxson into a folk hero. The more the media investigated the dead man, the more good things they found out about him.

"I always knew that the guy was a head, but it wouldn't have worked if I had narced on him." The guard looked guilty. "I still have to work with his friends."

"Sure . . ." Sash smiled and looked down at his watch. "Is there something I can do for you?"

"Oh! No . . . I saw the television reports and thought

that you should be the one to get this." The guard removed a medal from his coat pocket.

Sash saw immediately what the medal was, and he could feel the color draining from his face."Where did you find that?"

"I'm sure that it's *his*." The guard handed the Distinguished Service Cross to Sash. "We're supposed to turn this kind of stuff in to the main office when we find it . . ." He looked out the window. "*They* leave stuff under the wall all the time. We even found a Medal of Honor there one day. Do you know how much one of those would sell for?" The guard didn't expect an answer, and continued, "Anyway, I thought that you might want this . . . its's better than it ending up stored away in a box full of junk in some federal basement somewhere."

Sash took the offered medal and turned it over. "SSG ALEX P. JAXSON" had been carved in tiny letters on the back of the medal. "Thank you, officer . . . it was very kind of you to bring this here."

The man smiled. He felt better about the whole incident now that he had given the medal to the man's friend. "I'll get in a lot of trouble if they know that I gave that to you. I guess it would be some kind of evidence, but the police don't know about it. I saw it in the snow when I was talking to him the night before all of this happened."

"Thanks again." Sash went over to the bar and poured himself another drink.

The guard drained his glass and set it down on a nearby coffee table. He adjusted his jacket and looked at the carpet. "I've got to be going now. Thanks for the drink."

Bobby closed the door behind the National Park Service guard and ran back over to the bar, where his father and brother stood looking down at the beautiful red-white-and-blue ribbon with the bronze cross and eagle attached to it.

"Gosh, Dad! A real medal!" Bobby hopped up on one of the bar stools and nearly touched the medal with his nose.

"Yes, a *real* Distinguished Service Cross." Sash finished his drink and set the glass down. The thoughts flashing through his mind were traveling at a billion miles per second. He reached over and touched the cold medal and was transported back to Tong Le Chon and into the middle of the battle that had raged there twenty years earlier.

Billy Mills stepped out of the back entrance to the command bunker. Sash could see the blood from the wounded men covering the whole front of Mills's camouflage fatigues. Mills wore rubber gloves on both hands and was holding a piece of surgical rubber tubing that they used for emergency tourniquets. Sash lifted the dust cover of his M-60 machine gun and placed a fresh belt of ammunition on the receiving tray. He glanced back at Alex and saw his buddy down on one knee, holding a bloody machete in one hand. Alex had stopped the NVA advance through the main gate, and the muddy ground surrounding him was littered with hacked-apart NVA bodies. Sash pulled back the charging handle on his machine gun, sending a round into the chamber, and set the bipod legs of his weapon back down on the sandbags. A bright flash of light caught his peripheral vision and he looked back at where Mills was standing surrounded in fire. At first Sash thought that the sandbags were burning, and then Mills took his first step forward and he could see that the medic had been hit by a flamethrower and it was the man's hair and fatigues that were on fire. Mills stumbled over to the rubber fuel pods and leapt forward. The explosion leveled that portion of the camp, killing dozens of NVA soldiers who had been caught in the open. All of the commandos and Americans had been inside the fighting bunkers and were protected. The explosion had been the major turning point in the battle and had destroyed the main body of NVA who had gained entrance into the camp.

The image of Mills's burning body flashed back in front of Sash's eyes. He could see the man's flesh burning, the heat forcing the sergeant's arms and legs to contour and withdraw into unnatural shapes. The whole incident had lasted only seconds. Sash looked back at Alex and saw him staring at the burning pods. Alex had seen everything and miraculously had escaped injury from the explosion.

"Dad! Dad!"

Sash's eyes focused and he saw both of his sons staring at him with expressions of fear.

Bobby continued screaming, *"Dad! Dad!"*

Mary and Elizabeth came running out of the bedroom. "What is going on out here?" Mary's voice carried her fear.

Sash realized that he had slipped back into the past. "It's all right, Bobby." He hugged the ten-year-old. "It's all right."

"Dad, you looked so weird!" Bobby started crying. "I thought you were having a heart attack!"

"No . . . I'm fine." Sash felt the sweat that had saturated his fresh shirt. "Let me change my shirt real fast and we'll go." Sash pushed the boy away from him and looked over at the medal lying on the bar. He smiled and lifted Bobby up on the bar. "Here!" Sash pinned his war buddy's Distinguished Service Cross on the lapel of his son's suit coat. "I think your Uncle Alex would like it if you wore it today."

Bobby's face changed instantly into a wide-toothed smile.

"Sash?" Mary's face was filled with worry wrinkles.

He took her outheld hand. "It's fine, dear . . . just fine."

"Are you sure? We don't have to go, you know."

"Oh, but we *do*, my dear . . . we must bury the

dead." Sash went back into the bedroom to change into his spare dress shirt.

The ride over to Arlington National Cemetery was totally quiet inside of the rented limousine. Sash sat looking out the window. Bobby was absorbed in the medal hanging from the lapel of his jacket. Mary was crying, but she always cried at funerals. Elizabeth was watching her mother, and Alex was thinking about his few minutes with his Uncle Alex in the park.

Sash saw the media vans as soon as they pulled into the cemetery gate. The Jaxson story was the hottest human-interest story in the English-speaking world and Europe. Jaxson's story would have been only a small blurb in a local Washington paper if it hadn't been for the unique series of reports done on him by the television network as a follow-up to the war hero's obvious suicide.

The limousine was forced to park a quarter of a mile away from the grave site because of the people and cars. Sash was surprised at the number of people Alex's funeral was drawing, even for a media event. He looked out over the crowd as he held the door open for his wife and daughter.

"Gosh, Dad! Uncle Alex sure had a lot of friends!" Bobby spoke in awe of the thousands of people that had been drawn to the cemetery.

Sash could see flags snapping in the brisk wind that represented veteran groups from as far away as Alaska. The Washington police had requested—everyone started *requesting* things after the President himself ordered that Alex be allowed burial in Arlington—that there not be a funeral procession through the streets. Alex's sister had agreed to a small sermon at the grave site. It had been a very smart move.

A soldier from the Army's Old Guard escorted Sash and his family to reserved seats at the grave. Sash had never met Alex's sisters, but from what Alex had told him about having a *rainbow* family, he recognized them easily. He seated his family and then went over to where the eldest sister was sitting. "Keena?" She looked up at the distinguished man from under her veil. "Keena, I'm Sasha Maleko . . ."

There wasn't any hesitation from the fifty-year-old woman. "Oh, Sash! Alex spoke of you often, even after the war."

"He was a good friend . . . a very good friend, and we'll miss him."

"We?" The proud woman looked back over Sash's shoulder.

"Yes, my eldest son was named after your brother, and in fact Alex was his godfather."

"Where is he? I must meet my *godnephew*!" Keena stood, and Sash beckoned for his son to join them.

"You brought your whole family with you?" Keena could see them sitting a few rows away.

"Yes."

"Let's walk over there, I'd like to meet all of them." She smiled a tight-lipped grin. "Besides, I need to move a little to get warm."

Sash introduced his family to Keena, not realizing that the television cameras were recording the whole event. Keena saw the medal on the ten-year-old's lapel and reached over and touched it. She instinctively turned it over and read her brother's name engraved on the back.

"Someone dropped it off at our suite this morning —by rights it's yours, Keena." Sash knew that it would break Bobby's heart to have to give up the medal, but she was entitled to it.

Keena patted the top of Bobby's head and smiled. "It looks just fine where it is." She looked over at the tall teenager standing next to his sister and gasped. The boy looked so much like her brother that she nearly swooned. If young Alex's eyes had been emerald green, she would have screamed. She caught herself and thankfully touched the edge of the heavy veil that covered her face. "You must be my godnephew?"

Alex smiled.

"You do justice to my brother's memory."

A soft trumpet called alerted the assembly around the grave site that the funeral was about to begin.

Sash escorted Keena back to her seat and leaned over to whisper in her ear, "We'd like for you to join us for dinner tonight if you don't have to go right back to New York."

Keena smiled. "Thanks so much for your offer, Sash, but my sisters and I must return right after the funeral. Let's talk for a little bit afterward."

As Sash returned to his seat, he saw four faces that he would never have expected to find at Jaxson's funeral: Sanchez, Costello, Martinez, and Lopez. All of them had taken on the middle-aged build of successful men. Sash looked around and saw that the crowd was still milling and it would take a couple of minutes before they would settle down. He stepped over to a smiling Sanchez and held out his hand. The Puerto Rican grinned and shook it.

"It's good seeing you again, Maleko. You look like you've made a few dollars since Vietnam."

Sash smiled back at the man. "A dollar here and a dollar there, all add up. What brings you here?"

"Us?" Sanchez almost laughed, and then caught himself. "Alex and us were *partners*. He loaned the four of us enough money to start our own chain of Puerto Rican restaurants. We're going to open a franchise this year."

Sash shook his head slowly from side to side. Twenty years ago he would never have believed it.

"Yeah, Alex looked us up after the war and made the offer." Sanchez looked over at his well-dressed partners and smiled. "We weren't doing much of anything else, so we took him up on it, and we've done pretty good so far."

Costello looked at Sash and spoke in a somber tone. "We owe him a lot." His old gang members all nodded their agreement.

"I've got to take my seat. It was nice seeing all of you again." Sash left his former platoon mates and joined his family just as the priest started the eulogy.

The southerly wind had died down and the priest's voice carried all the way to the back of the crowd surrounding the grave site. The detail from the Old Guard had been totally outnumbered and had finally withdrawn to control the guests in the immediate area around the grave. None of them had seen so many people gathered at an Arlington burial since President Kennedy was buried—and even then, it was only the old sergeant major, who had been there as a private.

Sash tried keeping his eyes off the casket. He could make it through the funeral if he didn't look directly at the dark wooden box that contained the remains of his war buddy. He scanned the perfectly kept grounds of the cemetery, trying to locate a patch of snow. It had been only a couple of days since he had been sitting with Alex on the park bench surrounded by snow, but the warm southerly wind had melted all of it. Sash's eyes paused on a distinguished-looking man in his middle or late sixties. The man used a cane, but his back was still erect. His most noticeable characteristic was a thick white handlebar mustache.

The living legend sensed that someone was staring at him and searched the crowd until his eyes locked with Sash's. The heavy alcohol-created lines on his face pulled back into a tight smile and he nodded at the gentleman sitting with his family.

Sash didn't know why, but he liked the old man and nodded back.

The crowd had done well during the short sermon, mostly because they were paying more attention to everyone else gathered there than to what the priest said. It was the sad rendition of taps that broke through the hardest veneer, and a field of white hankerchiefs appeared. Sash fought it, but he felt the tears running down his cheeks. Bobby reached over and took his hand in his and gently patted it. Sash's thoughts switched from Alex and the Vietnam War to a much simpler thought: what had he done to deserve such a family?

The American flag was presented to Keena. She was the family's senior representative. Alex's mother had disappeared shortly after he had gone into service, and Keena had been left to raise her three sisters. It had been a hard struggle for her and she had passed up marriage to raise them. Once Alex had earned his medical degree, he supported her, and also ended up supporting his sisters' families at one time or another.

Sash saw the crowd milling around and wanted to walk over to the grave, a tradition at Russian burials, but hesitated because he didn't want to offend anyone, especially with the media present. It was the old man with the snow-white mustache who drew the camera lenses when he slowly walked over the lowered casket and dropped down on one knee to flip the edge of the imitation turf covering that side of the mound of black dirt. The old man grabbed a handful of the loose soil and dropped it on the casket. Sash could see the Special Forces crest pinned on the old man's lapel and knew that the old warrior had come to bury one of his own. A line of veterans formed, and they followed the old man, each throwing a handful of dirt on the fallen warrior's casket. Women dropped flowers in the grave as they filed past the hole in the ground.

The television cameramen were going wild trying to film the unscheduled event from different angles. The Alex Jaxson story had taken another twist. The gravedigger's backhoe would not be needed to fill in the grave.

"What a waste of a life." Mary sobbed the words around the hankerchief she held to her nose.

Sash wrapped his arm around her shoulders. "I don't know if that's true, dear. Look around you. There are a lot of people here who have come to pay their respects to Alex and what he represents—a lost generation of American warriors."

EPILOGUE

The old man with the white handlebar mustache waited in his car until the Old Guard detail had finished picking up the litter around the grave and left in their trucks. He sat for a couple more minutes just thinking about the young Special Forces medical trainee who had impressed him so much when he had beaten his buddy running the MATA Mile. The years slipped away and the old warrior felt young again sitting on the front seat of his car. He reached in the brown bag next to him on the seat and removed an unopened bottle of Jim Beam.

"Are you ready, Cowgirl?" The old man spoke to a large German shepherd resting on the backseat.

The dog lifted her head and whined softly.

"I want you to meet your grandfather's best friend." The living legend opened his car door and slipped off the seat. The instant he put pressure on his foot, a groan escaped from between his lips as the pain erupted from his hip joint, which had been shattered and put back together over forty years earlier after the battle at Anzio beachhead. The dog didn't respond to the groan; she had heard it too many times.

He took his time walking over to the deserted grave. The mound of fresh earth was covered with flowers and wreaths that had been sent from around the country. The old man could smell the heavy sweet fragrance coming from the thousands of roses in the crisp winter air. He paused and looked over toward the setting sun, holding his cane in his left hand and the bottle of Jim Beam by its neck in his other hand.

"We've got to visit Billy, too, over at the memorial before we head on back to North Carolina tonight, Cowgirl."

The dog nuzzled his cane hand.

He took a seat on a concrete bench located in a small grove of trees a few feet away from Alex's grave and unscrewed the top of the bourbon bottle. The living legend threw the cap over his right shoulder in an old Special Forces tradition that signified the whole bottle would have to be finished, and gave a quiet toast to the listening wind:

To those who have fought . . .
To those who have fallen . . .
To those who continue to fight . . .

He sucked down a quarter of the bottle before he stopped drinking and looked over at the grave. "Well, boy . . . you did good." The white mustache quivered. "You did real good."

The park bum watched the man with the cane from his hiding place in the trees. He had been there all afternoon watching the thousands of people who had come for the burial, and twice he had nearly been discovered in his hiding place. He watched the man with the large white handlebar mustache drink from the bottle of bourbon and felt a tremendous desire to leave his hiding place and panhandle enough money for a bottle of wine. He forced himself to ignore his body's selfish demands. He had promised himself something, and he was going to do it or die from withdrawal in the process.

The man with the cane stood up slowly and started

walking back toward his car. The park bum watched him pause next to the grave and say something that the wind was the sole witness to, and then slowly hobble back to the vehicle with the dog.

Cowgirl paused next to the door and looked back at the thick trees where the old bum was hiding. She whined and tried nuzzling her master's hand.

"What's wrong, girl? You sad?" He opened the rear door and she jumped in and instantly curled up on the backseat.

The white-bearded bum waited until the car had pulled away before leaving his hiding place. He went over the the concert bench and saw that the bottle of Jim Beam was over half-full. A smile spread across the old man's face and he held the bottle up to the sky and a passing bank of clouds. "Thanks!"

Darkness fell over the cemetery early. The park bum had nursed the bourbon and still had a quarter of it left. He was lying against the side of the dirt mound, using it as a backrest, and had tucked newspaper and flower boxes around his body to retain its heat. The sky was cloudless, making for a perfect winter's night.

The old bum from Lafayette Park patted Alex's grave and mumbled under his breath, "Don't worry, kid, I won't leave you alone out here on your first night."

There's an epidemic with 27 million victims. And no visible symptoms.

It's an epidemic of people who can't read.

Believe it or not, 27 million Americans are functionally illiterate, about one adult in five.

The solution to this problem is you... when you join the fight against illiteracy. So call the Coalition for Literacy at toll-free **1-800-228-8813** and volunteer.

Volunteer Against Illiteracy. The only degree you need is a degree of caring.